CROOKED HEART

CRISTINA SUMNERS

Bantam Books

CROOKED HEART

A Bantam Book / November 2002
All rights reserved.
Copyright © 2002 by Cristina J. Sumners.

BOOK DESIGN BY VIRGINIA NOREY

LIBRARY OF CONGRESS CATALOGING-IN-PUBLICATION DATA
Sumners, Cristina.
Crooked heart / Cristina Sumners.
p.   cm.
ISBN 0-553-80303-4
1. Police—New Jersey—Fiction. 2. Police Chiefs—
Fiction. 3. Women clergy—Fiction. 4. New
Jersey—Fiction. I. Title.
PS3619.U46 C76 2002   2002025589
813'.6 21

Published simultaneously in the United States and Canada

Bantam Books are published by Bantam Books, a division of
Random House, Inc. Its trademark, consisting of the words
"Bantam Books" and the portrayal of a rooster, is Registered in
U.S. Patent and Trademark Office and in other countries. Marca
Registrada. Bantam Books, 1540 Broadway, New York, New
York 10036.

PRINTED IN THE UNITED STATES OF AMERICA
BVG   10   9   8   7   6   5   4   3   2   1

WITH LOVE AND GRATITUDE
TO MY SUPERLATIVE PARENTS
—ALL THREE OF THEM

ACKNOWLEDGMENTS

This book would still be a stack of dog-eared pages in the back of my closet were it not for my amazing agent, Linda Roghaar, who took me from query letter to three-book contract in sixty-three days. Linda, remind me to thank you adequately when my head stops spinning.

Linda delivered me into the hands of a bevy of stunningly competent folks at Bantam Dell, to all of whom I am grateful (what a joy it is to work with people who know what they're doing). Above all I must thank Kate Miciak, whose enthusiasm for *Crooked Heart* exceeded my wildest expectations, and whose sage, funny, and utterly merciless editing has been both revelation and blessing.

In the embarrassing number of years between the first draft of this novel and the seventh (I think it was, but I may have lost count), which is what Linda and Kate saw, many people read the manuscript and kindly told me what was wrong with it. They were mostly right. Thanks to them, an amateurish effort gradually metamorphosed into Something Worth Publishing.

They are the proverbial too-many-to-name, but I'd assuredly get struck by lightning and rot in hell if I didn't mention Barrie Van Dycke, Lyle Meyer, and Susan Herner.

Buckets of gratitude must be poured over my splendid husband Colin and my wonderful son Tim, who managed to put up with having a Writer in the house, which I can assure you, if you've never had to do it, is a pain in the lower parts of the anatomy.

Finally, I herewith fulfill a promise a quarter of a century old: Thanks to Bill. He knows who he is.

CHAPTER 1

i

She knelt on the floor beside the body. Not to see if it was dead—she knew that already—but because something terrible inside her drew her down for a closer look.

The blood had stopped flowing. It lay in perfect stillness on the white tile floor, a glistening scarlet halo around the upper torso of the dead woman. The dress was white, too—or had been before the knife went through it. The knife now lay on the floor beside the body, oddly inconspicuous amid a gory miscellany of flatware and small utensils; every implement was as wet and as red as if it had been dipped in crimson paint.

The door of the dishwasher hung limp on broken hinges, pointing downward toward the body as if in mute apology. Three of the four small plates in the lower rack had slid from their places and lay in an untidy stack, facedown, where the cutlery rack had been before it had fallen to the floor. Like everything else within arm's reach, the rack and the plates in it were liberally splashed with blood.

She looked at the body, at the blood, at the knife. She thought she ought to feel something—anger, pity, remorse, anything—but no feeling came. Nothing except a fine buzzing that hummed in her ears and danced all over her body, as though an electric current ran through her skin. She did not seem to be able to move.

For how many minutes she remained kneeling, numbly gazing at the dead woman, she did not know.

Neither did she know how long he had been standing in the doorway to the hall. She had not heard him come. His presence had crept into her senses gradually, through the buzzing, until there came a moment when she knew, unsurprised, that he was there.

She tried to look up, but she did not want to see his face; her eyes instead found his hands, and that somehow was worse.

He started to say something, but only a voiceless whisper came. He stopped, cleared his throat, tried again, and this time spoke. But what she heard was a thin, pinched travesty of his voice, the ghost of his voice.

It said, "Do you have any of the blood on you?"

For some reason the pedestrian practicality of the question offended her. The flicker of anger broke through the buzzing paralysis, or at least loosened it slightly. He was cool? So would she be.

"There's a little on my skirt."

"Stand up before there's more of it."

She stood up. Too suddenly, for the room heaved; she put out a hand to steady herself.

"Don't touch that!" he cried.

She snatched her hand back from the countertop, half-expecting to see a bloody handprint on the white surface. *Like Lady Macbeth!* she thought wildly. Then reason reasserted itself. "Don't be absurd. My fingerprints are all over this kitchen. All over the house."

He made a motion in the air in front of his face, as though to clear something away. "Of course," he said. "I— Yes, of course."

There was a silence. She could no longer look at the body now that he was there.

"I think you had better leave," he said.

"Yes," she replied, still not meeting his eyes. "Yes, I believe it's time." She moved stiffly, carefully, toward the back door.

ii

Julia Robinson softly opened the door to her daughter's bedroom and looked in. She saw tumbled covers on an empty bed, and an empty chair by the window. Startled, she stepped into the room and said sharply, "Tita?" There was no one there. Julia turned and walked quickly down the hall to the bathroom. The door was open, the room empty. "Tita?" she called back down the hall, louder this time. No answer.

She hurried toward a narrow door, flung it open, and fairly shouted "Tita!" as she ran up a flight of uncarpeted stairs. The attic was a wide, low space tucked under the eaves, with four dormer windows peeking out at the treetops, one on each side of the house. Julia moved swiftly past stacks of cardboard boxes, an ancient set of golf clubs, and a standing rack of off-season clothes swaddled in plastic bags. She arrived at the area around the dormer at the back of the house, where a space had been cleared and a tiny, shabby living room created. A child's dresser supported a rag doll—obviously long retired—and an array of seashells; a sagging bookshelf held the annals of Narnia and Oz; beside an armchair of faded maroon stood a floor lamp in the dated trendiness of the sixties. In mingled exasperation and relief Julia looked down upon her daughter, asleep in the armchair.

Elizabeth Robinson, once and forever nicknamed Tita by a fond aunt, was ten years old. She had very short ginger hair, an elfin face lightly freckled, and a slowly abating case of the flu. She very rarely did what she had been told not to do, and for a moment her mother was completely puzzled. Then she saw the ballpoint pen resting in the slack fingers of Tita's right hand, and she understood. There on the floor, where it had fallen, was the spiral notebook, opened and folded back; the heading on the exposed page was FROM THE ATTIC. Below was half a page of neatly written lines, the first of which began with the notation *1:04 Monday*. Julia glanced at her watch. It was 1:47.

She felt a rush of guilt; she should have checked on Tita earlier; the child had been here most of an hour. Well, at least she'd remembered to turn on the little space heater. Julia switched the heater off and gathered her daughter in her arms, murmuring in a voice too low to wake her, "Come along, Chiquita, back to bed, whooo! You're getting heavy, in another year or two I won't be able to do this, mmmm, that'll be a shame, won't it. . . . It'll be a bigger shame if you've made yourself worse. . . . Next time when your silly mother says you can sit by the window with your notebook, she will be sure to specify your *bedroom* window. . . ."

iii

He sat on the floor, feet drawn up, head between his knees, arms wrapped tightly around his legs. He was on the floor because his legs had refused to support him another moment; he had his head between his knees so that he did not have to see.

Every few minutes his stomach revolted, but he had already vomited, painfully and thoroughly, in the hall, and now the spasms were only dry heaves. He waited until they stopped, and then he waited some more. It felt like an hour; it might have been four minutes. Finally, the fear of discovery grew greater than the horror of the task, and he began, with the help of the doorjamb, to struggle to his feet.

He found that his teeth were chattering, and he clenched them. It seemed to strain every muscle in his face and neck, but the chattering stopped, and from that minuscule victory he drew a feather's weight of courage. Still holding the doorframe, he bent to pick up the sheets he had dropped.

Clutching them hard against his chest, he forced himself to look at the disaster that lay on the floor, splashed like a crimson insult across a space heretofore impeccably white. It was vulgar, melodramatic, remote from anything she would have done or worn in life, an alien intrusion on her style. After the eternity of minutes he had had to get used to it, it still did not seem real.

The blood had grown darker and was beginning to thicken. If it dried, it would be harder to clean up. He moved his stiff legs and slowly approached the body. He pulled a single sheet out of the bundle of pale colors he carried and dropped it into the pool of blood beside the corpse. His hand hovered over the dishwasher rack that had come to rest almost on top of the wound in her back; he needed to push it back onto the door of the dishwasher, then close the door to get it out of the way. Simple enough, if only he could get his fingers to overcome their revulsion and actually touch the sticky red surfaces of metal and rubber. Before he could summon the will for it, an unwelcome thought came to him. Getting the dishwasher out of the way would be easy enough—he could do that in two seconds with one hand. But what about the body?

He would get blood all over himself.

He tried to think. Something like cunning, unfamiliar to him, stole across his mind. He stepped back to the kitchen table, laid the remaining sheets on it, and began to take off his clothes.

When he had stripped completely, laying his clothes across the table and his shoes under a chair, he again picked up the sheets and returned to the body. Without giving himself time to think about it, he reached for the dishwasher rack, shoved it back onto the sagging door, lifted the door, and closed it.

He knelt on the sheet he'd already dropped onto the pool of blood. His mind, which seemed no longer to belong to him, kept noticing color. The sheet he knelt on was a paisley print, a delicate blue and pink over which the dull red was slowly creeping. He dropped its mate over the blood on the other side of the body. The sheets ruined the color scheme, he thought absurdly, then wondered if this judicious detachment was what is called shock. The red and white might have been overly dramatic for her, but the darkening paisley transformed the scene into a common, ugly mess. How she would have hated it! He took a third sheet—flowers, this one, the color of peaches—and began to wrap it around the still-supple corpse.

She was as warm as a living soul. It would have been easier for him if she had been stiff and cold. As it was, the feel of her was too familiar, the flesh soft under his touch, as it had always been.

He slipped his arm under her waist and gently rolled her over onto her back. He was unprepared for her face.

Her eyes were open. Blood smeared her right cheek and temple where she had lain in it; blood was drying in her hair and in her eyelashes. He cried aloud and dropped her. Her left arm fell across his thighs, just brushing his penis.

Two things happened in two consecutive split instants: in the first, his body's attempt at the unthinking, primeval reaction; in the second, his mind's shrill veto. In a rush of horrified, irrational modesty he struck at her arm with the back of his hand, trying to knock it away without touching it, as one would a spider crawling across one's bare skin. He caught his breath on a sob, smothering panic with reserves of will he did not know he possessed, and continued his work with the sheets.

When at last she was completely enveloped, arms wrapped to her sides, dreadful face covered, he slid his right arm under her shoulders and his left under her knees and stood up. He took a step.

Memory, sudden as pain, struck his mind and slid into his heart like an oiled knife. With brutal Proustian clarity the hotel room materialized before him; he was naked; he was carrying her to the bed; she was laughing. He could feel the carpet beneath his bare feet, hear the Fifth Avenue traffic muted through the window.

He sank to his knees, pulled the awkward cloth-wrapped figure into a hopeless embrace, pressed his face against it, and wept.

CHAPTER 2

It was the frequently expressed opinion of the Rev. Dr. Kathryn Koerney that committee meetings were among the prime works of the Devil. She based this assertion on the ancient and orthodox doctrine that the Devil's chief mission is not (as is popularly believed) to make people wicked, but to make people miserable. On that criterion alone, she maintained, committees ranked right up there with income taxes and Pledge Week on PBS; when asked to serve on one, her invariable reply was "Life's too short."

When asked, however, to select, cast, direct, and produce a medieval mystery play for the church's annual patronal festival, Kathryn had fallen upon the assignment with glad cries of joy. It wasn't until six weeks later that they told her that as head of the Play Committee ("An entirely fictive body," she protested in vain), her presence was required at all meetings of the Festival Planning Committee.

The first of these was inching past the midpoint of its second hour. Kathryn had made out her grocery list, written a letter to her mother, outlined a lecture for the next day, and invented four really compelling reasons why she couldn't possibly make it to any of the subsequent meetings. At this point, however, she was passing from boredom to spiritual crisis, as she slid into one of her periodic fits of despair; these were normally characterized by thoughts such as *The Church is never going to be anything more than a club for dinosaurs and any priest with a grain of self-respect would abandon her priesthood and take up a more honorable profession, like prostitution or maybe gunrunning.*

Miss (never Ms.) Amalie Prescott, with the faint but unmistakable condescension that the traditional female displays when explaining to a man one of those Things That Men Don't Understand, was entirely failing to make her point to Mr. Carson Strothers; Mr. Strothers, with the saintly patience and gentle amusement that marks the traditional male who is listening to a woman Go On and On the Way Women Do, was utterly failing to convince Miss Amalie that he understood her point but disagreed with it anyway. Kathryn was aggravated with both of them, less for the time they were wasting than for their dull-witted smugness; neither had the wit to see that the other's attitude was an insult. Then the thought struck her that she was listening to the present Junior Warden and a former Senior Warden of the vestry. She made a note on a loose sheet of paper and slid it eight inches along the table to her right.

Tom Holder, who had been put in charge of security for the upcoming festivity on the unarguable grounds that he happened to be Chief of Police, looked down at the note. It said: *Is it true that in order to be elected to the vestry of this church, your income in millions per year must exceed your I.Q.?*

Tom strangled a laugh and wrote back, I'M *on the vestry of this church, thank you!!!*

Kathryn replied, still on paper, WHOOPS.

You'd have known that, Tom wrote, *if you ever came to vestry meetings.*

Kathryn reclaimed the paper and wrote, *I am paid by the seminary, I thank God, and not by this congregation. That means that around this church I do what interests me and I don't what doesn't.*

Tom loved it when she made weird sentences.

He responded, *I think you ought to come to vestry anyway.*

Give me 1 good reason. Give me 1 mediocre reason, even.

To keep me from being BORED TO DEATH.

Kathryn's eyes widened; the compliment was unexpected. For the first time in the exchange, she glanced at Tom's face. His bland gaze was focused on Amalie Prescott as though he were actually listening to her. Kathryn looked again at the note.

It pleased her. She had always liked Tom Holder. The questions he had asked in her adult Sunday school class the previous year had revealed areas of ignorance but never a trace of stupidity; moreover, he possessed that rarest of gifts, an open mind. She suspected he must be very good at his job, and to be good at one's job was one of the surest ways of earning Kathryn's admiration.

The admiration, apparently, was mutual. That was gratifying, but in an unaccustomed fit of discretion Kathryn resisted the urge to return the compliment, and wrote only: *I'll give it my fullest consideration.*

As this was the Rector's favorite way of saying "Not a chance," it drew a smile from Tom. However, he was also visited—belatedly—by a spirit of discretion, and decided it would be wise to let the exchange lapse.

It had required serious willpower to keep his nose pointed at Amalie while Kathryn responded to his last comment. But the only way he'd been able to get away with that remark was by making it (writing it) and then acting as if it weren't important and he didn't care what she said back. In fact, he hadn't the faintest idea what Amalie had said during that crucial twenty seconds; his entire concentration had been in his peripheral vision. Kathryn had looked at him, that much he knew, but what her expression had been he had not been able to tell. Nor could he tell much from her reply. Whether she was pleased, flattered, amused, offended, or utterly and completely indifferent, he couldn't say. All he knew was that it was incredibly stupid of him to even think about it.

You're old enough to be her father, he reminded himself. *You're forty pounds overweight and you're going bald. She's got college education coming out of her ears and the best thing you ever graduated from was high school. And in case you haven't noticed recently,* he told himself witheringly, *you're married.*

As usual, the thought of Louise plunged him into a moment's depression. Against it he marshaled—again, as usual—that reliable anesthetic, fantasy. For a few sweet seconds he was free, and fit and attractive, and Kathryn was laughing at some witty thing he'd just said. Now, *that* had actually happened once. Fantasy segued into memory.

Kathryn had been one of a lively group at coffee hour who appeared to be engaged in some sort of word game. What had gotten them started Tom never knew; when he had moved unobtrusively into an open space in their little circle, they were trying to make sentences out of the street names in Canterbury Park, in the order they occurred, north to south. The streets were all named after famous writers (the main cross street, inevitably, was Shakespeare Lane), but the game was turning more on bad puns than on literary criticism.

Tom, who was capable of punnery when inspired, nevertheless had little hope of scoring points in this contest; the subject matter and the audience (Kathryn, a lawyer, a university professor, and the professor's husband, who had recently retired from selling insurance to enroll in the seminary) were a bit intimidating— what if he said something dumb?

The lawyer was lamenting the order of the next two streets: "If we could just reverse those two, we could say, 'Austen is a Dickens of a writer.' " The professor and her husband greeted this with cries of "Tame!" and "Boring!"

Then Kathryn ventured, "Dickens is an Austen-tatious writer?" which had been greeted with acclaim by all, including the lawyer, whose own suggestion had been spurned. Kathryn added, "And *isn't* he! All frills and furbelows and gobbledygook."

Amid the chorus of protests that this opinion brought forth, Tom had somewhere found the temerity to say, "What's the matter? They give you a B in that course?" This had surprised a whoop of laughter out of Kathryn, and a whistle of appreciation, raised eyebrows, and "Touché!" from the others. Kathryn, still laughing, said, "Ouch!" then put her arm around his shoulders and gave him a quick squeeze, telling him, "You missed your calling, my friend. You should have been a psychologist."

She had then added, "Of course, a good cop would have to be something of a psychologist, wouldn't he?" and before Tom knew it, they were off and running on the more sophisticated aspects of criminology, deferring to him as the expert.

This was heady stuff. Besides being hugged by Kathryn (thank

God Louise had been twenty feet off, looking the other way), he was being included as an equal among intellectuals. He rarely had this feeling, especially at church. In fact, for years he had regarded the way he was treated on Sundays as God's way of keeping him from getting a swelled head from being The Man at the police station the remainder of the week.

Tom Holder's bailiwick was Harton, New Jersey, so his church—St. Margaret's Episcopal—was perched between an Ivy League university and a major seminary in a wealthy commuter town, which meant it attracted rather an impressive lot of parishioners. Everybody, it seemed, had either money or brains. Holder, laying claim to neither, was generally accepted as one of the pillars of the church simply because he had been there forever and he volunteered for everything. And when the Wall Street barons and the university professors found themselves face-to-face with him at coffee hour, they obligingly talked football.

Kathryn Koerney never talked football, at least not to Tom Holder, and that may have been the thing that first endeared her to him.

Kathryn had arrived in town the previous fall to take a teaching position at the seminary; she had a Ph.D. from someplace in New York City that Tom had never heard of but that other people seemed to be terribly impressed with. The Rector of St. Margaret's, always happy to have an extra priest he didn't have to pay, had invited her to teach the adult Sunday school class of which Tom Holder was a member.

Holder, one of the earliest in the congregation to have supported the ordination of women, had had his liberal views sorely tried by the Rector's previous assistant: The woman had been the

second (and much younger) wife of one of the parish million-
aires, and Tom had never quite shaken the notion that she treated
her priesthood as if it were some sort of hobby. Sure enough, she
had quit her job at the church a year after she started, saying that
her children needed her at home.

Then here came another woman, and before she ever showed
her face in the parish there were rumors she'd inherited a fabulous amount of money from her father; Tom had thought, *Not
again!* On her first Sunday he took one look at her—an attractive
thirtysomething, moving gracefully down the aisle in snowy vestments, her perfect chestnut hair putting shampoo commercials
to shame—and thought, *Debutante. Playing priest.*

But Tom was one of those unusual people whose opinions, however strong, are revised when they begin to clash with observable
fact. At the end of three months he had become one of Kathryn's
most vocal supporters. Then one day Louise had wondered, with
the air of one much imposed upon, why on earth he liked that
Koerney girl so much. The truth ("Because she's the first Ph.D. I
ever met who talks to me as though I'm every bit as smart as she is,
that's why") was obviously not an option. He said instead, without
enthusiasm, "Who—Kathryn? Oh, she's O.K., I guess." As soon as
he'd said it, he realized that "Who—Kathleen?" would have been
much better. Pity he hadn't thought of it in time.

After that, of course, he had decided that it would be wise to
talk to—and about—Kathryn less often. That wasn't too difficult;
after all, he got an hour of her every week in Sunday school. But
in the fall of her second year in Harton, Kathryn had asked to be
reassigned to a children's class, God knew why, and Tom was horrified to discover how much he missed her. At coffee hour he

caught himself trying to watch her out of the corner of his eye so he could go back to the serving table for a refill at the same time she did. Which was dangerous as well as foolish.

So he rationed himself: He spoke to her only on one Sunday out of every three. This was good from the standpoint of Louise, who seemed not to notice anything wrong, but bad from the standpoint of his feelings, which just got stronger. He began to think up good questions to ask Kathryn, so that when he joined the group she was part of, he had a way of getting her attention fairly quickly.

The trouble with this approach was that it meant she was always the one teaching, while he was the one learning. That was O.K., he didn't really mind that, but he longed for that wonderful feeling he had had the day she told him he was a good psychologist, and everybody had treated him like an expert. To make something like that happen again, there would have to be a conversation about something he was an expert on, and that meant crime and police work. But it had to be interesting. Stolen hubcaps and speed traps weren't going to do it.

And so it was that Harton's Chief of Police sat in a boring committee meeting and wished that somewhere in his jurisdiction, somebody would commit an interesting crime.

CHAPTER 3

i

How she had successfully driven to the airport she would never know. Every turn, every stop, had been negotiated for her by some automatic system in her brain, and as she pulled into a place in the parking garage and turned off the ignition, she realized she had no recollection of the journey at all. She might just as well have been driven by someone else while she slept. Now, however, she was going to have to do things, talk to people. Unless she just kept on driving, of course. She could do that; nothing said she had to get on that plane.

But she resisted the temptation to do the easier thing. This was harder, seeing people, being seen by people, but the plane was the better option; it would take her farther and faster.

She got out of the car and opened the back door to get the two pieces of luggage on the backseat, but she found to her annoyance that she couldn't pick them up. They seemed to weigh a ton. She tried first one, then the other, but all that happened was that her whole arm began to shake. She had been shaking when she first got into the car, but the tremor had stopped somewhere on the drive to the airport, and she had thought then that the worst was over. Obviously it wasn't. Shock, or perhaps guilt, had drained all strength from her. The hanging bag contained only dresses; it weighed only a few pounds. But it might as well have been lead. She tried for two more minutes, which seemed like thirty. All that happened was that her arm trembled all the more, her breath grew ragged, and she began to be afraid she was going to burst into tears.

Finally she swore in a voice loud enough to startle herself, stepped back from the car, and slammed the door. What the hell. She had a purse full of cash and plastic. She could buy clothes in San Francisco. She took several deep breaths to steady herself, and walked purposefully into the terminal.

It wasn't so difficult, after all. No one paid any attention to her. Why should they? Airports were crowded with people. All minding their own business. She attached herself to the end of the appropriate line.

She was wrong, in fact, in assuming no one would pay any attention to her. Being naturally modest, it did not occur to her that she was particularly worth looking at. Nor could she have expected the remarkable coincidence that occurred when she reached the head of the line.

"May I help you?" sang one of the ticket clerks, an unprepossessing young man with a large nose, an unflatteringly short haircut, and a smile perched neatly between the personal and the professional. "Yes, ma'am, what have we got here, Flight Three-twenty for San Francisco, Mrs.—Stanley! That's my name, too. Only mine doesn't have an E. Well, Mrs. Stanley with an E, would you like a window or an aisle? Mmm-hmm. All right, and how many bags will you be checking?"

Impossible to explain! She said with as even a voice as she could manage, "I'm not checking any bags."

"Carrying it all yourself, eh? We recommend I.D. tags for your carry-on luggage. May I give you a couple, or tag your bags for you?"

"No," she said a second too late to sound natural. "Thank you," she added. If only she could walk away now! But this stupid boy was still holding the ticket. She could stretch out her hand for it, then he would have to give it to her. But her hand might shake. Stifling panic, she said, "I don't have any carry-on luggage."

"O.K. then," he said after what felt like an eon, "here you go, Mrs. Stanley. That'll be Gate Thirty-four, boarding at two forty-five."

"Thank you," she replied woodenly, taking the ticket with a hand that considering the circumstances was surprisingly steady. She turned away as the boy called out, "May I help you?" to the next person in line.

Now all she had to do was find Gate 34. She could do that, it would be easy. After all, she wouldn't have to talk to anybody. As long as she didn't have to talk to anybody, she'd be all right.

ii

He had put the body in the basement. That was temporary, obviously; he would have to figure out what to do with it before it started to— Here his brain hit a brick wall and stopped. The body in its current state was very nearly more than he could endure. The state the body would be in after a few days was not something his mind could cope with even in the abstract.

The kitchen. He could think about the kitchen.

It was only blood, after all, and he had seen blood lots of times. Just never this much at once.

He stood in the kitchen doorway and attempted to think logically. He was still naked. There were smears of blood all over him, beginning to harden, crinkling stiffly when he moved. He looked at his clothes, still lying on the table. For the first time he noticed that her coat was draped over one of the chairs. He would have to put it somewhere. He couldn't do it now, any more than he could touch his own clothes, because he wasn't clean. He would need to clear up the entire mess, he decided, every drop of it; after that he could take a shower, and then he could get dressed. Then he could do something with the coat.

It helped him, somehow, to have arranged the nightmare into a list of chores. It was still a nightmare, but at least he knew what to do next. He surveyed the shambles that had been, in some previous lifetime dimly remembered from an hour ago, his favorite place in the house. The easiest thing, he saw, would be to put all the stuff that was on the floor into the dishwasher and run it.

He walked over to the dishwasher, being careful not to step in the pool of blood around it. *Dumbo*, he thought. *You're covered with the stuff. What does it matter if it gets on your feet?* Nevertheless the bare soles of his feet cringed at the moist red threat. Leaning over it, he opened the dishwasher door. It was unusually heavy in his hand, and when it reached its horizontal position it did not stop, but fell another several inches. He had forgotten the hinges were broken. He had also forgotten how bloody it was inside the dishwasher: as bloody as the floor.

He started to pull out the bottom rack—how much easier it was to touch this time! After what he had done with the body, this was child's play—but he found that the rack would not stay on the broken door. Unless held in place, it would roll off. This discovery cost him a plate, which slid out of the tilting rack, hit the floor in the middle of the thickening blood, and broke. The sudden movement and the noise made him jump as if he had been shot. He swore under his breath and shoved the rack back into the cavity of the dishwasher. He bent to pick up the pieces of the plate, then stood with them in his hands, at a loss. He couldn't just put them in the trash; there was blood all over them. After a moment he reached into the dishwasher and laid them carefully on the lower rack, more or less in the place where the plate had originally been. The smaller pieces fell through the gaps in the rack, clattering onto the basin-like bottom of the dishwasher. He swore again, started to reach under the rack to retrieve them, and then decided it didn't really matter.

He stooped to pick up the long, narrow cutlery rack that lay among the implements it had spilled onto the floor. One by one, as if picking up items of great delicacy, he placed them in the rack: a butter knife, some forks and spoons, a table knife, a plastic-coated spatula—the modest little tools of ordinary domestic life, now dark and tacky with gore. The large carving knife he came to last of all, out of some confused feeling that was part squeamishness and part respect.

When everything except the blood itself had been cleared off the floor and placed in the cutlery rack, he leaned over the sagging door, placed the cutlery rack in position, closed the dishwasher, and turned it on. As the machine began to hum, he emitted a shaky sigh of relief that wavered on the edge of a sob. He controlled it, and made himself consider the next step.

The blood. He had to clean up the blood.

CHAPTER 4

It was about seven-thirty in the evening when George Kimbrough at last got home. Every time he drove to New York City he swore he would not try to get home during rush hour. And every time, he would conclude his business toward the end of the working day, and be faced with a choice: Either he could drive home during rush hour, or he could select a pleasant restaurant, have an early dinner, and head for home after seven. The restaurant option was by far the more inviting, but frequently he was unable to find a colleague who would join him for dinner; they were tired and wanted to get home, or they already had other plans. The problem could have been solved by making dinner plans in advance with one of the said colleagues, but George didn't like making plans in advance; it was too much bother. He preferred to be spontaneous. And being one of those people who have never learned that the only way to change things is to start doing something differently from the way you have done it before, George persistently wound up in the middle of Manhattan at the beginning of the evening rush hour with not a prospective dinner companion in sight.

Of course he could have chosen to eat alone, but that was a possibility he never even considered. He knew, naturally, that other people dined alone, some of them frequently. He did not know how they did it. That was as far as he ever got in thinking about the matter: He didn't know how they did it. It never occurred to him to wonder why he was so averse to an activity most people had no serious problem with, even though they might not be enthusiastic about it. But the reason George Kimbrough did not fancy his own company long enough to eat a meal in a restaurant by himself was the same reason that he would never know *why* he had this particular aversion. He was positively allergic to self-examination. George needed at all times to be concentrating on work (his wife said he was a workaholic) or getting the full attention—preferably the flattering attention—of another human being. Left to his own devices, he became prey to a niggling anxiety that he never put his finger on because he was too busy denying its existence.

The reasonable person might at this point suggest that he could simply take a book or a newspaper into the restaurant with him and safely occupy his mind with reading. In fact, in his younger days George had been accustomed to doing precisely that. But once, in his middle thirties, he had dined in a restaurant that had serious pretensions to elegance, in the company of immoderately wealthy clients for whom he was redecorating a mansion on Library Place. Mrs. Wealthy Client had caught sight of a man a few tables away, dining alone and reading a book. "Look at him!" she snorted, inviting George to share her scorn. "Where does he think he is, a coffee shop in Oklahoma?" Mr. Wealthy Client had huffed, "Might as well have brought a newspaper."

George had never heard that it was ungenteel to read in a restaurant. Silently cursing his parents for never having taught him what was obviously an essential point of etiquette, he simultaneously thanked God (with whom he normally had little to do) that he had learned it before he'd made a fool of himself in front of these or any other important people. And from that day he had steadfastly resisted the attempts of his wife and friends to convince him that the Wealthy Clients had pulled this idea out of thin air and not out of Miss Manners or even Emily Post; he would have died (well, almost) rather than be caught with any reading matter in a restaurant.

So it was that George did his usual: He drove from Manhattan to Harton in the rush hour, swearing he'd never do it again. He also swore at every one of the countless cars around him, generously including not only the ones in which his own car was imprisoned, but the oncoming traffic as well (because they were having an easier time of it). In a leaden dusk they all slushed their way slowly past an endless parade of huge industrial plants, alike in their ugliness, hunching like malevolent hobgoblins over the tired earth they occupied, belching out unbreathable air. There was thus plenty of time for George to work himself up into a considerable ill temper.

"Grace!" he shouted as he let himself in the back door. "Grace, I'm home!"

There was no response.

"Grace!" he shouted again with an edge to his voice.

Silence.

Damn and blast the woman, where was she? As if he hadn't

had enough to contend with already! He took off his coat and threw it over one of the kitchen stools. Grace would hang it up later. She didn't have enough to do to keep her busy, anyway. He took a glass from a cupboard and ice from the freezer and went into the dining room, to the bar. Pouring himself a stiff bourbon, he went to the hall, stood at the bottom of the stairs, and shouted up them, "Hey! I said I'm home!"

Still getting no response, he began to prowl around the downstairs, steadily drinking the bourbon and refilling his glass periodically from the bottle he still carried. Finally he decided he would have to go to the totally unreasonable length of actually going upstairs and fetching Grace from the bathroom or wherever else it was she was hiding herself. He plodded grudgingly up the stairs and shouted some more. He looked in every room on that floor, but his wife was in none of them. He became, naturally, even more exasperated. She was supposed to be here. She was always here when he got home, and today she knew that he'd be driving back from the City, so she knew he'd be tired, so where the hell was she? Thinking he might have failed to see a note, he went back to the kitchen and looked where she usually left notes, on the countertop next to the refrigerator. There was nothing there. He looked over all the countertops in the kitchen and checked all the bits of paper stuck to the refrigerator door with magnets. At this point he noticed that there were no signs of dinner in preparation. He swore.

Still looking for a note, he went back to the dining room and looked on the bar. Then he went to his chair in the living room, where the mail and the evening paper would be waiting for him. There was nothing there, either. Not only was there no note explaining where she was, she hadn't even fetched the mail and the paper. Grace could be very inconsiderate at times. She *would* have to pick today for it.

He made himself sit down in his chair and think. What would be the reasonable thing to do next? Call next door, of course. Ask if Grace was there, and if not, did Bill know where she was? Or had Carolyn said anything, before leaving on her trip, about Grace going somewhere or doing something today? Yes, that was it, he'd do that.

He tossed off his fourth bourbon and rose, somewhat unsteadily, to go into the kitchen to use the phone. He dialed the number and stood staring out the window that looked over to the Stanleys' house, as if willing Bill to answer.

Next door, Bill Stanley was sitting in the exact center of his house, that is, halfway up the stairs. He did not have the faintest idea why he was sitting there, as opposed to somewhere sensible like the living room. He had gone to this place without conscious thought, and was sitting in it without being at all curious as to why he was there. He did not know, nor would he have cared if told, that he was hiding from the windows, all the windows, as if they were hostile eyes. What he did know was that his life lay about him in jagged fragments; if he moved carelessly, they would slash him, and he would bleed. He had had enough of blood.

When the phone rang, he jumped, and started to tremble. He counted. Four rings. He was afraid of it, that harsh braying; he wished it would go away. Five rings. He was not going to answer it no matter how long it rang. Seven rings. No matter how long.

There was not a single soul in the universe whom he wanted to talk to. Ten rings. His teeth were clenched, and he began to sweat. Jesus, thirteen rings!

Then it stopped.

George cursed at the phone and at both Stanleys. It didn't make sense that no one was at home, not at this time of day. Maybe their phone was out of order. His anger prevented his noticing what his eyes might have told him. From the Kimbroughs' kitchen window, five of the Stanleys' windows were visible, and none of them showed a light.

George stood for a while, considering. The next logical thing was to go over there, wasn't it? He left the kitchen by way of the back door, crossed his driveway, went through the gate in the hedge to the Stanleys' driveway, ran up the steps to their back door, and began to pound on it. But the door had a large glass panel in it, and at that point it would have taken more than temper to keep even George from noticing the obvious. No light shone on the other side of the door. He stomped back down the steps, marched into the middle of the driveway, and turned to survey the house. It was completely dark.

He swore loudly and long.

Meanwhile in the house, halfway up the stairs, Bill Stanley had heard the thumps on the back door, and his heart had contracted to the size of a child's fist. Then it began to beat so loudly, he actually began to fear that it would be heard by the person on the back porch.

The person on the back porch. George. It was probably George. He never wanted to see George again.

CHAPTER 5

Everybody at the station knew of the Chief's standing orders about calling him at home when he was off duty: They were never to hesitate to do so. Sergeant Fischer admired the Chief for this policy; he thought it showed a noble dedication to duty. Sergeant Rossi knew better. Not that Rossi was all that perceptive, but he, too, suffered from a home life in which any interruption would be welcomed.

When the phone rang in the drab little living room, it was just after ten o'clock. Tom Holder was sitting in the shabby armchair that had mercifully faded from its original poison green into something marginally more tolerable; he was reading, as was his habit, a paperback best seller, tuning out the noise from the television with an expertise born of long practice.

That night, however, his virtual earmuffs were being tested to an unaccustomed extreme. The squalid river of confessional talk shows oozed off the screen as usual, but for the past several

minutes the sludge had become both intellectually more respectable and harder for Tom to bear. The show in question, God
knew why, had temporarily forsaken interviewing neo-Nazi les-
bians who'd sold their grandmothers into white slavery in
Namibia and was instead inviting the audience to comment on
various film clips of the newly re-elected President of the United
States. That distinctive and detested drawl crawled into Tom's
consciousness despite his most desperate attempts to block it
out.

Tom Holder had been unable to bring himself to vote for any
man who had a bright, gutsy, attractive wife and who still couldn't
keep his pants zipped. On the other hand, Tom would die drunk
in a ditch before he would vote Republican, so he hadn't voted at
all. Not for President, anyway. And since all his life he'd poured
scorn on people who shirked that citizenly duty, he was now
stewing in a pot of custom-made guilt. The voice of the unfaith-
ful President now reminded Tom of his own defection from responsibility.

A few feet away on the sofa, as oblivious to the squirms of her
husband's conscience as she was to his very presence, Louise was
stretched out in an ancient orange bathrobe. She held the remote
control in one limp hand and a cigarette in the other; the ashtray
rested on her stomach. Tom had a fantasy, of which he was exceedingly ashamed, that one day she would fall asleep with a
cigarette and he would be summoned to the scene by the fire department to discover that he was a widower. In some versions of
the fantasy the whole house burned down, and he collected the
insurance and started a whole new life.

When the ring of the telephone interrupted the flow of soft,
Southern plausibilities from the man in the Oval Office, Tom

kept his nose pointed at his book and sat dead still, evincing no interest—another practice in his repertoire of survival skills. He had given up answering the phone years before. (Whenever he had gotten to it first, Louise had complained that he was trying to keep her from knowing what was going on.) Louise, without muting the television or taking her eyes from the screen, put the cigarette in her mouth and, with the hand thus freed, reached down to the floor where she kept the phone.

After a desultory hello from which all upward inflection had been scrupulously drained, she listened for a few moments, then extended the receiver vaguely in her husband's direction and announced, with the satisfaction of a pessimist who has been proved right, and in a voice clearly audible to the person on the other end of the line, "I knew it, they want you again, they have no respect for your privacy, do they, I don't know why you put up with it."

Tom took the phone without comment—he had also given up making comments years before—and said neutrally, "Yes?" After that he made listening noises for about a minute, then asked for an address, then said, "On my way. Meet me there," and hung up.

As he donned his coat, he answered a couple of Louise's non-questions ("I can't imagine what could be so important that a man would have to go out and work at this time of night, when you do this kind of thing I never know, do I, when you'll be home, it never said anywhere, did it, that you were going to be gone all the time") and ignored the rest. "Just business, dear. Missing person."

With that he was out, and closed the door behind him, welcoming the chill November rain as a companion preferable to the one he'd just left. He took a moment for the silent scream he allowed himself on these occasions, and then thanked God (with whom he talked regularly) for this escape. Whoever and wherever this Grace Kimbrough was, he blessed her and wished her well.

He remained in charity with her as he drove into the Kimbroughs' affluent neighborhood, peering through his windshield wipers at the big, comfortable-looking houses set well back from the streetlights in neatly landscaped yards. It had been years since Tom Holder had felt any envy of people with money—he had seen too many of them with their misery showing.

No, the people Tom envied were the ones who were happily married. According to his stringent standards, he hadn't met very many of them. When he did, he always wondered what it was that made the miracle; was it just luck that some people had made the right choice, when by all rights they should have been too young to know what they were doing? Or was it some special virtue in them, a quality he didn't have and couldn't understand? And if that was it, could that virtue be acquired? He had tried prayer. God, had he ever tried prayer.

His kindly feelings toward Grace Kimbrough suffered a setback when he and Sergeant Rossi were ushered into the Kimbroughs' living room. It was, Tom thought ungrammatically, the awfullest room he'd ever seen. No, he corrected himself, the awfullest *expensive* room he'd ever seen. A sofa of some extravagant style he couldn't name was upholstered in different shades of gold stripes and littered with fake-tiger-skin cushions. The black background of the wallpaper was scarcely visible for the profusion of mustard-yellow flowers on it. The carpet was patterned like a leopard, but here and there were clearings in the spots occupied by large pink roses. Where the coffee table should have been there was instead something like a giant round footstool covered in wine-colored satin with gold tassels. The curtains were an abstract nightmare of copper and black, and were literally too much; they fell lavishly from brass curtain rods, hit the floor, and frothed into piles of extra fabric on the carpet. The overall impression was one of barbaric extravagance; Tom thought that Attila the Hun would have loved it.

Rossi seated himself gingerly on a small black-lacquered chair just inside the entrance to the room, as though unwilling to commit himself further. His boss, a man of stouter heart, crossed to a large gold-velvet chair with ball-and-claw feet, parked himself on it as if perfectly accustomed to such surroundings, and decided he didn't care too much for the missing lady after all. But some of his preliminary questions elicited the information that George Kimbrough was an interior decorator, and no, his wife did not assist him, she had no talent at all in that direction; in fact, she couldn't produce a room like this (Mr. Kimbrough indicated their surroundings) if her life depended upon it. This immediately brought Grace back up in Tom Holder's esteem; indeed the irreverent thought came to him that maybe she had run away to escape her own living room.

Fifteen minutes' conversation with George Kimbrough, however, was enough to convince Tom that it was the decorator, not the decor, that had prompted Grace Kimbrough to flee. He reckoned he had discovered a kindred soul and fellow sufferer in her, and thought, *More power to you, dear, I only wish I had your guts.* He was also thinking, had been thinking ever since the phone call, that heaven had handed him his wish: an interesting crime. So it wasn't really a crime, maybe it was even better as a topic of conversation. Nothing violent, just a nice upper-middle-class housewife who had decided to make a run for it. He hoped they wouldn't find her too soon.

It appeared that in the two and a half hours that had passed since George Kimbrough had gotten home, he had been busily doing all the correct and sensible things.

"Well, first I looked all over for a note in case she'd left one," George had said to the two policemen sitting in his living room. Or more precisely, he had said to Holder; he ignored Sergeant Rossi. "I looked in all the possible places she might have left it, and then I looked in some impossible places. Trust me, there is no note."

"Yes, Mr. Kimbrough," said Holder pacifically. "And then what did you do?"

"I called next door. My cousin lives there with her husband. Name of Stanley. My wife and my cousin are good friends, hell, we're all good friends, so much running back and forth between here and there, you'd think it was one family." George managed a shrug and a pinched smile.

Holder's placid expression betrayed no clue, but his attention sharpened: hostility there. Kimbrough was being polite, but he'd had too much to drink—who could blame him, under the circumstances?—and he was losing a fraction of control over his less civilized emotions. Rossi, who was used to being ignored, was more or less returning the favor—which was why he was still a sergeant—and heard nothing in George's statement except the words.

"So I figured Grace might be there, but she wasn't. No one was, they weren't home. I should say, Bill wasn't home. Carolyn—my cousin, that is—left for California earlier today. So of course she wasn't there. Anyway, Bill wasn't home. It wasn't likely Grace'd be visiting anywhere else around here; we don't have a lot to do with the other neighbors; there was only one other place in the neighborhood where she might have been, and that's really too far to walk, but I called them anyway."

"Why would she have to walk?"

"I thought I told you, her car's in the shop."

"Mmm. Are you sure about that? Because it would make a lot of difference, whether she had a car or not."

"Of course it would, and that's why I'm telling you she didn't have one, and yes, I'm sure. We took it to the garage first thing this morning, and they said it wouldn't be ready till Wednesday."

There was a faint but—to Holder—unmistakable air of "I told you so" about this speech, mingled with a bit of "My God, the people I have to deal with." Tom's vague dislike of George Kimbrough began to be less vague, not least because he guessed that in the company of people whose opinions he valued, George would pass for charming because he would take pains to be so.

Gradually, with patience in the asking and impatience in the answering, they established that George had called the likeliest people, the less likely, the completely unlikely, the hospital, the Stanleys again without success, and finally the police.

"Yes, sir, that sounds very thorough. Does your wife ever call a taxi to pick her up when her car's in the shop?"

"Sure, if she has anywhere to go. I thought of calling the taxi companies, but I figured they wouldn't tell me if they'd picked her up."

"Well, I imagine they'll tell me," Holder said, "if I ask nice."

Rossi shot the Chief a quick look. It wasn't like Holder to wise off when talking to citizens.

George, always quick to take offense, took it. But before he could figure out exactly why the remark was offensive, the cop was talking again.

"Your next-door neighbors, Stanley, did you say? Is it unusual for them to be out of the house at this time on a Monday evening?"

"I'd say it was unusual for them to be out this late on any weeknight. Carolyn's a demon for getting to bed early."

"But Carolyn—Mrs. Stanley, I should say—she's gone to California?"

"That's right. San Francisco. On a buying trip for my firm, Elton Kimbrough Interiors. She'll be gone for a week."

"Have I got your name wrong, Mr. Kimbrough? They told me George."

"No, that's right. Elton was my uncle, he left the firm to me. And to Carolyn."

"Oh, I see. I was saying, would it be usual for Mr. Stanley to be out this late on his own, with his wife out of town?"

"Christ, I don't know, does it matter?"

"Maybe not. What about suitcases?"

"Suitcases?" George repeated as if he'd never heard the word.

"Well, since you've been so thorough," Tom said sweetly, "I thought you might have checked to see if any of her suitcases are gone."

George flung out his hands, as if beseeching God to grant him the patience he had no real desire for, and said, "Why the hell should she take a suitcase? She wasn't going anywhere!"

"Well, we don't know that, do we?" asked Tom with gentle malice.

Frostily George responded, "I know my wife, and I know what she would do and what she wouldn't do, and I can assure you, mister, that she did not pack a suitcase and leave town without telling me. She wouldn't do it."

Tom, obscurely pleased to have exposed Kimbrough's simmering hostility, uncharacteristically went on to expose more of it. "They might not necessarily have left town," he suggested.

"They?" George repeated blankly.

"Whoever she went with."

Rossi turned to stare at the Chief in astonishment. Holder himself was amazed at what he heard himself doing; he didn't think he had ever deliberately tried to alienate a witness.

He had certainly succeeded. All pretense of courtesy gone, George Kimbrough leaned forward in his chair and shook his finger furiously at his tormentor. "I'm not going to sit here and listen to nasty insinuations about my wife! I'll have you reported to your superior officer!"

Tom realized he was enjoying himself. "Two things, Mr. Kimbrough," he said with unruffled calm. "One, I'm not making nasty insinuations, I'm just a cop doing his job, and that means considering all the possibilities. Two, I *am* the superior officer. If you want to report me, you'll have to do it to the mayor. Now, why don't you just show me where Mrs. Kimbrough keeps her suitcases, and prove to me you're right? That's if you think you can tell if any of them are missing."

Later Holder would wonder what on earth had made him so cocksure Grace Kimbrough had run away from her husband; he had absolutely nothing to support that assumption except his own rapidly formed opinion that George Kimbrough was a husband well worth running away from. Later still he would recognize that what had prompted him to jump to this conclusion was the phenomenon psychologists call projection: He had "projected" onto Grace Kimbrough his own marital misery. And that, of course, was why he had baited George; he was punishing the man on Grace's behalf.

"I can tell you exactly how many suitcases she has," George was saying belligerently, "and I can tell you with absolute certainty if any of them are missing." At this point he was out of his chair and heading for the stairs, Holder hard on his heels, Rossi plodding along behind. "I gave her a new set of luggage for her birthday, seven bags, the whole damn set, every kind they made in that style; small, medium, large, carry-on, collapsible, dress bag, even a train case, for Christ's sake, and who uses train cases anymore?" By this time they were in the upstairs hallway. "There," George said, flinging open the door of a walk-in closet. "Count 'em."

Holder counted them: seven brand-new brown tweed bags with leather straps. His heart sank. He had really, badly, wanted this woman to be a runaway from a dreadful marriage. His quick sympathy for her, he now discovered to his dismay, had progressed to affection.

Doggedly, he tried to find a loophole in the conclusion that was drawing itself in his mind. "She might have taken one of her old ones."

"Gave them to Goodwill," proclaimed George with the air of one preening himself.

"She might have taken one of yours."

George rolled his eyes heavenward and then directed Holder's attention to the other side of the closet, where there was a matched set of five black leather bags.

"All there," Holder said without sufficient optimism even to make it a question.

"All there," George crooned.

"You realize, don't you, Mr. Kimbrough," said Tom grimly, "that if one or two of these bags was missing, then we could almost have assumed that your wife hadn't come to any harm, because we'd know that she left of her own free will."

George stared at him, and in that instant Holder saw him wonder if his wife was all right. But only for that instant. Then Kimbrough once again assumed the air of one who is inconsiderately used by others due to no fault of his own. "Of course she left of her own free will," he snapped. "She just didn't pack a suitcase to do it, that's all." Then suddenly it seemed as if Kimbrough, having endured all the pressure he could, suddenly broke. He burst out in furious bewilderment, not at Holder but at the world in general, "Where the goddamn hell *is* she?"

"Mr. Kimbrough," said Tom with a sigh, "we'll do our best to find out."

CHAPTER 6

As the Chief of Police put the machinery of investigation into motion, he refrained from informing George Kimbrough that Grace would not be considered officially missing until she'd been gone considerably longer than eight hours. If George got the idea he was getting special treatment, he might feel mollified. Tom preferred to leave him mad as a hornet.

Holder had phoned the station and set one of the junior officers onto the cab companies. He left Rossi to extract from George the names of all the people he'd called when looking for Grace; they would have to be called again. After all, it was quite possible that a friend of Grace's might have conspired with her to keep George ignorant of her whereabouts. The friend might lie to George but tell the truth once the police were involved. That was assuming Grace had run away, of course, which Holder no longer believed. As rapidly as he had formed the opinion that Grace had left her husband simply because her husband was eminently leavable, he had abandoned it. He had looked at all that beautiful new luggage sitting there untouched, and he had thought, *She's dead.* And the thought had filled him with aching melancholy.

This situation was something new to Tom. Not that he didn't regularly form impossible attachments. But the women he fell in love with—about one a year—were always "impossible" simply because they were married (as, of course, was he). But this one, he told himself with scathing contempt, this one wasn't just married, she was dead. *Way to go, Holder,* he thought. *Don't you think your fantasy life is getting a bit out of hand?*

That fantasy life was his chief survival mechanism, and he knew it. He had always been careful about it, always kept to the rules that made it safe: only women at church, never women at work (so as not to get distracted). Only women who were roughly in his league in terms of age and general attractiveness. Only women who were securely married. And never, never, never let the woman suspect that anything improper was going on in his mind. Well, he was keeping that last rule, at least, as far as Grace Kimbrough was concerned.

But he needed to get hold of himself and stop romanticizing her. She was not his kindred soul inspiring him with the nerve to break out of an unhappy marriage. For all he knew, she might even love that S.O.B. she was married to, even if he was so stuck on himself that his first and last reaction to his wife's disappearance was to be mad at her for putting him to all this inconvenience. Women loved the damnedest men. And if she was dead, well, then, she was a homicide victim and he should get along with his job without getting all maudlin about it.

He needed to ask around to find out when she had last been

seen. The neighbors on one side, the Stanleys, or at least the male Stanley, would have to wait, but it was after ten-thirty and the guy had to come home sometime. Unless, of course, he had run away with Grace! Hey, now, that was a thought. Despite himself, Tom felt a little spurt of hope.

He stood for a moment on the Kimbroughs' front porch, appreciating the night. He loved the dark. (In fact, he loved it because it is the place where the imagination is most free, but he didn't know that.) It had stopped raining, and the weather seemed a bit milder now that it wasn't hitting his face in drops. He took in a lungful of cool, damp air and looked around.

The Kimbroughs had a corner lot; their driveway ran onto the side street, and a streetlamp stood where the roads met. It illuminated the asphalt, wet and empty, but not much light filtered through into people's front yards because there were too many trees and shrubs. The deciduous trees, of course, were bare, but there were multitudes of evergreens. The houses were nestled in layers of dark vegetation, separated from one another by high, thick hedges. Even if Grace Kimbrough had disappeared in daylight, it was going to be difficult to find anyone who had actually seen anything.

On his right, across the side street, lived the Heseltines, Franklin and Mabel. Inquiries there revealed that they had been gone for most of the day and glued to the tube for most of the evening, and they were sorry, but they hadn't seen Grace Kimbrough recently. Similar tidings greeted him at the Forrester residence directly across the street from the Kimbroughs. It was at the house next door to the Forresters, directly across the street from the Stanleys, that Tom got the first break.

He had taken one of the uniforms, Roscoe "Rocko" Pursley,

along with him, so that people would be less skittish about opening their doors to a strange man at this hour of the night. But it was he who did the talking, of course, and it was therefore he who caught the brunt of the attention of Gloria Simmons.

She opened the door so promptly upon his ring that he suspected she must have been watching their approach, yet she affected surprise. The po-*leece?* Why, what*ever* could be the matter? She was wrapped in a lilac satin robe that might have been more becoming to her when her hair was its natural color and her breasts were at their original height. She was at the age that the writer of *Auntie Mame* once described as being "somewhere between forty and death," and any fool could see she wasn't going to go gentle into that good night. She offered Holder a handshake that was meant to be feminine but struck him as unpleasantly limp, and presented him with her name as though it were a personal gift.

She insisted they come in and sit down, which they did, in a room full of faded femininity and stale cigarette smoke. Ashtrays, all of them dirty and most of them full, cluttered every one of the little tables that flanked the sofas and chairs. Everything that was upholstered was pink. The lady of the house draped herself with elaborate sensuality across a white and gold liquor cabinet and simpered about not offering them drinks because she just *knew* they were on duty, weren't they? And what on earth could she do to, ah, assist them? At the word *assist*, she had aimed a look at Holder that somehow gave to that innocuous verb a heretofore unappreciated sexual connotation. Holder sighed internally. This was going to be tedious.

She was well named, he thought. She was a Gloria kind of person. Which made sense, he supposed. Presumably the mother who named her had also reared her to be this way. He tore his attention away from these ruminations and told her why they were there.

She bestowed on him what was obviously supposed to be a worldly smile. "Well, it just so happens I *can* help you with that," she said.

"Yes, ma'am?" Holder replied in his flattest voice.

With immense satisfaction she cooed, "I saw her this afternoon."

"What time was that, ma'am?"

"Oh, *dear,* I just *knew* you were going to ask me that, and *isn't* it silly? It's slipped my mind."

Oh God, she was going to make him wring it out of her bit by bit. "Well then, ma'am, could you say approximately what time it might have been?"

Gloria gave him a hurt look, lit a cigarette, and sucked the first lungful of smoke out of it. "Well, I'm *sure* I could remember, if you could just be *patient* with me." The hurt look gave way to a quavering smile that was intended to convey something along the lines of "poor little me."

Holder considered a moment. "Tell you what, Ms. Simmons—" He broke off as though dissatisfied with what he'd said, and then produced a tiny, conspiratorial smile. "Or may I . . ." He hesitated. "May I call you Gloria?"

"Why, certainly, Officer," she purred, unwittingly reducing Harton's Police Chief to the status of flatfoot.

Holder turned his smile up to match the magnitude of hers and continued. "Let's pretend it's a game, like on one of those game shows on TV. Let's pretend I know the answer, and if you can guess it correctly, you get dinner for two at Leboeuf's with the, ah, gentleman of your choice." This last phrase was said with such significance that Pursley regarded his Chief with awe.

It worked.

"That sounds *very* nice. I think I'm going to *like* this game."

"All right, then, Gloria Simmons"—Holder manufactured a twinkle, put it in his eye, and leaned forward in his chair—"are you ready for the question?"

"I'm *ready*," she assured him, also leaning forward, and exhaling smoke in Tom's face.

With difficulty he stopped himself from recoiling and asked, "At what time did you see Grace Kimbrough this afternoon?"

She puckered her face in concentration, then smiled in triumph and announced, "Just after lunch!"

"Very good, Gloria Simmons!" Tom was grateful that the part called for a broad smile at this point, because he certainly could not have done this any longer with a straight face. "And what time is just after lunch?"

Gloria closed her eyes and drew languorously on her cigarette in a manner she clearly fancied seductive. After a pause so pregnant it was a wonder water didn't break, her eyes reopened and focused on him like rifle sights in mascara. "I looked at my *watch*," she uttered. "It was *exactly* seven minutes after one."

"Fan*tas*tic!" Tom shouted. "Gloria, that was the right answer! And now for the grand prize—"

"What's the grand prize?"

Holder looked her in the eye and said deliberately and with great meaning, "Anything you want."

"Oh, *good*!"

"*Where* did you see Grace Kimbrough, what was she doing, and what did she say?"

"Well, she didn't *say* anything, I just *saw* her."

"And where was she?"

"Coming out of *her* house and going into the house just across from here, which belongs to the *Stanleys*."

"She went into the Stanleys' house?" Tom had unintentionally fallen out of character and back into Efficient Policeman.

Gloria pouted a bit at Holder's desertion, and sought to recapture his manly attention by being useful. "Well, she's *always* going into their house, you know, just *constantly*, I mean a person can't help *noticing* a thing like that, and drawing her own *conclusions*." Being useful seemed to work, for there was no denying that the policeman was glad to hear this.

"Oh, Gloria," he breathed, "you don't *know* how helpful this is." A strangled sound emanated from Pursley, and Holder, under the guise of uncrossing and recrossing his legs, managed to kick Pursley quite painfully on the ankle.

Gloria was gushing, "Oh, I'm so *glad* I can be *helpful* to you. I mean, of course I wouldn't say anything to anybody else, because I'm just *not* a person who *gossips*, that's just not the way I *am*, but I mean *you* have to *know* these things, don't you? Because you're the *police*."

Holder assured her earnestly, and even honestly, that this was an attitude he didn't always meet, and he was glad to have found a citizen so willing to share her knowledge. After that his compliments became less honest but no less effective, as Gloria worked her way through two cigarettes and her meager store of knowledge. As facts go, it was nothing to write home about; she was convinced that Grace Kimbrough and Bill Stanley had been "carrying *on*," but of course she could offer no proof for her convictions; it was just obvious from "the way they *were* together." Did she see them frequently? Not really, not very often, but it had been going on for *years* and *everybody* knew, of course, except the spouses, who were always the *last* to find out these things, weren't they? And it was a *complete* mystery to Gloria why the thing had started in the first place, because *why* Grace could be interested in such a dumpy little man as Bill Stanley when she was married to a *fabulous* man, really, *so* handsome *and* charming, Gloria just didn't know.

As far as Grace's movements on that day were concerned, Gloria had seen her come out her own front door, cross her yard to the Stanleys' house, and, Gloria was pretty sure, let herself in with a key. Unless the door was unlocked. Anyway, Grace had certainly not rung the bell and waited to be let in. She had just walked right up and gone in. This had happened just after one o'clock, *exactly* at one-oh-seven. Had Bill Stanley been there at the time? Gloria couldn't say, really, although she could make a good *guess*. How about Mrs. Stanley? Gloria couldn't say that either, and on that question no guesses were forthcoming.

It wasn't much, but it was highly suggestive. Of course, what it was suggesting was precisely the thing Tom Holder wanted very badly to believe: Grace had bolted with her lover, who was the guy next door, whose wife was conveniently out of the way on a plane to California. Of course there were some serious problems with that theory. To consider those problems, Holder needed to extricate Pursley and himself from the web of Gloria Simmons, and he did so, not without difficulty.

She made her last play at the front door, laying an insinuating hand on the sleeve of his coat, saying, "You're a *very* distinguished-looking *man*, you know; *nobody* would *ever* guess you were a *police*man."

It was clear that she meant this as a compliment, which confirmed Holder's opinion of her intelligence—or lack thereof. He couldn't stand stupid women. A brief vision of Kathryn Koerney flickered across his mind.

As Gloria's front door closed behind them, Holder and Pursley went back down the walk, Holder murmuring gently to Pursley, "If you ever, and I mean EVER, tell any of that to ANYbody, I will personally bust your ass so bad, you'll be singing soprano in the nearest church choir."

Pursley laughed out loud. "But, sir, it was great, I couldn't believe it when you—"

He broke off as they simultaneously stopped dead at the curb. In front of them, across the street at the Stanley residence, a light had come on in one of the downstairs rooms.

CHAPTER 7

Bill Stanley had needed thirty seconds' worth of light to locate a bottle of gin, and then he had switched the light off again. Originally, he had let the house grow dark because there had been no particular reason to turn on any lights; all he was doing was sitting on the stairs. But after a while the dark had seemed natural to him. Not comfortable; nothing would ever be comfortable again. But it seemed somehow fitting to be in the dark.

Finally, however, cold and inactivity combined to bring his bodily discomfort to a level where he noticed it. Painfully he unfolded himself and stood. He tried to stretch, and found his limbs were full of cramps. Also he was cold. A blanket, maybe? No. Something to drink.

He moved stiffly down the stairs, still in the dark, and made his awkward way first into the dining room and then to the sideboard, which was used as a liquor cabinet. Here he had discovered he needed the light, but it hurt his eyes, and he turned it off again as soon as he had what he was looking for. Now he needed a glass, but the glasses were in the kitchen.

He didn't want to go into the kitchen. It was clean now; the blood was all gone, but still, as he approached the open doorway his steps slowed, then stopped. He stood for a moment and considered the problem.

Why didn't he just drink out of the bottle? He could do that. Yes, there wasn't any reason why he shouldn't drink straight out of the bottle. After all, it was a bit late for being civilized, wasn't it?

The doorbell might have been a bomb, the way he jumped. In the wake of the sound, he hunched against the nearest wall, his arms crossed over his chest in a vain attempt to subdue the pounding of his heart. The gin bottle, which he still gripped in his right hand, was pressed by his left arm so hard against his ribs that it would have been painful if his mind had not been too occupied to notice. He braced himself for the second ring, so there was no reason it should have made his heart contract again, but it did. But now all he had to do was wait. Whoever it was would go away, thinking there was nobody home. He forgot that he had just turned a light on and off again.

Out on the front porch Tom Holder was losing patience. "What do you think, Pursley? Is there somebody home here or not?"

Pursley said dubiously, "Maybe it was one of those timer things people get to turn their lights on when they're gone."

"So why did the light go out again?"

"Lightbulb burned out?"

"Could be, but I'm not convinced." Holder pounded on the door with his fist. "Come on, man, open up!"

From the house there was nothing but dark and silence.

Tom thought for a minute. "I have an idea. Come on." With Pursley behind him, he descended the steps and set off across the wet grass and through a break in the hedge, back to the Kimbrough house. There the door was opened by George Kimbrough, who looked every bit as irritated as he had been when Holder had seen him an hour earlier.

"I'm sorry to bother you again, Mr. Kimbrough, but do you have a key to that house over there?"

"Yes, but why do you want it?"

"We're getting worried about your neighbor not coming home," Holder lied. "We'd like to take a look around."

"I thought you were supposed to be looking for my wife."

"Yes, sir, we are. We were thinking, what if Mrs. Kimbrough went over there this afternoon and fell or something and hit her head? She could be lying in there unconscious, and if we wait for Mr. Stanley to get home, well, who knows when that'll be?"

From Kimbrough's face it would have been obvious to an idiot what he thought of this idea, but he did not immediately refuse Holder's request. He considered it, then, as if humoring a four-year-old, dug into his pocket and produced a ring of keys. "This is the one you want. No, on second thought, I'd better go with you. I wouldn't want them to think I was letting a bunch of strangers loose in their house." He stepped out onto the porch, pulling the door closed behind him. "Your man's in my kitchen, monopolizing my phone," he announced as if he were scoring a point against Holder.

Sergeant Rossi was probably talking to the station, getting an update on the results of the phone calls to friends and taxi companies. "You have call-waiting, I assume?" Tom inquired mildly.

"Of course," Kimbrough snapped. "Doesn't everyone?"

"Well then, at least we know that if your wife calls, she'll be able to get through."

"Not if there's already somebody on the call-waiting. She'll get a busy signal." Again, as if scoring a point.

Holder had an equable answer for this, but didn't need it because they had arrived at the Stanleys' front door.

Bill Stanley, meanwhile, had gotten as far as the foot of the stairs on his way back to his perch, and consequently was only a few feet away from the front door when George Kimbrough put his key in the lock. The doorbell had been a threat, and Bill had been terrified by it. But this—someone actually coming into the house—was a disaster of such magnitude that he wasn't even frightened. He was simply paralyzed.

George opened the door, saying, as he switched on the hall light, "I don't mind you looking around, but please don't touch— aah!" This last was a cry of alarm as he literally walked right into Bill, who stood, swaying slightly, in the middle of the hall, squinting in the sudden brightness and looking exceedingly blank.

"Jesus Christ, Bill!" Kimbrough exploded. "What are you doing in here in the dark? Scared me to death!"

Bill made no reply, but looked past George to the unknown man behind him. Then he saw the uniformed policeman.

Tom Holder cast a swift glance at Stanley, stepped around Kimbrough to get to him, and took his elbow in a sustaining grasp. "Mr. Stanley? Sorry to bother you, but Mr. Kimbrough here has a bit of a problem, and we hope you can help us with it. I'm the Chief of Police."

Holder's grip on his arm was not enough. Stanley instantly turned the color of putty and the gin bottle slid from his slack grasp. He fell heavily against George, who caught him with an ill grace and angry exclamations.

"Ease him down to the floor," commanded Holder. They did so, Holder nearly losing his balance by stepping on the bottle Stanley had dropped onto the carpet. When they had laid him on his back, Holder told Pursley to elevate his feet; Pursley, finding no convenient object of the right size, squatted on the floor, thrust his hands under Stanley's ankles, and lifted them to a height of about eighteen inches.

"Water," Holder said succinctly to Kimbrough. George stared at him stupidly. "Water," Tom repeated. "You know: kitchen, glass, water. For your friend here."

George turned on his heel and stalked down the hall toward the back of the house.

Holder leaned over to get a whiff of Bill Stanley's breath, then began softly slapping his face and saying meaningless encouragements to him: "There you go, come on now, wake up, you're O.K."

When George got back with the glass of water, Stanley was just sitting up; Holder took the water and held the glass to the man's blue lips. "Here, have a sip. Make you feel better."

Stanley obediently sipped. His gaze was confused, but he seemed to recognize Kimbrough. "George," he said.

George responded, "Uh, yes. You all right, Billy? Have you got the flu or something?"

Stanley slowly gathered his wits. "That's right," he said finally. "Got the flu. Sorry about all this. Very embarrassing. Here, let me get up."

He insisted on staggering to his feet, but permitted the two policemen to take his elbows and walk him into the living room. Tom was intensely interested in Bill Stanley, and took time for only a fleeting glance around the room. That was enough to tell him that he liked Carolyn Stanley's taste better than George Kimbrough's; the room was a beautiful blend of soft colors. It wasn't until he looked around for a place to sit that he discovered it was all rather gently intimidating, its pastel perfection so clearly unsuited to harsh feet and heavy hands that he was afraid to touch anything.

They had deposited Bill in an armchair, and George had turned on a couple of lamps. "Billy," George complained, sinking gracefully onto the sofa, "what the hell were you doing here all by yourself in the dark?"

Bill Stanley was discovering that it was indeed true what the old proverb said about necessity and invention. "Came home from work," he said, "not feeling well. Must have fallen asleep on the couch."

If it weren't for the gin bottle, Holder would have believed him. The guy looked genuinely sick. "Listen, Mr. Stanley," he said, gingerly seating himself on a delicate straight-backed chair, "I'm sorry you're not feeling well, but we have a problem on our hands that won't wait. Have you seen Mrs. Kimbrough today?"

Had he seen Mrs. Kimbrough today. That was rich. "No," Bill said.

"We think she may have come into this house in the early afternoon." Stanley said nothing. Holder tried again: "She didn't meet you here?"

"No."

"What time did you come home from work?"

Stanley rubbed his eyes and thought for a minute. He shook his head. "Early. Can't remember what time."

"Mr. Stanley, I know you're not well, and I really hate to bother you, but this is very important. Mrs. Kimbrough appears to be missing."

"Grace? Missing?"

"Yes, Grace!" exclaimed George indignantly. "Blast her, anyway. I've tried everywhere; nobody knows where she is. I was hoping you'd know."

Bill shook his head again. "I'm sorry. I have no idea where Grace is."

It was well done, Holder thought. It was almost convincing. "I understand from Mr. Kimbrough here that your wife left this afternoon to go to California."

There was a pause, then Stanley nodded.

"Did you drive her to the airport?"

"No, she always dr—she always drives herse—" The final syllable was virtually inaudible; Stanley seemed to freeze for a moment, and his face, already pale, went positively white.

"She always drives herself?" Holder asked, wondering what on earth had triggered that reaction.

"Yes," Stanley answered weakly, then more firmly: "Yes."

"Something upset you, Mr. Stanley?"

"No, uh, no, I'm just, uh, not feeling well."

Holder chewed his lip, trying to think of a way to break through Stanley's really very effective defenses, but failed to come up with anything he could do without breaking the law. He shrugged mentally and went on. "What time did your wife leave for the airport, Mr. Stanley?"

"Uh, let me think. George? You'd know that better than I would."

"The last time I saw Carolyn," George said promptly, "was at lunch. Then she left for the airport, and I left for New York to meet with some of our importers."

Holder asked, "Was she going to drive straight to the airport?"

George shrugged. "I suppose so."

"She had her luggage with her already? I mean, in her car, so she wouldn't have to come home to get it?"

"I didn't think of that," George admitted. "I don't know."

"Mr. Stanley?" Holder asked. "Do you think she took her bags with her to lunch? Or came back here?"

"I really have no idea. And I can't understand," he groused, "what difference it makes. To where Grace is, I mean."

"Mr. Stanley, sir, I'm just trying to figure out if maybe your wife came back here before she drove to the airport, because if she did, she might have seen Mrs. Kimbrough when she was here, and Mrs. Kimbrough might have told Mrs. Stanley something about where she was going or what she was doing today."

"Oh. I see. Well, I'm sorry, I still can't help you."

"Might I suggest," George said cuttingly, "that if you want to find out if Carolyn saw Grace today, the simplest thing to do would be to ask her? She's probably there by now; why don't we just get on the telephone and call her?"

Holder looked at Stanley. "O.K. by me. Mr. Stanley?"

"Uh, sure. I've got the number somewhere."

"Don't bother, Billy, I've got it." George pulled a tiny leather book out of his breast pocket and leafed through it. "You there," he said to Pursley, who had been standing inconspicuously off to one side. "Bring me that phone."

Pursley was agreeable to a fault, but his eyes narrowed for a second. Then he fetched the phone from its table and walked it over, trailing the cord carefully behind him, to the table at Kimbrough's elbow. There he deposited it without ceremony or comment and returned to his prior place.

George gave Pursley a scarcely audible "Thanks" without looking at him, and punched eleven digits on the phone. "She always stays at the Mark Hopkins," he said complacently to no one in particular as he waited for the hotel to answer.

"Hello? Could I please speak to Mrs. William Stanley, I'm afraid I don't know her room number." There was a short silence. "Really?" said George, his eyebrows rising. He looked at his watch. "I'm calling from New Jersey. What time is it there? That's what I thought. Well, she ought to be checking in any minute now, and could you please leave a message, it's very important. Tell her to call—one moment, please—shall I have her call here, Billy?" Stanley sketched a gesture of indifference. "Have her call home, please. Right away. Yes. Thank you very—"

Tom Holder was standing in front of him with a hand extended. "May I?" he said with a courtesy ever so slightly exaggerated.

Kimbrough said into the phone, "Please forgive me, I've been interrupted," and handed the receiver to Holder.

Holder identified himself, said it was an emergency, asked for the manager, and agreed to settle for the night manager.

"Good evening," said an efficient voice in Holder's ear. "This is Stephanie Wilkoff. May I help you?"

Holder identified himself again, and Ms. Wilkoff—rather apprehensively, Holder thought—expressed the hope that there was no trouble having to do with the hotel.

Holder set her mind at rest by describing the situation briefly, and asked if there was a way to guarantee absolutely that Carolyn Stanley would get a message to call home the instant she arrived at the hotel.

"Certainly," replied Ms. Wilkoff, whose relief was audible. "I will tell the reception clerk to keep an eye out for her, and I'll do that immediately. She'll get that message as soon as she checks in. And to make absolutely sure, I can put a note on her entry in the computer, that's if she made a reservation."

Holder said, "Mr. Stanley, did your wife make a reservation?"

Stanley started to reply, but Kimbrough interrupted with "*Weeks* in advance."

Holder relayed this information, and Ms. Wilkoff asked him to wait just a moment. After very much more than a moment, she came back on the line.

"I'm sorry to keep you waiting so long," she said, "but she wasn't in Reservations, so we looked in a few other places. Are we talking about a Mrs. William Stanley, with an address on Austen Road, Harton?"

"That's her."

"Well, I'm really sorry to tell you this, but I don't think we're going to be able to help you. I believe Mrs. Stanley must have changed her plans; the reservation was made in October, but it was canceled this morning."

"Canceled?"

"Yes, we got a phone call this morning." There followed a silence so long that Ms. Wilkoff said, "Hello? Are you still there?"

Holder shook himself, apologized, said all the polite things, hung up, and returned to his chair.

"Do you mean to tell me," said George, "that Carolyn canceled her reservation at the Mark Hopkins?" He made it sound as though it were Holder's fault.

"Looks that way to me. Mr. Stanley, did your wife say anything to you about where she was staying?"

"Uh, no. As George says, she always stays at the Mark—"

"She should have told *me* if she was going to stay somewhere else," sputtered George, outraged. "How in the hell am I supposed to be able to find her if I don't know where she's staying?"

"Good question," Holder replied unexpectedly. "You don't know where she's staying, Mr. Stanley here doesn't know, either. Is there anybody who does?"

Thus challenged, Kimbrough produced: "Patricia Clyde. My secretary." He pulled the little address book out of his pocket again, consulted it, picked up the phone, and tapped out the number.

"Patricia, my dear—" But once again Holder was standing over him with hand stretched out. "There's a gentleman here," said George with the faintest trace of emphasis on the word *gentleman*, "who would like to talk to you. Please be as helpful as you can." He handed the phone to Holder.

"Ms. Clyde, my name is Holder, I'm the Chief of Police. I'm here with Mr. Kimbrough because his wife appears to be missing. We're at—"

"Missing? Grace Kimbrough?" It was evident from the voice that Patricia Clyde had been asleep and was striving to wake up.

"That's right. We're at Mrs. Stanley's house, Mr. Stanley's here, too, and we're trying to find out where Mrs. Stanley is staying in San Francisco. We need to ask her if she's seen Mrs. Kimbrough today."

There was a three-second pause before Ms. Clyde said, "I'm sorry, I can't help you."

It was not merely curt, it was guarded. Holder asked carefully, "What do you mean by that, ma'am, you can't help us?"

"I mean exactly what I said. I don't know where Mrs. Stanley is staying."

"You're aware that she canceled her reservation at the Mark Hopkins?"

"Yes."

"Mmm. That's interesting; you know, Mr. Stanley and Mr. Kimbrough both, they didn't know anything about it."

To this Ms. Clyde said nothing. *God, talk about pulling teeth,* Holder thought. He soldiered on. "How did you get to know about it?"

"Mrs. Stanley asked me to cancel it."

"*You* canceled it?"

"Yes."

"You made the phone call to California?"

"Yes."

"And that was this morning?"

"No. Early afternoon."

"And when," said Holder with the persistence of water dripping on stone, "had Mrs. Stanley asked you to do this?"

"At the same time."

"Oh, you mean she asked you and you did it immediately."

"Yes."

"But she didn't tell you to make other reservations for her somewhere else?"

"No."

"Was she still intending to go to San Francisco?"

"Yes."

Holder swore mentally but kept at it. Eventually he gathered that Carolyn Stanley had come back to the office after lunch and before she went to the airport; she had asked Patricia Clyde to call the Mark Hopkins and cancel her reservation, said she hadn't decided where she would stay, and promised to let Ms. Clyde know when she arrived there. It took him five minutes to get that, and he wasn't even sure if it was true. It was clear that Ms. Clyde regarded him as the enemy.

"So she hasn't called yet?" he asked.

"No," said Ms. Clyde, and then, surprisingly voluble, added, "She wouldn't call tonight because she knows I go to bed early." There was an unmistakable edge to her voice.

Holder kept his irritation hidden. He said politely, "Well, I'm sorry we had to bother you. When you hear from her, let us know, would you? As soon as possible?"

"Yes," said Ms. Clyde, lapsing back into the monosyllabic.

And that was the last useful thing Tom Holder heard on Monday night.

CHAPTER 8

i

There was no one in line at the reception desk. Was it an odd hour to be checking into a hotel? Would she be conspicuous? She told herself not to be paranoid. No one in the elegant lobby could see the clouds of guilt, the nightmare visions that clung to her.

She had done very little thinking on the long flight west; so little had gone through her mind, in fact, that the destination arrived as a surprise. One of the effects of shock, she supposed. But one thing she had decided, and that was to go to the Mark Hopkins despite the cancellation. She would just tell them she'd changed her mind. No, better: She'd pretend to know nothing about it, insist they'd made a mistake. Insist they give her a room anyway. She stepped up to the desk and opened her handbag to take out the folder from the travel agent.

"Good evening, ma'am," said the desk clerk with a smile.

"Good evening," she replied, although she was unable to

summon a smile in return. She extracted from the folder a typed confirmation of the reservation and handed it to the man behind the desk.

"Thank you," he said pleasantly, and tapped a few keys on his computer. After a few seconds he stared at the screen in some puzzlement. He tapped some more keys and waited, still looking puzzled. "This is funny," he said.

"What?"

"Well, it looks like there's been a little mix-up here. The computer says this reservation was canceled."

"Canceled? There must be some mistake."

"Yes, there must be," he agreed lightly. "But never mind, it's no problem." He glanced again at the confirmation slip, tapped at his keyboard once more, and consulted a rank of keys behind him. "Here we are," he said, plucking one like a ripe fruit. "This is a nice room, has a wonderful view of the city. Would you like this on your credit card, Mrs. Stanley?"

"Yes, please," she said, opening a slim folder of white snakeskin and extracting a gold American Express card.

The clerk ran the card through his machine and handed it back to her, lifting his other hand to signal a bellhop. "Thank you, Mrs. Stanley. Enjoy your stay with us."

"Thank you," she replied automatically, and followed the bellhop up to the room with the wonderful view of the city, which she failed to notice. The bellhop had watched her at the reception desk, and being wise beyond his years, did not attempt any chatty remarks.

Once in the room, she actually remembered that bellhops expect to be tipped, so she tipped him, and thanked him, and he left. She stood motionless in the center of the room. She realized suddenly that she had no idea what to do next. Up until then it had all been fairly straightforward; the path, so to speak, had been marked. But now what?

She stood for several minutes, until she noticed she was standing. Then she sat down in a chair by the window. She turned her face toward the glass because it seemed like the thing to do, but she did not bother to focus her eyes on the impressive sea of fog-blurred lights below her.

She had always thought of herself as a good person. Not a saint, of course. Definitely not a saint! But she had always thought her sins had been minor, forgivable. Like most people, she believed in God but had never done much about it; God was a presence somewhere in the background of life, vaguely in charge of right and wrong. She had always felt that he did not disapprove of her too seriously. The unhappiness she had known in her life had been her own stupid fault; it would never have occurred to her to consider it as some sort of punishment from above.

But now that things had gone so horribly, disastrously wrong, divine punishment began to look like a real possibility. Not that she was afraid of going to hell, it wasn't that. The punishment wasn't coming in the future, it was happening now. The disaster itself was the punishment. It was as though God had been sly, luring her into thinking her little sins were negligible in the great scheme of things, then without warning stunning her with consequences so dire that she could not bear to think of herself as having contributed to them. God seemed suddenly sneaky, and mean. Always before, a distant but benign presence. Now an enemy. A shattering transformation.

Bill, too, had undergone a shattering transformation. He, too, had been a benign presence—though hardly distant. She had thought of herself as a good person, but she had always thought of Bill as a better one. So kind. So true. She had trusted him absolutely. She had been wrong.

Beneath the shock, beneath the unbearable guilt, another emotion had been growing in her so imperceptibly that she was only then becoming aware of it. Anger. She was angry at him. How could he have done this thing? How could he have done this to the love they had shared? How could he have committed this appalling betrayal? More than anything else, she discovered, she was angry at him for deceiving her about the kind of man he was. Had he not deceived her so badly, none of this would have happened. Had she known what he was really like, she could have stopped it all before it had begun. She remembered kneeling by the body in the kitchen, staring at his hands. There had been no trace of red on them, but now in her emotional memory she saw them covered with blood.

She had put a vast distance between herself and him, which is what she had intended to do when she caught the plane. Now she realized with dismay that it wasn't enough. He was still with her. Covered all in blood, he was part of her, inside her. His presence occupied her like a hostile army, filling her, too, with blood. She felt contaminated, defiled. She couldn't stand the thought of him. She couldn't stand the thought of herself.

She stood up, left the room, and went looking for the hotel bar.

ii

The service had started normally enough. The Rector was rushing the congregation, as he always did, through the Nicene Creed, but people were getting more and more behind and it was getting pretty messy. Kathryn was trying to strike a compromise, but more people were coming up from the sacristy to the altar and things were getting out of control. Some of them were people from that afternoon's festival committee meeting, and they were still carrying on, with scrupulous politeness, the squabbles they'd had in the meeting. There didn't seem to be a congregation at all at this point; everyone was up by the altar and they were all priests. Kathryn found herself listening to Miss Amalie and Carson Strothers, who were once again failing, at great length, to communicate. She began to lose her temper, and was just choosing the words she would use to let them both know what self-important buffoons they were, when the Rector caught her by the arm and tugged her back to reprimand her. They argued heatedly, while Tom Holder (also vested as a priest) kept intervening, whether to arbitrate or to keep score, Kathryn wasn't sure. By this time it was Tom, not the Rector, who was gripping her arm, and he was urging her to sit down in one of the choir pews. The pew was deeply cushioned, and the hymnal racks were full of large, beautiful volumes of Chaucer. She took one of these out and opened it, but instead of the expected medieval handwriting that she could have read easily, the manuscript was written in a seventeenth-century script she could not make out at all. She asked Tom Holder to help her, and handed the book to him. He began to read *The Canterbury Tales* to her, at first from the book, and then the book was no longer there but he was still quoting Chaucer, and she was sinking into the cushions. Her vestments had come open, and she was wearing only her underwear. Then she felt the buckle of his belt bite into the soft flesh of her abdomen, and she realized he was on top of her.

Now she was in familiar territory. Now she knew what was happening, what was going to happen. She explained, as she always did, that this would have to be a matter of holding and being held, no more, but when she finished the explanation she found that he was kissing her breasts. This was exciting to her and for a moment she thought she would let him make love to her. Then she remembered he was married, and she began, as she always did, to protest that they shouldn't be doing this. But all the while she was letting him kiss her breasts, and move his pelvis rhythmically against hers, and she felt the orgasm coming. It came, and as always, it almost waked her for a moment; for an instant she was alone in her own bed, then the dream pulled her back again. Now he was trying to enter her, and she began to fight him, crying that they couldn't, they shouldn't, he was married, it was wrong. Finally she broke free of him and ran—out of his living room, out of his house, across his yard. And now here were the roses. She ran into the thorny branches, battling to get through them; they dragged at her as they always did, they tore her skin, and then some of the branches became his hands, pulling at her, tearing at her, until finally from her silent throat she produced a real cry, and awoke.

Shit, she thought. *What did I do to deserve that?* She was accustomed to thinking of the dream as a sort of punishment, as she always dreamed it when she had permitted herself to become attracted to a man to whom she had no business being attracted.

And it was that man, the one who was making her feel guilty, who usually appeared in the dream. Unless it was *the* man, the original man, the one in that dreadful encounter that was the original source of the dream. But to the best of her knowledge, she wasn't particularly interested in anybody just now. She most certainly wasn't interested in Tom Holder. The Rector had also been in the dream, of course, and she did think the Rector a very agreeable man with a sharp wit and a gorgeous profile. If he had been the man she had almost made love to, the dream would perhaps be understandable.

But the star spot had been occupied by Tom Holder, and Kathryn thought Tom Holder was about as sexy as Donald Duck. It wasn't so much that he was middle-aged as that he was middle-aged gone to seed; overweight and balding and shabbily dressed, he looked like a man who had given up on himself as a sexual animal twenty years ago. Well, given the woman he was married to, perhaps that wasn't to be wondered at.

But the point was that Kathryn wasn't attracted to Tom. So she hadn't done anything to deserve the dream. Like a child wrongfully punished, she felt a burst of righteous resentment toward the erring authority figure. This aggravation, mingled with the sour emotional aftertaste of fear, provoked a wordless grumble in the general direction of the Deity as she rolled over and burrowed deeper into her pillow. The prayer was wordless because if she'd been forced to articulate it, it would have come perilously close to "I don't know what the hell you think you're doing," and even for Kathryn that would have been a bit egregious.

Kathryn bestirred herself just enough to rise up on one elbow and take a sip of water from the glass on the bedside table. The dimly illuminated dial of her alarm clock told her it was just a few minutes past one. Plenty of time left to get a decent night's sleep. *But don't* DO *that to me,* she prayed angrily, *when I haven't done anything to provoke it!*

iii

The conventioneers, after the manner of their kind, had taken over the bar. Clusters of men with name tags on their lapels shouted shop at one another and vied for the attention of a scattering of name-tagged females. Explosions of laughter became more frequent, and the hunt expanded to the other unescorted women in the bar. The last lingering traces of the day's business having been washed away with the second round, preparations were being made, with the third, for the business of the night. Women who were not interested beat a strategic retreat; women who were began the delicate process of conveying that information to the men of their choice.

There remained at a corner table one woman alone, oblivious alike to the retreat of her fastidious sisters and to the surrender of the more willing; oblivious, even, to the seemingly unignorable clamor that filled the room.

She was no longer young, but it was not for that reason that she remained unapproached by any of the conventioneers. She would be called beautiful at sixty; at forty-six she could stir the blood of any man past adolescence. Among the roisterers at the other tables there would be, from time to time, the nudge of a manly elbow and the lift of a knowing brow, a sideways glance and a murmur of appreciation. But not the most intoxicated man in the room ventured into her impregnable solitude.

Her armor was neither scorn nor indifference, but something harder and colder than either. One of the conventioneers, more sensitive or less drunk than his fellows, was struck by a sudden fancy. *It's grief,* he thought. One does not, however, confess to one's drinking buddies that one is lapsing into psychology; he shook off the thought and turned his attention to the man from Ohio, who was recounting the peculiar history of the call girl and the left-handed bus driver.

The woman finished her third drink and seemed to decide it was enough. She signaled the waitress, signed the check that was presented to her, and rose somewhat unsteadily to her feet. Bar drinks were stronger than the occasional drinks she had at home, and she never had three. Very carefully, she walked out of the din of the bar into the more subdued noises of the hotel lobby. The night, she knew, would be dank and uninviting; she decided to go for a walk.

The doorman's offer to call a taxi was refused with the automatic courtesy that clings to some people under any circumstances whatsoever. (It is said that Marie Antoinette, stepping up to the guillotine, accidentally trod on the headsman's toe, and murmured, "Pardon me.") From his post at the curb the doorman watched the woman as she walked slowly away from the hotel, and wondered whether her husband had left her, or she had left him.

The city was submerged in an all-enveloping fog. The street-lamps were soft, subaqueous moons in the moist gray air; lighted windows shone from invisible buildings, rectangles of diffuse light floating in the darkness. Headlights of cars swam past her with the sibilant sound of tires on wet streets.

For some reason she was glad of the damp, the chill, the featureless sky. If it had been a lovely evening—crisp air, shining stars—she would not have been able to endure it. As it was, she had walked into the shrouded dark as if it were a friend. A quotation stirred in her memory, something about being one with the night. A cliché, of course. Bill would know.

The sudden recollection of Bill as a lover of literature—not a violent stranger—struck her with a pain so fierce that she actually staggered. Or was it just the alcohol? What a fool she was! Had she really thought that scotch would do it? Would wash him away? Would drive him out of her?

In all of this she was in her own world, oblivious to the small stir of activity in her wake.

Her sympathetic observer, the conventioneer who had sensed that the cold wall around her was grief, had seen her leave the bar, and in a spurt of unaccustomed madness had followed her out into the lobby. He saw her walk toward the entrance and go out. He cudgeled his brain, ducked back into the bar for a minute, and emerged with a borrowed cigarette lighter.

Out at the curb he looked around for her, certain that he could catch up with her. It did not even occur to him that she might have taken a taxi, because her whole attitude bespoke a person who has nowhere to go and nothing to do. Sure enough, there she was; she had gone only about thirty yards. "Excuse me," he called, sprinting after her. "Hello, ma'am?" He had to get almost within arm's reach of her before she seemed to discover that the shouts were addressed to her. She turned and looked at him inquiringly, saying nothing. *Christ, he thought, doesn't she talk?* He made much of pretending to huff and puff a bit, as if trying to catch his breath before speaking. "I don't usually do a quick run after two vodka tonics," he said, laughing. "I'm sorry to yell at you like that, but I thought you'd probably forgive me. You dropped this in the lobby." Confidently, he held out to her a slender gold Cartier lighter.

She took it from him, peering at it in the darkness. "No, I'm sorry," she said, giving it back to him. "It's not mine."

He was incredulous. "Not yours? But I could have sworn— Are you positive?"

"Quite," she replied flatly. "I don't own one. I don't smoke."

"Oh," he said, apparently crestfallen. "I could have sworn— Well, I guess I'd better turn it in to somebody."

As if aware that she had sounded ungracious, she added, "But thank you for, well, for the thought. It was kind of you to come after me."

"Oh, no problem. I was coming out for a walk anyway. The bar was getting pretty unbearable, all that smoke." He smiled. "I don't smoke, either," he said, trying to make it sound like a bond between them. And then, when she did not respond to him in any way, he asked desperately, "Do you mind if I walk with you?"

She did mind, of course, but being more experienced in courtesy than in honesty, she was incapable of telling him so. After a few moments when no inspiration came to her, she said, "If you like," and turned to resume her slow pace. "I must tell you, however, that I'm not very good company right now."

"I don't mind."

They walked for a while in a silence that was, he judged optimistically, not wholly uncomfortable. He had come this far, and was pleased, but he had yet to win a smile from her. He realized that he had an insane desire to make her laugh. Not as any sort of credit to himself; he wanted only to break open the shell of misery around her and let her out into the free air.

"My name's Mike," he ventured. "Mike Slattery."

They walked a few steps in silence, then she started to say something at the same time that he said, "It's O.K. You don't have to tell me."

She shook her head slightly. "I don't mind. Carolyn Stanley."

He stopped and held out his hand. "Glad to meet you, Carolyn."

She took his hand, gathered courage from somewhere, and said, "Thank you, Mike."

For a moment she looked directly at him, and the naked despair in her eyes struck him like a physical blow, so that he gave a little gasp.

"Are you all right?" she asked.

His facade broke. "Ca—Carolyn," he stammered, "please don't be angry. I know it's none of my business, and you don't have to tell me, you don't have to tell me anything"—he had gathered her hand in both of his and held it firmly—"but whatever it is, I want to help. Please let me help, don't say I can't. Please—"

It was the kindness that undid her. She had held herself together, had she but known it, buttressed by the indifference of the strangers around her. Instantly her defenses crumbled, her breath caught in her throat, and she began to sob, great, racking sobs that shook her whole body.

When he held out his arms to her, it was an instinctive reaction. No thought of seduction entered his head: He wanted only to soothe her grief, to take the hurt away.

She, too, moved as if by instinct; seeing his open arms, she stepped into them, laid her head upon his shoulder, and wept uncontrollably.

He held her close, patting her as one would a crying child, wondering what to say. Some deep wisdom told him that "Don't cry" would be an asinine thing to say to anyone in such pain. So he said, "Cry all you want to. All you need to. It's O.K."

Finally, the sobs abated, and she stood quiet in his arms for a few moments. Then she lifted her head from his shoulder and said unromantically, "I'm afraid I need a tissue."

"Oh. I don't think I—"

"It's all right, I think I have some in my bag." She stepped back and opened her handbag.

He let her go, without regret. He had not been holding her for his own pleasure but for her comfort, and if she no longer wanted or needed to be held, then that must mean she was feeling a little better. Or stronger.

"I'm terribly sorry," she was saying in obvious embarrassment, as she dabbed at her eyes with an embroidered handkerchief and then blew her nose in it. "I don't normally burst into tears all over total strangers."

"But we're not strangers. We've been introduced."

"So we have."

She began walking again, slower even than before. In order to have time to get acquainted? *You dreamer,* he thought. Still, there was a chance. After a while he offered, "I'm from Cleveland. Here for a convention on computers in insurance."

They walked on in silence.

"Was that the wrong thing to say?" he asked finally.

She was thinking. Perhaps he really could help. The necessity of making conversation would occupy her mind. But it had to be conversation that didn't carry her back to what she had run away from. She laid a hand on his sleeve and they stopped. "Could we—could we make an agreement? Let's not—" She searched for a way to say it. "Let's not do all that information people always do, the same old stuff about where are you from, and what do you do, and all that. Let's make a deal to just—" Again she searched for the right words. "To just do trivia."

"Trivia?"

"Yes, I mean things like, oh, who's your favorite singer, that kind of thing."

"O.K.," he said agreeably. "I think I can handle that. Pavarotti. Who's yours?"

"I like opera, too." She sniffed, recovering from the tears, but determined not to lapse back into them. "But I think I'd have to say that Domingo is my favorite. He's a much better actor." This being a commonplace observation among music lovers, she produced it without the effort of self-examination. But to continue the conversation along these lines would be unwise. A topic like opera could all too easily get into emotions. So she said, "Next question. Your turn."

"O.K. Hmmm, let's see. What's the best movie you— No, what's the worst movie, the very worst movie you ever suffered through?"

The corners of her mouth tightened in the veriest ghost of a smile, and he felt a disproportionate surge of triumph.

"That's a good one," she acknowledged. "Let's see, what was that awful thing with Dudley Moore and Liza—oh, I know, *Arthur 2*. Never trust a sequel."

"Yeah, *Arthur 2* was a real dog. But I think the worst I've ever suffered through—" He paused a moment, and then continued: "Come to think of it, when I think of movies I've suffered through, I think of the good ones."

"You suffer through good ones?"

"Yeah, sometimes. I suffered like mad all the way through *The Godfather.* I kept thinking, this is a brilliant movie and I can't wait for it to be over."

"Why?"

"You'll probably think I'm a real wimp, but I couldn't stand the violence. Since when is it supposed to be entertaining to see some guy get shot in the eye? Carolyn?" For she had come to an abrupt halt.

Not realizing she was doing it, she held a trembling hand out to him. He took it and held it in both of his. She started to walk again. He kept her hand, tucking it into the crook of his arm, and she didn't seem to mind. She said as evenly as she could, "I agree with you. Absolutely. I can't even stand violence that's supposed to be funny."

"When I was a kid, all my friends loved the Three Stooges. But I got really tired of watching those guys hitting each other."

"Oh, yes. I have never understood why people hitting each other was funny. I couldn't stand Laurel and Hardy, either."

"The fat one was always bullying the skinny one."

He was doing nothing but telling the truth, but it was working, he knew, better than any line he could have invented. She was beginning to become just the slightest bit animated. Almost as if she were beginning to enjoy herself, at least just a little. It might work. He might be able to break through the grief after all. He pursued his advantage. "I guess I didn't like that because I was skinny myself when I was a kid."

At some point in the ensuing discussion of cruelty in comedy, they turned their steps back toward the hotel. She could have said "Let's go back," or "I'm getting chilly" or a dozen other things, but there was no need. He could have said "Would you like to come up to my room for a nightcap?" but again, there was no need. The talk about the unattractiveness of violence got them through the lobby and onto the elevator without either of them having to say anything about where they were going or what they were going to do next.

In the elevator the conversation died, but that was all right because there were other people there. At his floor he gestured as if to say *Ladies first*, and she stepped out of the elevator without any visible hesitation. He led her a short way down the hall, stopped by a door, opened it with his key, and again gestured for her to precede him, all without either of them saying a word or meeting the other's eye.

He was holding his breath. Once in the room, surely he would have to say something? No, even then the magic held. He helped her out of her coat and dropped it over a chair. She immediately turned and came right into his arms, just as she had done out on the street, only this time she was not crying.

Even as he kissed her, however, his conscience stirred. She was so vulnerable; he was taking advantage of her. He pulled gently away from her kiss, took her face in both his hands, and whispered, "Are you sure you're not going to regret this?"

She looked at him. "No," she answered quietly. "I couldn't possibly regret anything more than I'm already— Never mind. Anyway, I haven't got any regret left, I've used it all up."

"You're sure?"

It was almost with a trace of impatience that she said, "You don't want to, do you?"

"Not want to? Oh, God!" He gave a shaky laugh. "Oh, God, yes, I want to!" And then, striving for a lighter tone: "But will you still respect me in the morning?"

She laughed. She actually laughed.

He was exultant. He had done it, he had made her laugh. It was what he had wanted all along, but he could not have told her that. She wouldn't have believed him, she would have thought it a line, a ploy to get her—

Where he had her now. In his arms, pressing against his growing hardness. Allowing him to stroke the silk of her blouse over her breasts. Lifting her hands to pull the pins from her dusky hair. Coming to him, giving herself to him, an unlooked-for miracle. It was the reward for his good intentions. He had wanted more than anything else to lighten her sorrow, to take it from her, and he had; and now he took from her the silken blouse, and released the lace brassiere, and touched a softness finer than the silk. It was not just desire, no, not just desire, but breathless gratitude that filled him, that swelled in him as he lost himself in her, as his senses swam in her fragrance, in the glorious perfume of her.

And she also, feeling the body's urgency, lost herself in it, and for the first time since her world had ended in blood on a white tile floor, forgot the blood, forgot the body of the woman who had been her friend, forgot the dreadful sight of him standing in the doorway, forgot everything that had followed her relentlessly across the miles, forgot the fearful images in her mind, forgot, forgot.

iv

It was the deep of the night. It should have been completely tranquil. The noises, the furtive movements, fell like stains on the serenity and ruined it. One sleeper, pulled from her bed by the sweat of a breaking fever, heard and watched. She took in every terrible moment of it, until at last it was finished, and the noises pulled slowly away into the dark.

Julia Robinson was sleeping soundly. Then gradually, she became aware of small, icy hands shaking her shoulder, and an unintelligible babbling that became, as she struggled up from sleep, the voice of her ten-year-old daughter, demanding that she call the police.

v

She lay quietly in his arms, and he was content. She murmured something.

"Hmmm?" he asked.

"I said, I just remembered."

"Remembered what?"

"The lighter, that little gold lighter you tried to give me. You forgot to turn it in at the desk."

"Oh, yes, the lighter."

"Some woman is going to be frantic."

He chuckled. "No, I told her I'd give it back to her tomorrow."

Thinking she had not heard him correctly, she turned her head to look at him and asked, "What?"

He kissed her on her perfect nose. "I probably shouldn't tell you this, but I borrowed it from a friend of mine in the bar. I had to have *some* excuse to start talking to you." He was so sure she would laugh, share the joke with him, that when he got no response from her he assumed she had not understood him. "I saw you in the bar, down at the end by yourself. I thought you were the most beautiful woman I had ever seen in my life." He could have added *and the saddest*, but he was afraid that if he mentioned the sadness, it would come flooding back. "So I said to myself, How can I meet that gorgeous woman?" He did not add *and take away her pain.*

"I see," she said neutrally, and turned her face away.

He had blundered. "I'm sorry," he said softly into her hair. "I thought you would think it was funny."

She did not say anything.

"Carolyn? Are you angry at me?"

After a pause she said, "No, I'm not angry at you."

It was true. Her anger was at herself. She had been a pickup, a common, vulgar pickup. She had thought—God, how could she have been so stupid?—she had thought he was a gift from heaven, a little miracle from a God who was not, after all, her tormentor, but who knew how bitterly she felt her guilt, and had given her a way to purge herself of the man who was in fact her tormentor. What better way to erase a man from your body and your soul than to let another man take his place? A charming man who disliked violence even on a movie screen. An honest man, making an honest mistake, trying to return an expensive toy to its proper owner. But there had been no miracle, and no mistake. Wrong! *Her* mistake.

"I'm so sorry," he said.

She turned her face back to him long enough to plant a swift kiss on the corner of his mouth. "Don't worry," she said, snuggling deeper into the sheets and making no move to free herself from his embrace. "I think I'm just tired. My body clock thinks it's three A.M., you know. I'll probably think it's funny in the morning."

And so they slept.

But in the morning she was gone.

CHAPTER 9

Twenty-two hours. Grace Kimbrough had been gone for twenty-two hours, they had been on it for about nine hours, and they were nowhere. She was dead. She had to be. It was stupid to waste time hoping she wasn't.

Tom Holder had wished, the previous afternoon, for an interesting crime; the recollection of that wish now filled him with a guilt he knew to be unreasonable. No desire of his, expressed or unexpressed, had caused her death. So why did he feel so bad about it?

Because of Kathryn, answered a voice in his head. He was not immediately sure what that meant. Then suddenly he saw what a fool he'd been. For the better part of a year he had actually allowed himself to believe that his attraction to Kathryn was light and insignificant, that all he ever wanted was the satisfaction of knowing she returned just a fraction of his interest. He didn't want her for a lover, after all. Surely his reaction to her was normal and permissible, thwarted only by Louise's unreasonable jealousy.

But now he saw clearly for the first time how far over the line into his fantasy life his feelings had strayed. She didn't fit the profile for his regular make-believe lovers, so he had been able to pretend to himself that he didn't seriously want her. But he did. Oh, shit, he did. And that was where his guilt was coming from.

He escaped from this unhappy revelation by dragging his mind back to the matter at hand. Grace Kimbrough. She was dead and it was his job to do something about it.

He thought he had a pretty good idea of who killed her, but he had not one bit of evidence. Worse: He could not even establish that there had been a murder. They needed to find the body, obviously, and until they did, he was more or less stuck.

There was a faint possibility that a forensic search of the Kimbroughs' house might yield something useful, but George Kimbrough's response to a mild suggestion that the police "take a look around" had been uncivil bordering on violent. His compliance could be forced only with a search warrant and there was no evidence to persuade a judge to issue one. Besides, Holder didn't believe that Grace could have been violently done to death in that over-decorated residence without George's noticing something out of order when he got home. The removal of her body would have left one of the gold tassels crooked, or something.

With a sigh, Tom shuffled through the unhelpful results that were coming in from the routine inquiries. Although he was personally convinced that he wasn't dealing with a runaway— runaways generally take suitcases—he was still obliged to check out the possibility that Grace had left the neighborhood under her own steam. As her husband had said, she hadn't driven away in her own car; Reilly's Garage had verified that Mrs. Kimbrough's green Volvo had been on their premises all day Monday—and was, in fact, still there. Nor had she taken a local taxi. Both the local cab companies had had pickups within a few blocks of the Kimbrough house on Monday, but they had all been checked out and none of them was Grace Kimbrough.

Checking the buses would be harder, of course, as you had to count on the memory of drivers who had dealt with hundreds of people that day. That was a bush that Holder didn't want to spend a lot of time beating; bus service was scanty through Canterbury Park, and he could not picture the wealthy—all right, moderately wealthy—Mrs. Kimbrough leaving home by walking half a mile to the bus stop, with or without a suitcase. He had dispatched a couple of underlings to make inquiries at the terminal, but he knew they wouldn't get anywhere.

What he needed was something, anything, that would get him a search warrant for the Stanley house. It wasn't enough that the guy fainted on sight of the police. Correction: It was enough for Holder, who had been there and seen it, but it wouldn't be enough for a judge.

So where was he? He had the victim at the scene, thanks to Glamorous Gloria. The next step was to get the suspect there.

By his own admission, Bill Stanley had come home from work early, though he had steadfastly refused to remember the time he had done so. Clearly, then, what came next was to check out the place where he worked.

At this point Tom had a little talk with himself. He was running on four hours of sleep and he was seriously tired. If someone else drove him, he would have ten or fifteen minutes to concentrate on unclenching all the muscles that had been gradually tightening since the moment when he had seen Grace's luggage the previous night. On the other hand, if he drove himself, he would have ten or fifteen minutes on his own.

That thought made the decision for him. At work, he was almost constantly dealing with other people; at home, Louise's querulous voice stalked him from room to room until he hated the rooms themselves, the very house they comprised. Any threat of fatigue was utterly outweighed by the promise of ten blissful minutes of privacy. So he drove himself.

Once outside the station parking lot, he was in the small and incredibly congested downtown area. He was not much bothered by heavy traffic; he had learned years earlier that if you allowed the traffic to get to you, you only wound up twice as stressed. So when you got caught in a long line of cars going slowly nowhere, you took several deep breaths and studied your surroundings.

It was a drizzly day. Light rain fell, then stopped, then fell again. In spite of the weather, the old stone buildings around Peller Square managed to look as dignified and self-satisfied as they always did. The Orange Inn was no fake-antique watering hole, it was circa seventeen hundred and something, and it always pleased Holder to look at it. Those responsible for its restoration and modernization had possessed historical sensitivity, impeccable taste, and a great deal of money. Every time Tom saw it, he thought how satisfying it was to look at the work of people who knew what they were doing.

The line of cars he was a part of had inched its way past the back corner of the square and suddenly encountered the suburbs. The cars in front of him seemed to melt away in all directions, and in a couple of minutes Holder was cruising along at a comfortable twenty-five miles per hour.

Rackman-Stanley Real Estate was in a small shopping center with parking barely a step from the door. Inside, the office had that indefinable but unmistakable look of having been Done (capital D) by a Decorator (capital D), but not, thank God, by a Decorator with Something to Prove. The deep pile carpet was dark enough not to show every trace of mud, which was sensible in this climate, and it had a good pad under it. The walls were some forgettable color, and hung with large watercolors of sumptuous if botanically inaccurate flowers. The effect was more humane than George Kimbrough's house and more approachable than the Stanleys'.

The reception area was presided over by a damp-looking girl flaunting conspicuous symptoms of a bad cold. Her appearance was made all the more unprepossessing by a mane of sandy-blond hair that looked to Holder like it hadn't been combed in a week. He knew that messy hair was supposed to be fashionable these days, but he had not gotten used to it and he didn't plan to. Being put off by the hair, he further decided that the girl's bronze eye shadow was hardly suitable for the office, besides emphasizing unattractively the watery state of her eyes, and her fingernails were a positively revolting shade of brown. She should spend some of her makeup money on getting that lopsided tooth fixed. And if she was all that sick, why didn't she just stay home? At that point he noticed he was being crabby (if only mentally) and immediately atoned for it by giving her his friendliest smile.

He got a small, brave smile in return, and a "May I help you?" that hinted at the sore throat the sufferer was nobly trying to disguise.

"Yes, please, I'm looking for Bill Stanley," said Holder, who was doing no such thing.

"Oh, I'm so sorry," the girl said, actually sounding sorry, "but Mr. Stanley won't be in today. He's home with the flu." This last was said mournfully, as though inviting Holder to see for himself what deplorable condition the firm was in.

"That's too bad," Holder lied, giving himself points for having this figured out in advance. He took one of the chairs in the small waiting area and settled into it with a comfortable sigh, as though glad to get a load off his feet.

Tom Holder's techniques were more sophisticated than his vocabulary. He could not have described his smile as guileless, but it was, and it got better results than slow torture. He told the girl his name, and looked at her inquiringly.

This tactic was hugely successful; not many people are interested in a receptionist's name. "I'm Vickie Baskin," she said, momentarily forgetting to suffer, and responding with a warmth she usually saved for men of approximately her own age.

"I'm Chief of Police," Holder remarked as if it were quite a commonplace thing to be, and pulled out his credentials with a silent prayer that her goodwill would not evaporate. It didn't, quite, but it was instantly diluted by surprise and the merest hint of caution. "About Mr. Stanley's next-door neighbor," he continued. "You know about that?"

"No, what?" Her ignorance seemed genuine.

"Well, the Stanleys live next door to some people named Kimbrough."

"Yes, I know, they're—" Here Vickie was interrupted by a fit of coughing, the tenor of which erased any lingering doubts Holder might have had about whether the girl was really ill. "Sorry," she rasped when she had gotten it under control.

"You should be home in bed," Tom said sympathetically.

"Yes," she croaked, "I know. I'll probably leave in a little while, I only came in just in case— Never mind. It isn't important." She waved it away, whatever it was, with the lacquered nails of one hand, while with the other she opened the desk drawer and extracted a box of cough drops. She shook one out, carefully unwrapped it, and laid it on her tongue as devoutly as if it were a Communion wafer. She then plucked a pale green tissue out of a box on the desk and dabbed ineffectually at her nose.

Holder resumed. "I was saying that the Stanleys live next door to the Kimbroughs, and you were saying you knew that."

"That's right," she said, nodding weakly. "The Kimbroughs are Mrs. Stanley's cousins. Well, I mean, he is. Mr. Kimbrough." It sounded like "Bister Kibbrough"; her nose was beginning to stop up.

"That's right. You know Mrs. Kimbrough?"

"I've bet her."

" 'Scuse me? Oh! You've met her." Holder noticed that under Vickie Baskin's long-suffering nose, her small mouth had tightened ever so slightly. "What'd you think of her?" he asked as though pleased to discover that she might help him out on this baffling topic.

This blunt inquiry was clearly unexpected, and for a moment she stammered. "I—uh, well, I dode really dough her like a fred, you dough, just—uh, I just bet her."

Tom hid a smile, and said with genuine concern and in his best Dutch-uncle tone, "Vickie, you poor thing, you really ought to go home."

"Oh, I'll be all right, but—could you excuse be for a biddit?"

As Tom said "Sure, no problem," she wavered to her feet, scooped up the entire box of tissues, dragged her handbag out from under the desk, and vanished down a narrow corridor. This gave Holder a chance to get a good look at her retreating legs, which, he was forced to admit, were not bad. In his youth he had admitted to being a leg man. That was before he had married a beautiful set of legs that were attached, as he later discovered, to the most depressing woman in the state. Belatedly he wondered if the stopped-up nose had been an excuse, and the girl had really retreated in order to figure out what to say—or not to say—about Grace Kimbrough.

Vickie reappeared six minutes later with a wan smile. "Well, that's better. At least I can talk without sounding like a joke."

"You sound fine. Ah, if you don't mind my asking"—*as if that would stop me,* he thought—"how did you happen to meet Mrs. Kimbrough?"

"It was at the Christmas party last year," she said as she resumed her seat at the desk. "You know, the company Christmas party. Bill's—I mean, Mrs. Stanley was out of town with her cousin on some business trip, so Mr. Stanley brought her instead. Mrs. Kimbrough, I mean." Vickie sniffed.

If she had pounded the desk and declared in ringing tones that she disapproved, she could not have made herself more clear. Holder was intrigued. Ms. Baskin did not have the look of a prude, so it seemed unlikely that her objection was on moral grounds.

"She's missing, you know." He said it in the manner of one who drops a pebble in a pond in order to observe the pattern of the ripples.

"Mrs. Kimbrough?"

"Mmm-hmm."

"*Missing?*"

"That's right. Since about one o'clock yesterday afternoon."

Vickie Baskin sat perfectly still for three full seconds. Then she said, "How terrible." It was so patently false that Holder for an instant wondered if she was even trying to sound sincere. He waited, hoping she would reveal something more either by word or expression, but she merely looked at him with watery eyes unfocused, forgetting even to look miserable. It was as though she had been switched off. Tom let the silence lengthen.

Finally she reanimated. "Sorry," she said with a noise that in a healthier respiratory system would have been a self-conscious laugh. "It's just such a surprise, you know. It's not—well, you *hear* about things like that, but you don't—" She waved her hands, as if they might waft her meaning over to Holder without the assistance of words.

"That sort of thing always happens to *other* people," Holder agreed with an understanding smile. Would she smile back?

She did. "That's exactly it! It happens to those people you see on the ten o'clock news, it doesn't happen to *real* people, like me."

There was enough shrewdness in this reply to make Holder decide that he had miscalculated Vickie Baskin's intelligence. *It's that damn hair,* he thought. *Any woman with hair like that ought to be a bimbo.*

As though realizing she had slipped out of her part, Vickie pulled another tissue out of the box and held it waveringly in the immediate vicinity of her face, as though to cope with any unexpected behavior on the part of her mouth or nose. She asked sadly, "How can I help you?"

Holder explained that they were trying to establish when Mrs. Kimbrough had last been seen, managing rather adroitly to suggest, without actually lying, that Bill Stanley had not yet been questioned about his movements on the previous afternoon.

It was pie. In fact, it was so easy that Holder began to be a little suspicious of it. Vickie readily answered his every question about Bill Stanley's comings and goings the previous day: Bill had left the office a few minutes after one, shortly after taking a brief phone call from his wife, saying he was on his way home and didn't want any calls there. Vickie spoke with absolute conviction about all these details, and even brought out the observation that it was extremely strange for a real estate agent (accustomed to working from home as well as office, and both in and out of regular business hours) to tell his receptionist to hold his calls. "It made me wonder," she said, looking Holder sapiently in the eye and taking time to create a significant pause, "if something was wrong."

Amazing, Holder thought. She was actually enjoying herself. The trace of caution with which she had greeted his identity as a policeman—Holder had judged it about average; most people greeted cops that way—was now nowhere in sight. He had told her about something very serious indeed, and instead of growing more cautious, she was blooming right under his nose, unfurling like a tawny morning glory in the sun.

When it was over, Holder found himself back in his car without any very clear idea of how he'd gotten there. It was obvious that Vickie Baskin had instantly assumed the worst about Grace Kimbrough. Wishful thinking? Pleased at the elimination of a rival? A rival in fantasy only, Holder judged; Vickie, when she spoke of Bill Stanley, did not have the air of possession with which a woman speaks of her lover. No, Ms. Baskin was one of those who love unrequited, happy only to serve in small ways. She knew exactly when Bill had left the office, because his comings and goings were of paramount importance to her. Holder felt sure that if he'd asked her what Stanley had been wearing yesterday, she could have obliged right down to the color of his socks.

Interesting that the girl had been jealous of Grace Kimbrough but not of Stanley's wife. She had spoken of Carolyn with warmth, making plain that Carolyn was the sort of nice person who took time to be polite to the receptionist.

What was interesting to Tom was that it confirmed the normality of a phenomenon he had noticed in himself more than once. When he was carrying on one of his make-believe love affairs—he would not think about Kathryn, he refused to think about Kathryn—he was violently jealous of any man to whom his paramour paid any attention—except her husband. For some reason the husbands never bothered him.

And the wife didn't bother Vickie Baskin. But the girlfriend! That was a different bucket of trout.

So he filed that as normal—any behavior that echoed his own was by definition normal—but there was something else he couldn't fathom. He was utterly certain that Vickie Baskin would lie through her crooked teeth to protect Bill Stanley. And he was equally certain she had not lied. A cop had come around asking her questions about the disappearance (and presumed death) of a woman who might have been, for all Vickie knew, Stanley's lover. And instead of shutting up like a clam, or getting suddenly vague, she had unhesitatingly given him an exact report of

Stanley's movements. She had made not the slightest attempt to defend his privacy against police inquiry.

"Why, why, why?" Holder asked his steering wheel. Receiving no answer, he sighed, started the car, and drove thoughtfully back to the station.

CHAPTER 10

Kathryn Koerney stepped out of the small rock-walled building in which her seminars were held, acknowledged the casual farewells of a couple of her students, and scrutinized the sky. It had the uninspiring appearance of leftover oatmeal. It was not, however, letting fall with anything at that moment, so she tucked her umbrella under her arm and set off down the sidewalk in the direction of Main Street.

It was a pleasant walk despite the unfriendly sky and the damp winter landscape. Harton was an exceptionally pretty town, particularly at its center; a charming shopping district bordered the campus of the university, and the seminary nestled in a residential area notable for magnificent trees and equally magnificent bank accounts.

Possessed of trees, bank accounts, and a tenure-track job at the seminary, Kathryn walked through her all-but-perfect world and felt profoundly grateful. A half-remembered verse from the Psalms flickered across her mind: something about the lot falling to one in a good ground. What was that wretched line? *Either of my little Baptists,* she thought with a sigh of envy, *could spout that verbatim—with chapter and verse.* Or did Baptists only memorize the *New* Testament? She would have to ask them at the next seminar.

Her mouth twitched in a suppressed smile; the comeback would be good, probably good enough to provoke a few inter-denominational catcalls from the one Episcopalian, two Congregationalists, and seven Presbyterians who made up the rest of the class. That particular seminar frequently turned into an ecumenical free-for-all, with the different denominations cheerfully attacking one another's absurdities with all the vigor of the Monty Python gang shouting "Your mother was a hamster" at one another. Kathryn deliberately conducted the seminar in a manner that encouraged this sort of debate, and every time they all dissolved into howls of laughter, she was once again convinced that there was hope for the Church Universal.

She walked past St. Margaret's Church, a fair imitation of Victorian Gothic, right down (or up) to the gargoyles on the bell tower. The parish wags maintained that the gargoyles, being Episcopalian, were glaring in the direction of the mostly Presbyterian seminary, and in point of fact they were right. Kathryn wondered if the architect had done it deliberately. The parishioners of St. Margaret's were sadly outnumbered; the town of Harton, like its seminary, had been dominated by the Presbyterians since the time of Cotton Mather. Now, *he* would have known that psalm!

She was walking past the churchyard gate she had entered the previous day on her way to the committee meeting. Glancing at it, she remembered the exchange she'd had with Tom Holder, and that, of course, made her remember the dream. She was accustomed to having that nightmare whenever she felt guilty about something in her sex life, but since her sex life at the present was, alas, virtually nonexistent, she was at a loss to explain why she had had the dream last night. It obviously had something to do with that written conversation she'd had with Tom. Well, then, starting with that: What had she been feeling?

She had felt . . . angry. Rebellious against the waste of her time. Frustrated by her boredom. Contemptuous of Carson and Miss Amalie. So she had concocted that jibe and shared it with whoever was handy, as a way of venting her anger. Was that it? Yes. She'd been angry. But how did that anger get transmuted into the sexual guilt that was surely the trigger for the dream?

Back to the drawing board. O.K., she had been angry, she had made up a pretty savage joke to express that anger, and then shared it with whoever— Hang on. Suzy Norton had been sitting on her left. Why had she passed the note to Tom and not to Suzy? As Kathryn was no self-deceiver, the answer to this question struck her almost at the moment she asked it. She had given the note to Tom because he was a man, and she liked him, and she wanted him to think she was witty. Not just that. A private joke is an intimate thing, be the intimacy ever so slight, and she had wanted to have that intimacy with Tom rather than with Suzy because Tom was a man.

He was a man, moreover (she continued ruthlessly), for whom she felt not the slightest sexual attraction, which meant that she had been—really, she was afraid she was going to have to call it flirting—she had been flirting with this man who was not very interesting to her, perfectly willing to make herself interesting to *him*. She had been, in short, collecting scalps. And she had succeeded, hadn't she? A very neat little compliment she had elicited from him, most gratifying to the ego.

Well, there was a certain satisfaction in knowing the answer to the question *Why the dream?* But the answer was hardly comforting. It all went back to an ego that seemed insatiable; it appeared that she could never get enough admiration from the opposite sex. She wondered if it had anything to do with her father. She decided to think about it later.

All this self-examination transpired in the course of one block, bringing her out onto Main Street close to the building that doubled as City Hall and Police Station. This edifice, despite being the only modern building within half a mile, was handsome enough, and managed not to jar the serenity of an area in which nothing else had been built in the last sixty years. She waited for the pedestrian crossing light (to do otherwise on Orange Street is suicide), crossed the street, turned right, and within a scant minute had arrived at the tastefully restored storefront occupied by Elton Kimbrough Interiors.

Stepping inside, she saw that the woman at the reception desk was on the phone. Kathryn smiled and lifted a hand in silent greeting before depositing her umbrella, handbag, and attaché case on the nearest chair.

The woman at the desk was explaining to the caller, with a courtesy so flawless it was really rather quelling, that Carolyn wouldn't be back until next week. Patricia Clyde warmed up perceptibly at the sight of Kathryn, however; she returned her smile, made an apologetic gesture at the telephone, and lifted a finger to indicate that she would be off it in one minute.

Ms. Koerney was not their wealthiest client (although if they rated customers in terms of dollars per year of age, Kathryn, at thirty-four, would have been close to the top of the list), but she was one of Patricia Clyde's favorites. She had won Ms. Clyde's undying affection by calling one day to ask when she could come in to see Carolyn when she could be assured of "not running into that loathsome man." As this description precisely tallied with Patricia's opinion of the firm's male partner, she had been deeply pleased. She had also been surprised. She had had a vague notion that members of the clergy said only nice things about people.

She had thereafter defrosted her formidable civility by a couple of degrees when dealing with Ms. Koerney, and had even, after a few weeks, yielded to Kathryn's repeated entreaties to call her by her first name. Kathryn remained modestly unaware of the magnitude of the conquest she had made, and assumed—incorrectly—that Patricia Clyde unbent to all the Kimbrough customers once she got to know them.

Having heard that Carolyn was not in, Kathryn knew that her errand would have to wait until another time, but she thought it would be rude to leave before Patricia got off the phone. She therefore studied the upholstery of an armchair near the window, on which sapphire dragons swam through roiling turquoise seas among random eruptions of coral like great anemones. She wondered if she dared put something like this in her library, and decided she probably didn't.

Patricia was off the phone. "I'm so sorry—"

"Yes, I heard you say she's not here. It's not urgent, I just thought I'd drop in. I really should have made an appointment."

"Would you like to come in next week?" Patricia asked, flipping the page of an appointment book.

"Yes, thanks. About this time again? It's about the chairs in the library, Carolyn was quite right, I should have—damn." This last was delivered *sotto voce*, and was prompted by the opening of the door to one of the inner offices.

For a moment George Kimbrough posed, framed by his doorway, inviting admiration of a custom-made suit, a hundred-dollar shirt, and an Italian silk tie. "*Doctor* Koerney!" he exulted, the facetiousness a dozen times more intimate than the use of her first name would have been.

"Hello," said Kathryn without even a pretense of enthusiasm. "I was just leaving, I came in only to make an appointment." She turned and moved to reclaim her things from the chair by the door, but not quickly enough.

George caught up with her and dropped an arm lightly across her shoulders. "I'm so sorry Carolyn wasn't here to meet you," he said, managing somehow to imply that it was both impolite and inefficient of Carolyn.

"It's of no consequence," Kathryn replied, lapsing into the archaic syntax that George Kimbrough for some reason always prompted in her. She bent to gather her belongings with an involuntary twitch of her shoulders that should have shaken off his arm. Not easily discouraged, he merely slid his hand to the back of her neck and kept it there as she straightened and turned toward the door. She thanked God that both a coat collar and a clerical collar were between his hand and her skin.

With his other hand he fingered the shoulder of her raincoat. "Ah," he said appreciatively, "there's nothing to beat a true Burberry, is there?"—letting her know that he could recognize one without a glimpse of the signature plaid of the lining, something

Kathryn couldn't do. She thought she would never be able to enjoy the coat again.

She escaped to the sidewalk before she actually started shuddering, but it had been a close call, and she strode down the street as though pursued by lice.

Halfway down the block somebody said, "Who are you so mad at?" and she realized that one of the approaching pedestrians had stopped in front of her. She looked up from the pavement and saw Tom Holder.

Her heart gave a little hop, which she diagnosed as embarrassment; at the same time her scowl broke into a spontaneous smile. "Oh, hello, Tom. Nobody. It's nothing. Wasn't that the ghastliest meeting you have ever had the misfortune to attend?"

"It wasn't that bad," Holder replied truthfully; in fact, their exchange of notes had been the high point of his week, but of course he wasn't about to say that.

"It was unspeakable," she contradicted, determined not to be too amiable. The tactic backfired; Tom laughed. *I've got to get away from him*, she thought.

I've got to start a conversation, he thought. It seemed too good to be true. He wanted an interesting crime to talk to Kathryn about, and first here came the crime, and then here came Kathryn. Perfect timing. If only he didn't blow it. He said, "I was on my way to talk to some people. I've got a missing person on my hands, and it's beginning to look bad."

"Oh, of course, you're working, aren't you? You can't stand around yattering about committee meetings. I won't keep you." She was already going. "See you in church," she said with a wave of her umbrella.

So sudden and so unexpected was the disappointment that Tom almost cried after her to stop, and was incapable of making any sensible reply. *Damn*, he thought, watching her hurry away.

He had one comfort: She had not gone off like that because she was not interested in his company. Her last speech had been an apology, and she had stepped back out of his path as if she had been intruding on him. She had been embarrassed. Amazing. What on earth for, he wondered. But at least embarrassment beat all hell out of indifference. He turned to resume his original course. Elton Kimbrough Interiors was supposed to be right about here. Ah, there it was.

His first impression when he walked in was of a beautiful woman with ivory skin and a faultless profile. When she turned from her computer screen to greet him, however, Holder thought her less attractive for some reason, and her cool "May I help you?" made him instantly long for Vickie Baskin. He knew that the polite skepticism of her greeting indicated that she had classified him—in a single, accurate glance—as a person of insufficient means to be a Kimbrough customer. Tom wondered if she thought he was a salesman, and decided not to waste any friendly overtures on her. He identified himself in a businesslike manner, allowing her a closer inspection of his badge and I.D. than Ms. Baskin had deemed necessary, and asked her if she was Patricia Clyde.

"Yes. We spoke on the phone last night." Her manner indicated that she was entirely too well bred to say "You woke me up last night."

"That's right," Holder replied amiably. "You said Mrs. Stanley was supposed to call you to let you know where she had decided to stay. Has she?"

Ms. Clyde looked at her watch, regarded Holder with what looked like a combination of pity and sarcasm, and informed him that it was seven thirty-eight A.M. in San Francisco.

"I thought she might have called later last night."

"As I *believe* I told you last night," uttered Ms. Clyde, icicles hanging from every word, "she knows I go to bed early." Holder paused a moment to get hold of his temper.

"All right, then, just let me know when she does call. Meanwhile, maybe you can tell me whether we're wasting our time trying to talk to her. What we want to know is whether she saw Grace Kimbrough yesterday afternoon."

At the mention of George's missing wife, some flicker of emotion crossed Ms. Clyde's careful face, but it was frozen over so quickly that Holder was unable to identify it.

"Yes, I understand that," she answered repressively, "but I can't help you."

"Well, can you at least tell me whether or not Mrs. Stanley went home after leaving here, before she went to the airport?"

"Yes."

Holder gritted his teeth. "Yes, you can tell me, or yes, she went home?"

"Yes, she went home," said Ms. Clyde, a schoolteacher explaining something simple to a dull-witted child.

"Wonderful. My heart sings. What time did she go home?"

Ms. Clyde was not amused. "She left here at twelve forty-five."

"You're very sure of that." Holder was openly skeptical.

Ms. Clyde's hackles rose ever so slightly, as he had intended they should, and she proceeded to demonstrate the accuracy of her information. "She was worried about the time. She looked at her watch as she was going out the door, and said she was running late, she should have been on her way at twelve-thirty and it was already a quarter to one."

"Now, that's the kind of information I like to hear," Tom replied with a smile, knowing it would irritate her. "That's very useful. O.K., so she went home at twelve forty-five, so she got there, when? About one?"

"Before that. It doesn't take fifteen minutes." Ms. Clyde was observably cross.

"Would she have been there long? When was her plane?"

"Three o'clock."

"Three o'clock?"

"Yes."

"She was cutting it close, wasn't she?"

Again, implied criticism produced corroborative information: "Mrs. Stanley allowed plenty of time, but circumstances were beyond her control. She didn't know she would have to come back here before she went home to get her bags."

"So she'd be in a hurry and wouldn't be there long?"

"Yes."

"Well, the time's close enough, it's still possible she saw Mrs. Kimbrough, so we're going to have to talk to her." When he got no response, Holder took a card out of his pocket and held it out to her, saying, "Look, here's my phone number at the station. Call me as soon as you hear from her." Ms. Clyde sat with her hands folded on the desk and made no move to take the card from him. He put it down on the desk with a snap and said, "Better yet, have her call me."

He didn't exactly slam the door when he went out, he just shut it very firmly.

CHAPTER 11

i

Patricia Clyde watched through the front window as the police-man walked away, and let out her breath as if she had been holding it for some time. She remained perfectly still, staring at the edge of the window where Holder had disappeared from view. Finally she looked down at the card he had left on her desk, but made no move to touch it.

The door to George's office opened and he emerged. "I was on the phone. Who was that?"

"The Chief of Police," she said.

"Christ! And you let him go? Didn't you stop to think I might be just a little bit interested in asking him where my wife is?"

The sarcasm was wasted on Patricia, who was inured to it. She watched dispassionately as George bounded across the room and out the front door to look urgently up and down the street.

He returned looking petulant, and having received no answer

to his question, repeated it, standing imposingly before Patricia's desk and glaring down at her.

Patricia was unimpressed. She inserted a floppy disk into the computer, lying to him without looking at him. "I assumed that if he had anything to tell you, he'd have asked for you."

"If he didn't have anything to tell me, why was he here?"

Patricia moved the mouse and clicked it. "He wanted to know if I'd heard from Carolyn yet. I haven't."

"Oh," said George, ever so slightly deflated. "Well, if he comes again, you tell me, all right?"

"Certainly," she said, moving and clicking the mouse twice more.

God, what a bitch! he thought. "Well, I'm going to be in Carolyn's office for a while, I've got to find those notes on the Sorenson job."

She didn't acknowledge this at all, but laid her perfect manicure upon the keyboard and began to type.

Like a better man before him, George abandoned the struggle. He went into his partner's office and closed the door behind him. Then it struck him for the first time that it was in his power to fire Patricia Clyde. This thought cheered him considerably. He didn't know why he hadn't thought of it before. He began to go through Carolyn's desk.

ii

Tita Robinson's father made his way across Peller Square in that wetness of air that is just barely too indefinite for the name of rain, remembering that he had heard a British friend call it

Scotch mist. He reflected that he could do, at this point, with a little less mist and a little more scotch.

Normally, he appreciated Peller Square, and was grateful that his accounting firm was located there among the two-story stone and wooden storefronts and the trees planted by some town council long dead. He had grown fond of the huge statue of the panther and that smaller, more recent sculpture not far from it, the life-size bronze student sitting on a small step, reading a bronze book and eating a bronze hamburger. Some people didn't like it. He couldn't imagine why; he had laughed out loud when he'd first seen it.

But he wasn't laughing now. At Main Street he turned right into heavier foot traffic and began dodging umbrellas. He passed more stone and wooden storefronts, more trees, but without appreciation. Why did these silly people have their umbrellas up in such a light rain, anyway? They were a menace. Why didn't they just wear rain hats like he did?

To say that he went on his errand reluctantly would be an understatement, but he saw no alternative. For ten years he and his wife had exercised certain eccentric theories about child rearing, and the results, so far, had been highly satisfactory. One of these theories held that a child is a human being in much the same way that a person of—say, thirty-five—is a human being; it followed that a promise made to a child must be kept with the same diligence appropriate to a promise made to an adult.

It made no difference that the promise in question was excruciatingly silly, and had been extracted from him while his daughter was nearly hysterical and in the grip of a high fever. It was still a promise. It is to his fatherly credit that although he cringed inwardly when he considered what he had to do, it never once occurred to him that he could merely refrain from doing it, and then lie about it when he got home.

Storefronts and umbrellas had thinned out. He walked across the broad brick expanse in front of City Hall, ascended the wide steps, pushed through one of the half-dozen sets of glass doors that together constituted the front wall of the building, and re-coiled from the subtropical efficiency of the central heating. He was in a spacious lobby, in which a decorator, as expensive as he was unoriginal, had grouped mushroom-hued chairs around a scatter of severely Scandinavian coffee tables, and polished off the job with a discreet forest of *Ficus benjamina*. The plants were the size of small trees, and stood in wooden tubs with brass rims. There was an air of understated wealth about the place, and a vague, unarticulated comfort crept into his reluctance.

He glanced around, and headed toward the right rear corner of the room. There the word *Police* hung suspended in the air, painted in large black letters on an immaculately invisible glass wall. A handle and hinges, likewise suspended, announced the presence of a door; he took a deep breath and pushed it open. Fortunately, the man at the desk appeared friendly and not too busy. It was still with some embarrassment, however, that Jim Robinson introduced himself and began to unfold his improbable tale.

iii

Oh, God, the phone again. Yesterday he had not answered it. Yesterday there had been no one in the world to whom he would willingly have talked. But today was different. Today there was just one, one person of all the billions on the globe, one voice he wanted to hear, that he had to hear. It had become a necessity, that too-familiar, that undervalued voice. Surely she would call, she had to call. And this might be her. The phone rang again.

But what if it were someone else? What could he say, what on earth could he possibly say? What—oh, God, what if it was George? Four rings.

He did not know how he had survived that dreadful conversation last night. Trying to act as if nothing was wrong. Acting not only for the policeman's benefit, but for George's as well. He was terrified that George had seen through him, that George knew there was something very wrong indeed. Seven rings.

But what if it wasn't George? What if it was—eight rings. He snatched the receiver off the hook and covered the mouthpiece with his hand. He listened.

A couple of seconds' silence, then a voice, the wrong voice, said, "Hello?"

He hung up.

iv

Tom Holder sat at his desk, working his way through a roast beef sandwich, a large mug of black coffee, and three powdered-sugar doughnuts. Normally he enjoyed his food, but the only thing that had happened all morning was that the pile of negative reports had gotten fatter, and the knowledge that he was getting precisely nowhere had rendered his lunch tasteless. Grace

Kimbrough had been missing for twenty-four hours. When the phone rang, he grabbed a tissue and spat out a large mouthful of doughnut and white sugar, dropped it into the wastebasket without regret, and picked up the receiver.

"Yeah?"

"Patricia, ah, Clive? On line two, sir."

About time. "Great," he said, and punched the second button on his phone. "Ms. Clyde! Where's Mrs. Stanley?"

A hesitant voice, peculiarly unlike the formidable Ms. Clyde's, said, "I don't know."

Holder's eyebrows rose. Had the iceberg thawed?

It had. The iceberg, in fact, was exhibiting marked symptoms of humanity. Patricia Clyde was actually unsure of herself. She confessed, as though she had taken some sort of liberty, that at noon she had called the office in San Francisco where Mrs. Stanley had a nine o'clock appointment. "She hadn't arrived yet, and I left a message for her to call our office as soon as she came in. I said it was urgent," said Ms. Clyde apologetically, as though nothing as melodramatic as urgency should be allowed to sully the hallowed dignity of Elton Kimbrough Interiors. There was a pause, during which Holder could have sworn he heard the woman swallow. "When I hadn't heard anything by twelve forty-five," she continued, "I called them again. Mrs. Stanley wasn't there. She had not kept the appointment, and she had not phoned to break it or reschedule it."

Holder felt duty-bound to suggest that Mrs. Stanley might be running late, but he knew somehow that Ms. Clyde would say, "She's never late," and she did.

"Mmmmmm," said Holder profoundly.

After a brief silence Patricia Clyde ventured, "I, ah, did something else, which perhaps I should just mention. It was very foolish of me," she said, fortunately unable to see the look of disbelief this admission brought to Holder's face, "but I suddenly thought that perhaps I'd better check to see if she had gotten to San Francisco at all. So I, ah, called the airline and, ah, said it was an emergency, and I needed to know if Mrs. Stanley had caught the three o'clock flight yesterday. I managed to get through to someone who knew something."

You would, Holder thought.

"She said that the flight had been fully booked, with a waiting list, and she remembered quite definitely, she said, that they hadn't been able to board any of the standbys because there were no—what they call no-shows. So Caro—Mrs. Stanley *is* in San Francisco, but I don't know," Ms. Clyde admitted bleakly, "where she is or why she's behaving this way."

Holder made some reassuring noises at her, trying not to sound as if he were getting rid of her as fast as possible, which in fact he was. When he hung up, he leaned back in his chair and closed his eyes. Was she telling the truth?

He would bet on it. In the Kimbrough office Patricia Clyde had been unmistakably hostile; on the phone just now she was worried. A little frightened. So Carolyn Stanley was not keeping her appointments in San Francisco, and she had yet to tell anybody where she was staying. That this unusual behavior had nothing to do with what had happened to Grace Kimbrough, and was merely a coincidence, Holder refused to believe.

He ran a tentative timetable over in his mind, and found it good. Now to get the S.F.P.D. working for him; best to do that through the District Attorney's office in Trenton. No, before he called Trenton, he'd better confirm that Carolyn Stanley had indeed been on that plane.

He reached for the phone, suddenly apostrophizing himself as a card-carrying idiot for not making this call sooner. Of course, the only thing remarkable that Carolyn had done prior to this morning was change her hotel reservation—a minor detail. But anything unexplained, no matter how minor it seemed, should have been looked into. He was slipping up. Just because he was so sure of Bill Stanley! No. That wasn't it. He realized with an inward cringe that he had been largely ignoring Carolyn Stanley because he was unhealthily preoccupied with Grace Kimbrough.

He swore comprehensively at himself until the airport police picked up their phone and rolled cooperatively into action for him. The airline was happy to verify that Mrs. Stanley had boarded the aircraft, stayed throughout the flight in the first-class cabin, and had spoken politely to the cabin crew as she disembarked in San Francisco. The hostesses, one of whom sounded mildly intelligent, had nothing interesting to contribute.

Not so the young man who had waited on Mrs. Stanley at the check-in desk.

"Yes, sir, positive. You see, my name is Stanly, too, except I spell mine without the E, so I mean, how could I forget?"

"Can you describe her?"

"Sure can. Ah, mid-forties, I'd say, brown hair, maybe black, pretty good-looking for a woman her age, I thought."

The faint trace of condescension in this last remark was not lost on Holder, who was mildly amused by it. "Did you notice anything in particular, anything unusual about her?"

"Oh, yeah, yeah, I did. It was really funny, I mean, I would have remembered it even if her name wasn't Stanley."

"What was really funny?" Holder asked, struggling not to hope for too much.

"Well, she didn't have any luggage."

"Didn't have any luggage?"

"Yeah, no luggage. She had a six-day round-trip to San Francisco, and I asked her how many bags she was checking and she said she wasn't checking anything, and I was surprised, I mean, I thought she meant she had carry-on, and she didn't look like the type, you know?"

"No, I don't know. What type?"

"Well, lots of people have carry-on for a weekend trip, but for a whole week, usually the only people who do carry-on are businessmen. Commuter types, you know, who fly a lot. Or students with backpacks maybe. And this lady, well, I mean, she didn't look like she was used to schlepping her own bags, you know?"

"No, I'm sure she's not. So she carried her bags on the plane?"

"No, sir. It was like, that's what I thought when she said she wasn't checking anything, but then I said, could I give her some I.D. tags for her carry-on, and she didn't have any. She just took her ticket and walked off, I mean, I thought it was really *weird*."

Holder thought it was really weird, too, and he thought about it for the rest of the day without being able to come up with a satisfactory theory to account for it.

V

The sergeant at the desk had been surprisingly sympathetic, and having nothing better to do had entered into the spirit of things with enthusiasm. Jim Robinson had left the police station with a sigh of relief and a typed document in his pocket. This he had immediately taken home to give to his daughter for her signature, thus convincing her that she was being taken seriously. The serenity that fell on Tita upon signing this document had been, her father judged, well worth the over-long lunch break and the embarrassment. He and Tita's mother had conferred and assured themselves that they had done the right thing.

And that would probably have been the end of the matter, but for the workings of a mischievous Providence, which decreed, first, that Jim Robinson's quaint notion of honesty should extend to mailing the signed statement back to the police station; second, that the United States Postal Service should effect a crosstown delivery in less than twenty-four hours; and third, that Sergeant Fischer should be scheduled for his annual physical that Wednesday morning, and thus be away from the station when the mail was delivered.

CHAPTER 12

i

The envelope was marked "Attn: Sgt. Fischer," but as Fischer was not in, and the envelope showed no signs of containing anything confidential, it was opened in due course by the department clerk.

Due course came screeching to a halt as the clerk read the statement of Ms. Elizabeth Robinson. He goggled. He gulped. He started to call Sergeant Martin. He stopped. He rose, walked down the hall, knocked at a door, entered when commanded to do so, and without a word laid envelope and contents in front of Chief Holder.

There were two pieces of paper: a small sheet of bone-colored notepaper with a brief handwritten message, paper-clipped to a sheet of plain bond, eight and a half by eleven, whose contents had been word-processed and printed.

The note said simply "*Sgt. Fischer— Many thanks for your kind assistance.*" It was signed by a James Robinson.

Holder read the attached statement twice, in rising incredulity, his eyebrows first ascending halfway to his hairline—or to where his hairline had been two decades before—then lowering and gathering into a knot over his nose.

"Get Fischer," he demanded of the clerk who hovered uncertainly by the door.

"He's over at the medical center, sir, it's his day for the physical—"

"Get 'im on the phone."

It was said of the Chief that he never lost his temper, and he never shouted at subordinates, but the tone of his voice made it unnecessary for him to add any instructions to hurry. The clerk hopped to it.

The crisp voice at the other end of the line explained to Chief Holder that Sergeant Fischer was in X ray, in much the same manner that a Buckingham Palace official might inform a caller, with implacable regret, that the Queen was in Scotland.

Holder remarked conversationally that he didn't much care if Sergeant Fischer was buck naked with pins sticking in him. "I want him on this phone. And," he added without heat, "I want him now."

Sergeant Fischer was produced.

"Yes, sir?"

"Fischer, I am holding a statement dated yesterday, apparently prepared by you, signed by Elizabeth Dawes Robinson of Four twenty-nine Dickens Street."

"Oh, my God!" Fischer was instantly apoplectic. "I didn't know he was going to bring that back to the station! Listen, sir, ignore it. I mean, it's just a joke; well, no, not a joke really, you know I wouldn't make a joke like that, I mean, it was just to humor the kid. And the guy, too, I mean, her father. It was him that came to the station. This Elizabeth kid, she's only ten years old, and she's been sick. She dreamed all that stuff. Her father, he's just, like, trying to humor her, and he—"

"If he thinks she dreamed it, why did he report it?"

"Because he's crazy," said Sergeant Fischer bitterly.

"How crazy?"

"Well, not really crazy, I mean—"

"Why don't you get back here and tell me what you mean."

"Well, uh, sure, yessir, they'll be through with the X rays in just a minute and then I'll be right back."

Chief Holder, with the utmost courtesy, made a suggestion regarding the disposition of the medical center's X rays, and further suggested that Sergeant Fischer move his anatomy back to the station without further ado. "I want to hear every little word," Holder said, "of your conversation with this James Robinson."

"But, sir, I keep telling you, the kid's sick, she's got a hundred and three degrees, nobody thinks she really saw anything, she was just—"

"Fischer," his chief interrupted with the patience one uses in addressing the mentally challenged, "what would you say is the biggest thing we're working on right now?"

Fischer changed gears with an all but audible grind. "Uh, well, this Kimbrough woman."

"And the Kimbrough woman lives where?"

The sergeant, mystified but game, dredged up the address out of Monday's mental notes. "Uh, Four twenty-two Austen Road."

"And where was she last seen?"

"Entering the residence of Mr. and Mrs. William Stanley at Four twenty Austen Road," Fischer recited.

"And what part of town is Austen Road in?"

"Uh, Canterbury Park."

"And this kid who's sick lives on Dickens Street, and what part of town is that in?"

Fischer whispered, "Oh, shit."

While he was waiting for Fischer to return to the station, Holder put in a call to the Township Development Office; could they send over somebody with a plat map of Canterbury Park, showing the house numbers on the lots? They could.

He wondered if he'd been too hard on Fischer. Would he himself have caught it if it hadn't been for "Austen is a Dickens of a writer, Dickens is an Austen-something writer"? Now, that was something to talk to Kathryn about! He was about to wrap up a homicide that was fancy enough for TV, and right in the middle of it was something he could reasonably label as a clue he got from Kathryn. He felt a little thrill of anticipation, and was instantly ashamed of himself.

Sorry, Grace, he thought. He noticed for the first time what the dead woman's name was. Well, that was where forgiveness came from, wasn't it? From God's grace. So maybe she wouldn't mind that he would use her death in ways that were pleasant to him. After all, she was already dead, had been dead probably since Monday afternoon, forty-odd hours now. There was nothing he could do about that except gather evidence against the man who had killed her. It pleased him to imagine that she approved his actions, and that she felt, as he had, a kinship of spirit between them based on common misery.

She had found an escape from her misery, and it had proved fatal. Would she mind, he suddenly wondered, that it was the man she had loved who would suffer for this crime rather than the man she had stopped loving, the man who so clearly loved nobody but himself? Had she forgiven Bill Stanley, who must have killed her in a lover's passion? And if so, would she forgive the husband who had driven her into Bill Stanley's arms?

How much grace could they expect of Grace?

ii

Young Ms. Robinson, meanwhile, was like the character in P. G. Wodehouse, who, if not precisely disgruntled, was nevertheless very far from gruntled. It was most annoying being cooped up for so long.

She had come home from school the previous Thursday puffy-eyed and listless; her mother had taken her temperature and promptly put her to bed, bribing her to stay there with several musty volumes of Nancy Drew. These Mrs. Robinson had hastily dug out of an attic storage box full of her own childhood memories, and Tita, recently graduated from Oz, had found a new passion.

When the Friday visit to Dr. Collins, whom Tita liked because she was pretty and funny, resulted in the sentence of a full week in bed, Tita had at first resigned herself happily to her incarceration.

Comfortably tucked up in bed, or in the old armchair in her attic, she had devoured *The Sign of the Twisted Candles* and was halfway through *The Secret of the Old Clock*. The problem arose when she became, inevitably, fired with the spirit of emulation. How could you detect anything if your mother wouldn't let you go outside?

Her mother, understanding Tita's frustration, had on Saturday presented her with a very official and adult-looking spiral notebook and a new pen. The idea was that she should observe what she could out of her window, and write it down. "Even quite small facts can be important," explained the inspired Mrs. Robinson. "If you write them down, with the times they happen, then even though you can't solve a mystery right now, at least you'll have had some good practice for later, when you get well."

Tita Robinson, who never failed to focus the full fury of her attention on whatever project was at hand, had no objection to practice. She was soon regretting, however, that the largest trees along the back fence were evergreens; if they had lost their leaves like the other trees, she would be able to see more. Still, there were patches of lawn, and fence, and neighbors' houses, that showed through spaces between the branches. On Saturday she was able to record on page one of the notebook the comings and goings of Mephistopheles, the neighborhood's largest cat, and she had noted which of the Henson children had played in their backyard. Sunday afternoon there had been more cats and more Hensons, and every now and then Tita was able to make a note on the movements of some temporarily visible adult.

Unfortunately none of these movements looked the least bit suspicious. Everything was normal and boring—until Monday night. Monday night had not been boring.

On Tuesday morning her mother had taken her to see the doctor again. Tita was shocked to discover that Dr. Collins could be as dumb as her parents. Since her parents weren't usually dumb, it was all very strange and frustrating.

Her parents, meanwhile, were worried. They were obliged to

pretend to take Tita's story seriously, since the child became dangerously excited when anyone attempted to convince her she had imagined or dreamed the whole thing. The Robinsons hoped that when her fever subsided, she would be able to face the truth more equably. Meanwhile, they were going to have to figure out what to tell her when she asked what the police were doing about what she'd reported. It wouldn't have been a problem, except for that Robinson eccentricity that held that you shouldn't lie to your children.

They need not have fretted. To Tita's early-Wednesday-morning inquiry her mother returned a perfectly honest "I don't know." Before Tita got around to asking again, her mother knew more than she wanted to.

"What do you mean, you need to talk to my daughter?"

The hostility fairly crackled down the wire. It did not surprise Tom Holder; he would have been more surprised by its absence, and he knew that its source was fear. "Now, Mrs. Robinson, I don't want you to get the wrong idea about this, and there's no reason to get upset, but the statement we've got here from your daughter, that's something we need to look into."

Mrs. Robinson, stunned, said hurriedly that it was just a dream or something, and the child was ill, and surely her husband had explained all that?

"Yes, ma'am, he did. But, you see, there's a—well, problem we're working on now that, uh, concerns that area right around where you live. It's not a homicide, I can tell you that." That was at least technically true; officially at this point it was still just a report of a missing person. "But there are certain things, certain facts, we need to know about. Now, your daughter may not have seen what she *thought* she saw, but it looks like she did see something. If we can figure out what that something was, well, that'll give us some information we need to have. So I need to talk to her as soon as possible. I'd like to come over now, if that's all right with you."

"But she's sick! She gets terribly excited when this is brought up, and we can't allow her to make herself more sick than she already is. Can't you—you'll have to wait a few days, till her fever's gone down."

"I'm sorry, ma'am, we can't wait." There was an unfriendly silence at the Robinson end of the line. Holder persisted. "I really am sorry, and I understand how you feel. Believe me, I'll be extra careful. A witness that's only ten years old, and is sick, I know that's a special case. I'm coming myself, I wouldn't trust this to anybody else."

At this point James Robinson would probably have buckled in the face of superior force, but mothers are made of sterner stuff. Tita's mother said coolly, "I'm sorry, I didn't catch your name?"

"Holder. Tom Holder. I'm the Chief of Police."

"Yes, I heard that bit. Mr. Holder, do you have children yourself?"

Across Holder's mind there flashed the worst part of seven years, compressed into instants: the frustration, the doctors, Louise's tears. "No, I don't," he admitted quietly.

"What experience do you have in dealing with ten-year-olds?"

Holder perceived that further assurance was going to be necessary. Of course he could just roll right over her objections and come anyway; he could even threaten her with Interfering with an Officer in the Performance of His Duty. But that wasn't how you did things when you were dealing with respectable citizens, and it wasn't Holder's style, anyway. Furthermore, Mrs. Robinson had succeeded in stirring up an uncertainty he had so far kept submerged at the back of his brain.

Children, to Tom Holder, were something other people had, and other people dealt with. They were small, incomprehensible beings who made clumsily adorable angels in the Christmas pageant, and damn nuisances of themselves when they played in the street. He had never had any conversation with one that had not been brief and trivial. So how was he supposed to pick the truth out of this kid's brain, when it was so mixed up with imagination and a high fever that even her parents hadn't believed her?

An idea broke over Tom Holder like a great light.

"Tell you what, Mrs. Robinson," he said. "Suppose I bring along a special consultant."

CHAPTER 13

Chief Holder's special consultant, having no idea she was shortly to be cast in that role, was perched on her kitchen countertop, having a spirited disagreement with her housekeeper about predestination. Mrs. Warburton was calmly sticking slivers of garlic into a roast, and maintaining a position that Kathryn stigmatized as hopelessly Calvinistic. As Mrs. Warburton was a staunch Presbyterian, this was not altogether surprising, and was certainly nothing new; all the major doctrinal wars of the Reformation were regularly refought, with the greatest good humor, across the kitchen at 34 Alexander Street. The Rev. Dr. Koerney persisted in believing that Mrs. Warburton might have made a splendid Anglican, if only somebody had gotten to her in time.

Mrs. Warburton, possessing the native shrewdness to have divined that her first responsibility as Kathryn's housekeeper was to act as little like an employee as possible, serenely resisted conversion, together with half of Kathryn's other ideas, and ran the household very much as she pleased.

Her domain was a pre-Revolutionary house on the sleepy residential street that bordered the seminary campus; a completely unremarkable structure in itself, peering decorously through its maples at its more imposing neighbors, it was impressive only to those who happened to know the going rate for eighteenth-century houses on Alexander Street. Unfortunately, most of the members of St. Margaret's Episcopal Church fell into this category.

Kathryn, in whom innate good taste was hopelessly entangled with a lively dread of being thought nouveau riche, would have been appalled to discover that her house and its contents constituted one of the hot topics of parish gossip, and that an invitation to that house ranked as no mean status symbol. Had she known, she might have been sufficiently mortified to stop entertaining altogether, and that would have been a pity, for Helen Warburton regarded the elegant little dinner parties she was privileged to concoct as the high point of her job.

She was busy being unimpressed by Kathryn's excoriation of Calvin's doctrine of Total Depravity, when the phone rang. Kathryn answered it. It was Tom Holder.

Damn, Kathryn thought, *what have I started?* "Hi, Tom, what's up?" He had never called her, and she couldn't imagine any quirk of church business that would require him to; he must be making excuses to talk to her.

Preliminary courtesies out of the way, Tom asked, "You teach the fourth-graders in Sunday school, don't you?"

"That's right."

"Fourth-graders are ten years old, right?"

"Most of them, yes. Why?"

"I have to question a ten-year-old girl, and it's a very delicate situation, and I don't know a damn thing about kids. I've got a nerve calling you, I know, I'm sure you're up to your ears, but I really could use some help and I can't think of who else to ask."

"Ah, Tom, by 'delicate situation' do you mean she's been molested?"

"Oh, no! No, nothing like that. She's a witness to something, and it's really important."

Kathryn was both relieved and embarrassed. She'd been so sure she had troubled Tom's serenity, attracted him, lured him into a flirtation. And now it turned out that the man was only doing his job. *God, what an unbridled ego I've got*, she thought, inwardly wincing. Aloud she said, "Why, sure, I'd be glad to help if I can, but you know that I know less about police work than you do about kids."

"I don't think that'll matter. Have you got some time right now?"

"Astonishingly, yes; the scheduling gnomes at the seminary gave me Wednesday mornings off this semester. Shall I come up to the Cop Shop?"

There followed a lively game of "After you, Alphonse," Kathryn operating on the assumption that it would be more polite for her to traverse the three blocks to the police station than to ask Tom to venture out on such a dismal morning, Tom suddenly confronted with the opportunity to see the inside of the fabled house and feeling it would be presumptuous to invite himself. But on the other hand, wasn't it rude to ask Kathryn to come trekking through the drizzle to do him a favor?

Landing by some miracle on the alternative both actually

preferred, they agreed that Tom was to be at Kathryn's in ten minutes. Kathryn hung up the phone and turned, grinning, to Mrs. Warburton.

"Warby," she announced importantly, "I am about to entertain a man I genuinely enjoy, without his incredibly tiresome wife, thank you, and tea for two"—she paused to execute a little shuffling dance step—"would be appreciated." She made a face. "Only he probably prefers coffee."

Mrs. Warburton smiled imperturbably. "Don't worry, dear; if he comes often, you'll have him trained in no time."

CHAPTER 14

Tom Holder, feeling a twinge of disappointment to have the door opened to him not by the high-toned housekeeper of whom he'd heard awed reports but by his cheerfully informal hostess, relinquished his raincoat to her, and while she hung it in the hall closet, looked around him with a curiosity restrained by good manners. He noted a wine-colored Oriental rug on the hardwood floor and an Oriental runner of a different shade going up the stairs, before his attention was riveted by the most amazing mirror he had ever seen.

It was half as big as a Ping-Pong table; the frame alone was a foot wide, and gold, and carved six inches deep with snaky tendrils of impossible trees; birds lurked among the curlicues, and cupids writhed coyly at the corners, holding the concoction together with garlands of carved gold ribbon. Holder's work had taken him, from time to time, into some lavish homes, but even by Harton standards this thing was remarkable. He was utterly unable to explain to himself why he didn't like it; he knew only that it reminded him vaguely of indigestion. Kathryn was watching him stare at it; he had to say something. He managed to get out, "That's quite a mirror."

"My mother sent it to me," said Kathryn neutrally.

He looked at her expressionless face, then back at the mirror, then back at Kathryn. He took in the discreet pinstripe on a charcoal-gray suit with a two-button jacket and a full skirt, the gray clergy shirt topped by a stiff white collar, and the small gold loops in her ears. He was visited by a stroke of that intuition that was the chief reason Kathryn admired him. "You don't like it," he said.

The deadpan look burst into a laugh. "I loathe it," she confessed heartily. "But what can you do? Mother sent it and said, 'Just the thing for your front hall.' "

"And she'll give you grief if she comes and sees it's not here."

"Oh, no, she wouldn't say a thing. She'd smile and be charming and go away with her visit ruined."

She had led him into the living room, and he fairly blinked from surprise. There was not a single thing in the room that was grand or expensive-looking. The biggest item, not counting the sofa, was a tall cabinet-like thing of some pale wood—pine, he thought; the old paint had been removed and nobody had bothered to put on a new coat; the knotholes showed. Tom liked it. He liked the sofa and chairs, too, though they weren't even a matching set.

He didn't know whether he was relieved or disappointed; Kathryn Koerney's famous house!—and it was perfectly ordinary. He walked innocently across a carpet, the sale of which would have paid off the mortgage on his house, dropped into a chair that cost more than his car, and said approvingly, "Nice room."

His hostess beamed. "The fell hand of Mother has not come near it! Thanks, I'm glad you like it. Ah, here's tea. Don't panic, there's coffee, too—" Kathryn paused in dismay as she registered the dazzle of silver that Mrs. Warburton was bearing. The pause gave Mrs. Warburton the opportunity to tell Chief Holder not to get up and Chief Holder the opportunity to get up anyway. Kathryn pulled herself together.

"Warby, this is Chief Holder; Tom, Mrs. Warburton. Maker of the second-best mandelbrot in New Jersey, and oh, my, what a plateful we have here."

Mrs. Warburton, long accustomed to Kathryn's exaggerations, set the tray down on the coffee table and extended her hand to Tom with a pleasant how-do-you-do. He shook her hand, wondering suddenly what this woman's status was. In all those wealthy homes his business had taken him into, he had observed the nuances and conventions that governed the behavior of people with servants, and he knew very good and well that you don't introduce your servants to your guests, your servants don't shake hands with said guests, and your servants certainly do not call you by your first name—this woman was telling "Kathryn" that she would be in the kitchen if anything else was needed. Tom was confused.

Kathryn was well aware that Mrs. Warburton was a presence not easily categorized, but she never offered any explanation. Having ascertained that Tom did indeed prefer coffee, she poured for him, supplied him with cream, sugar, and mandelbrot, kicked off her shoes, sat cross-legged on the sofa, and demanded, "What about this ten-year-old girl? I'm dying of curiosity."

Holder was noting but not appreciating the dexterity with which she had managed to assume a tomboyish posture without revealing so much as a knee. He decided that he didn't like full skirts. But he had business to attend to.

"Well," he said, "if I start with the ten-year-old girl, you'll think I'm crazy. I've got a sergeant thinks I'm crazy already. Mmm. Good coffee. Let's start with Monday. You realize all this is confidential."

"I never heard it. Tom who?"

"Right. Monday, ten P.M., a guy calls the station. Says he doesn't know where his wife is."

He began a succinct, orderly report of Monday night's events, discreetly referring to the people involved by first name only. At least when he started he was succinct. But soon it dawned on him that he might never get another chance to sit in Kathryn's living room like this, acting as if he belonged there, and he began to include minute details and to succumb to digression.

"Seven of the damn things, every size they made! Who would want seven different kinds of suitcase, I ask you?"

Kathryn shrugged. "Somebody who wants people to know how much money they have."

Tom decided to take a chance. He leaned back in his chair and examined Kathryn through narrowed eyes. "Let me see. You have . . . four, I think, matching suitcases, five at the most, but you never use more than three of them at the same time because you don't want to look like somebody who owns that mirror out there."

Her jaw went slack, and she stared at him for several seconds before saying, with quiet emphasis, "That's scary."

Tom's heart flipped over. He had gotten to her, seen inside her, and she hadn't realized until then that he was capable of it. He looked into those solemn, slightly widened eyes and saw in them his credit rising like mercury in a thermometer that has been un-expectedly dropped into hot chocolate.

But he had to say something. The moment was delicious, but it was lasting too long. It was getting heavy.

"Scary, yeah," he said, waving a dismissive hand. "We're sup-posed to be scary in my business, they give us lessons in it." He grinned at her.

She laughed, and the moment was gone. But that was O.K. It had happened, and he had it, and he could keep it.

Fifteen minutes later he was summing up. "So that's all we got, Monday and Tuesday both. And you can't take out a search war-rant on somebody's house just because he's sleeping with the woman next door and he faints when he sees a cop."

"Search warrant? What, did he bury her in the basement, or something? Shades of Hitchcock!"

"No, no." Holder waved away Alfred Hitchcock and similar nonsense with half a slice of mandelbrot. "The search warrant is for evidence she was killed in the house and afterward her body was carried away in their van. You're about to find out about that. What'd you say this stuff is? It's like a cross between cookies and toast."

"You like it? Mandelbrot. It's Jewish, and no, Mrs. Warburton isn't Jewish, but her best friend is."

"I love it. Never heard of a Jewish woman with a best friend who was a Gentile, I thought the Old Testament wants them to hate us and the New Testament wants—well, provides lots of ex-cuses, anyway—for us to hate them."

Kathryn whistled. "Tom Holder! Not one Christian in a thou-sand has noticed that the New Testament is full of anti-Semitism. I'm wowed."

Tom tried to look modest, and failed. "You're a cop in Jersey, you get to be an expert on racism. Hang on, if you know that, too, why didn't you ever say so in the adult Sunday school class?"

"Oh, right. 'Ladies and gentlemen of St. Margaret's, the first thing you need to know about the Bible is that there's a lot of crap in it.' "

Tom choked on his last bite of mandelbrot, and pounded the chair arm with appreciative glee.

"It's not," Kathryn continued, "the sort of thing you say to scaredy-cat Christians, of which there were about half a dozen in that class."

"See your point. I didn't know anybody still said 'scaredy-cat.' "

"That's what my uncle the rancher used to call me when I wouldn't go into the barns because of the rats." She smiled. "So he gave me his gun and taught me how to shoot them. Weren't we talking about search warrants, and how you can't get one?"

"Oh, yeah. This is where you and the ten-year-old girl come in. Missing woman lives on Austen Road, ten-year-old girl lives on Dickens Street. Ring any bells?"

"Afraid not," Kathryn admitted, displeased with herself for not knowing the answer.

"Austen is a Dickens of a writer? Dickens is an Austen-something writer?"

Kathryn laughed. "Austen-tatious writer. Fancy your remembering that!"

He thought, but did not say, *I remember everything you say.* Instead, he told her about James and Tita Robinson, and in conclusion picked up a zippered vinyl folder, opened it, drew out a sheet of paper, and with a bit of a flourish, handed it to her.

CHAPTER 15

This is a true and accurate account of the events of the night of Monday, November 7th. I was asleep in my bedroom. I woke up feeling hot. I got out of bed and opened the window and looked out at the backyard. There were suspicious sounds in the driveway of the house behind us. I put on my slippers and robe and went downstairs and outside. I climbed the back fence and looked over. I saw somebody back out our neighbor's camper van from their garage, but they didn't have the headlights on. He stopped the van and got out and opened the back door of it. Then he went to the house and came back after a minute carrying the body of a woman. He put the body in the back of the van and backed the van out of the driveway, still with no headlights. I went back into the house and woke my parents up and told them to call the police.

In the space at the bottom a careful childish signature had been written over the typed name, Elizabeth Dawes Robinson; under the name was the address on Dickens Street, then yesterday's date.

Kathryn wished the hollow feeling in her stomach would go away. Unwilling to play the squeamish female, she assumed a detached manner and said, "Now, according to your Sergeant Fischer, the girl's parents don't really believe she saw all this happen, but the father reported it because he promised the child he would."

"Yeah, one of Fischer's problems is that he believes what people tell him."

"Ah. You think the father does believe it?"

Tom chewed mandelbrot. "I think he half-believes it, and doesn't want to believe it, and is making up excuses not to."

"Umm. And the two major excuses he's got are, one, the kid is running a hell of a fever and is therefore delirious or dreaming, and two, this particular delirium or dream is brought on by a surfeit of Nancy Drew stories."

"A what?"

"Excess of Nancy Drew stories."

Tom was pretending to rummage in his pockets. "I meant to bring my dictionary with me," he muttered. Kathryn blew a raspberry at him, which delighted him hugely. "Yeah, however you say it. Those are the reasons he gives, and they're both bunk. The real reason is that nobody is going to believe that one of the neighbors has croaked the woman next door unless you show them movies of it."

Kathryn, thinking of Professor and Mrs. Allanby next door, and wondering what evidence it would take to convince her that violence had taken place amid that clutter of sheet music and gardening catalogs, admitted that she saw the point. She added, "There is one thing, strictly minor. The kid's supposedly dreaming about murders because she's been reading Nancy Drew. There aren't any murders in Nancy Drew."

"But I thought—they're mystery stories, aren't they?"

"Yes, but nobody ever gets hurt. The crimes Nancy Drew investigates are things like forgeries and theft. Fake antiques, stolen wills. No murders." Kathryn smiled. "I speak with authority, and not as the scribes! I read every one of them when I was that age."

Tom smiled. "I knew I'd come to the right place."

"Don't expect too much. I'm a theologian, not a cop."

"Not to worry, I'll tell you everything you need to know in the car."

In the front hall she took both their coats from the closet and handed him his. She got into hers without a move from him to assist her; she was used to unnecessary courtesies from older men, and mentally granted him points for having the wit to perceive that that stuff wasn't called for in dealing with a card-carrying feminist.

Tom, meanwhile, having captured his prize, was fairly glowing with pleasure at the prospect of spending time with her. He was so elated, in fact, that he forgot his manners. *Oh, damn,* he thought as they drove away from her house, *I should have held her coat for her.*

CHAPTER 16

Tita Robinson, in honor of Chief Holder's visit, had been allowed to put on a robe and sit on the living room sofa, on the condition that she keep her feet tucked into a blanket. This was hardly dignified, but it beat giving testimony in bed, and she accepted the compromise philosophically. The Robinsons, conferring by telephone after Holder's call, had agreed that Jim should stay at his office and that they should not ask their lawyer to be present; the less fuss made, the calmer Tita was likely to be.

And Tita was very calm, disconcertingly so. Her feverish anxiety about the business had settled into a mild impatience the moment her mother had told her the police were coming to talk to her. For reasons hard to define, this change in mood made Julia Robinson all the more fearful that what her daughter had been chattering about was not, after all, a fantasy, which in turn made her all the more insistent, as she ushered the policeman and the priest into the house, that it was. Holder made noncommittal noises.

They were led into the living room, and a thin child with freckles and ginger hair disentangled herself from a blanket and stood up to greet them. Her mother, too late to stop Tita from rising, refrained from correcting her, gathered up the blanket, made introductions, and stood ready to wrap Tita up again when the courtesies were over.

Tom Holder, in a flash of inspiration, offered a hand, and Tita solemnly shook it. "And this is my associate, Kathryn Koerney."

The child turned to Kathryn, eyes bright with curiosity and hope. "Are you a detective?" she asked.

Kathryn hesitated. To answer yes would be dishonest; on the other hand, "No, I'm a Sunday school teacher" seemed hopelessly flat. "I've never been one before," she said confidentially, "but Chief Holder wants me to work with him on this problem, so this is my first case. We're hoping you can help us."

"I hope so, too," Tita replied with dignity, allowing her mother to re-cocoon her in one corner of the sofa.

Gracious, thought Kathryn, *I didn't know they made them like this anymore.* "O.K., then," she said, settling into the other corner of the sofa while Holder placed a tiny tape recorder on the coffee table, switched it on, and took a chair a discreet distance away, "let's start with your name, I like to get names right. On your statement it says Elizabeth, but your mother calls you Tita?"

"That's right. It's sort of Spanish, short for Chiquita. And Chiquita," she added in the unmistakable tones of one who has endured much, "does *not* mean banana!"

Kathryn did not smile. "I know it doesn't, it means Little One. I had a Spanish nickname myself when I was growing up"— Julia Robinson silently awarded Ms. Koerney a point for not saying "when I was a little girl"—"my uncle used to call me Trina, because my name in Spanish would be Catarina." The spark of a joke leapt in Tita's eyes; Kathryn saw it, remembered horrid times in first grade, and said brilliantly, "And if you tell me it's short for latrine, I'll put slugs in your bed!" Tita giggled, and several muscles in Kathryn's stomach relaxed fractionally.

"O.K., now, Tita. The first thing we need to do is read your statement, just to be sure it's all correct." Tom had fished it out of his folder and handed it to Kathryn, who read it aloud in a matter-of-fact voice, as though bodies in camper vans were as unremarkable as tomatoes in the kitchen. "Is that all right?"

"Yes, except it doesn't say who it was. I wanted to put that in, but Daddy said the policeman said it would be better not to." The policeman, in fact, had agreed with James Robinson that there was no point in risking a lawsuit. "I don't know why. I don't think it's better not to, do you?"

"No, I agree with you. We better put it in. You could see who it was, then?"

"Yes, it was Mr. Stanley."

Flicking a glance at Mrs. Robinson, Kathryn held her breath for an instant. Would the mother protest? No, the mother would not; Julia sat as though carved in marble, out of Tita's line of vision, and the only change that came over her at the mention of her neighbor's name was that the line of her lips became a little tighter. *Good for you*, thought Kathryn, and then: *God, let me do this right.* "Good. It's good that you recognized him. Now, let's start from the beginning. You opened your window. What did you see?"

"Well, from my window you can't see the Stanleys' yard, because of the trees, so I just saw our yard."

"Can you see the Stanleys' garage?"

"No, there's a really big tree in the way there."

"So what made you think something was happening?"

"I heard their garage door open."

"Ah. And how did you know that the noise you heard was the Stanleys' garage door?"

"Because it squeaks. Johnny Hivers, he's this boy lives two houses down, he says it sounds like a cat when it opens and a moose when it closes, but I think he's just trying to be cool. I don't think he knows what a moose sounds like."

"Does it sound alike, then, opening and closing?"

"No, it really does sound different. That's why I knew it was opening. It was the meow sound."

"Good. So you heard the garage door open. What made you think something was wrong?"

"The garage light didn't come on."

"Would you have been able to tell if it came on? I thought the tree was in the way."

"It is. But you can tell anyway. You can see it on the branches. Once when it was snowing they turned on the garage light and you could see the snow on the branches. It was really neat, like a Christmas card. That's how I remember you can see the light, I remember when it was snowing."

"Excellent," said Kathryn with complete sincerity. "Then what?"

"Then I heard a noise like something falling over, or maybe like tripping over something, I'm not sure. But it was a"—Tita wrinkled her nose—"an *accident* kind of noise, if you know what I mean."

"I know exactly what you mean," Kathryn assured her with a

smile of delight and a split-second prayer that when she had children they would be just like this one.

Gradually, then, detail by detail, she coaxed the story out of
the girl: down the stairs, out the door, across the yard, and up the
fence, to the point where Tita had watched the van back out of
the garage.

"Was it coasting out, or was the motor running?"

"The motor was running. I heard it start when I was climbing
the fence, and thought somebody was stealing one of the
Stanleys' cars. And then, when I saw it, I *really* thought somebody was stealing it because it was all dark, they hadn't turned
the headlights on. But then it backed out to the middle of the
driveway and stopped and somebody got out."

"You saw him getting out?"

"No, I just heard him. The corner of the garage was in the way.
I could see the side of the van, but I couldn't see the driver's side,
you know?" Kathryn made a listening noise. "So then he walked
around to the back of the van and opened the doors. I heard that,
too. I mean, I didn't see it. Then he went into the house and
that's when I saw him."

"And that's when you first knew who it was," Kathryn said
halfway between a statement and a question. This was the important bit, this was what Tom urgently needed. She simply
mustn't screw it up. She simply mustn't fail. "How did you know
it was Mr. Stanley?"

"I just recognized him."

"There was light enough to see his face?"

Tita paused, obviously puzzled. "I guess so," she said slowly.

"Think carefully, Tita. You first saw him when he walked from the back of the van toward the house. So you knew then that it was a man."

"Yes."

"Did you think, Oh, it's Mr. Stanley?"

There was a pause. Kathryn let it lengthen.

"That's funny," said Tita finally. "When he was walking toward the back door, I thought he was going to steal something from the house and put it in the van."

"Ah. And did you still think that when he went into the house?"

Pause. "No, when he went into the house I knew it was Mr. Stanley."

"Why?"

The child's face puckered into heavy thought, and for nearly a full minute of silence Kathryn forbore to prompt her. Finally a light broke across Tita's face. "I know! It's the way he goes up the steps. Mr. Stanley always goes up in two big steps, you see. There are four steps, and he goes up them two at a time. Every time. And he puts his hand on the rail and he kind of pulls himself up when he does it, like he needs help, because he's kind of short, you know? It looks kind of funny, really, like he really has to try hard, I don't know why he does it that way. But he always does, so I knew it was him. You see?"

Kathryn permitted herself a glance at Tom, who raised his eyebrows and pursed his lips—an expression Kathryn correctly interpreted as appreciation. She muttered silent thanks to God and returned to the witness.

"That's brilliant, Tita. So Mr. Stanley went into his house. Why did you decide to stay on the fence, watching?"

"Because I still thought it was funny. You know, no lights and everything. I wanted to see what would happen."

"So what happened?"

"Well, after a minute the door opened and he was there again, only now he was carrying something big. That was all I saw at first," said Tita wisely, demonstrating that she had caught on to the rules of the game. "I didn't see at first it was a body, just a big thing. Then, when he got down the steps, he turned toward the— Oh!" This last was a cry of consternation.

"What is it?"

"I just thought. Mr. Stanley doesn't have a special way of going down steps, he just goes down them sort of fast, like lots of people. But he couldn't go down them fast because of this big thing he was carrying."

Kathryn looked into a thin face full of trouble. "Yes?"

"But don't you see? I said it was Mr. Stanley coming out, but that's only because it was Mr. Stanley going in. I mean, this man came out and I just thought, It's Mr. Stanley coming out again, and I was looking at the thing he was carrying and trying to figure out what it was, but you see I can't prove it was Mr. Stanley carrying it, because there's nothing like that thing with the steps to prove it."

Kathryn looked to Holder for instructions, and got an infinitesimal shake of the head, which she interpreted to mean "Let it slide."

"O.K., Tita, we'll be very careful and just say that a man came out carrying something."

"Yeah, it was big and it must have been heavy because of the way he was moving, real slow."

"How was he holding it?"

"Over his shoulder. It hung down in front and back. He had trouble getting it out the door, you could tell, 'cause it was so big and it looked like it was hard to carry. But he got it out, and then he came down the steps real slow, and then when he got to the bottom of the steps and started to walk across to the van, then I saw. Because then I could see him sideways, you know, and I could see that the part that hung down in front of him was legs. Ladies' legs."

CHAPTER 17

Kathryn went right on saying "very good" and asking calm questions, but the knot in her stomach made her thankful there wasn't much more ground to cover. The body had been carried to the back of the van, and once there, both it and its bearer were out of sight, leaving Tita nothing to report but noises. These, obviously, had signified the putting of the body in the van, the closing of the back doors, and the opening and shutting of the driver's door. Then the van had backed out of the driveway, still lightless, and Tita had run to waken her parents.

The interview concluded, Holder packed up his tape recorder and murmured his appreciation to Mrs. Robinson while Kathryn congratulated Tita on her powers of observation. Holder then asked if they might have a brief tour of the premises. Tita insisted that she was well enough to show them the spot where she had climbed the fence, but her mother, released suddenly from her frozen silence as if by the click of the stop button on the tape recorder, gathered herself together with visible effort and asserted Authority. Tita could not go outside; her mother would show the visitors the approximate place, and Tita could stand at the window and gesture to indicate a more exact location.

It was not highly conducive to the dignity of the Chief of Police, standing in various experimental spots before a fence and being directed to right or left by the silent semaphore of a ten-year-old girl through a closed window, but Holder's charity for Ms. Elizabeth Robinson was at that point boundless, and besides, zeal for the chase consumed him. He would have crawled around on his hands and knees at Tita's direction, and scarcely have noticed that it was hardly the sort of thing he was accustomed to.

In any event, the spot was located to Tita's satisfaction after a minimum of back-and-forthing. Then, since the fence was of that woven board variety that even a middle-aged policeman and a female priest can scale without difficulty or broken fingernails, they both climbed up just high enough to peer over into the backyard of the William Stanley residence. The layout was exactly as described, the garage hiding part of the driveway, the back steps—four high—in plain sight. Holder grunted his satisfaction and descended to ground level. Kathryn remained on the fence for a moment, bothered by something.

"What is it?" Tom asked.

"I don't know. Something . . . something I can't put my finger on."

Tom climbed back up beside her and ran his eye over the scene, but could find nothing wrong with it. "Beats me," he said.

Kathryn shook her head. "Beats me, too. Oh, well, never mind, I don't suppose it's important."

When they returned to the house, Tita, triumphantly back in

the limelight, led them upstairs to her bedroom. From her window they verified the non-view of the Stanleys' backyard and nodded sagely over it as though it mattered.

Tom turned away, but again Kathryn lingered. "What is it now?" he asked. After a minute she sighed, and admitted that she hadn't the foggiest idea. Holder, still game, and with the greatest respect for Kathryn's intelligence, went back to the window and looked again. Nothing. Kathryn shrugged, laughed at herself, and waved a dismissive hand. "Come on," she said, "let's go."

Chief Holder and Ms. Koerney then took their leave, shaking hands with the witness at the door to her bedroom, and being escorted out of the house by her apprehensive mother.

Once back in the car and safely out of Mrs. Robinson's hearing, Tom erupted in something approaching glee.

"Fantastic!" he bellowed over the roar of the starting engine. "Did you hear that kid? Did you hear her? Not one witness in a hundred—hell, not one in a *thousand*—would've seen what she did, that business about not knowing for sure it was Stanley coming out because there was nothing like the steps to prove it. Fantastic!"

"Do you think it wasn't Stanley coming out?"

"Oh, no, of course it was Stanley, had to be. Unless he was carefully backing the van out of the garage so somebody else could come cart off the corpse, and I'll believe that when I see pigs fly. Oh, no, it was Stanley. The only reason it's important, the kid saying she wasn't sure, is that it proves how good she is. She said she saw it, then by God she saw it!"

He breezed through the next two blocks in a silent glow of satisfaction, so pleased with Tita Robinson that he temporarily forgot about Kathryn Koerney. Kathryn sensed that his thoughts were elsewhere, and in that brief emotional vacuum her lifelong hunger for attention raised its ugly and familiar head.

"Uh, Tom?" she ventured. "When I asked her about the back-door lock—you know, you told me to see if I could figure out if she'd been fever-muddled or clear-headed, and I thought maybe little details like that—"

"Oh, sure, sure." He waved it aside, not dreaming that the Rev. Dr. Koerney wanted to be patted on the head and given a gold star. "No question. Clear as a bell. All my witnesses should be so sick." He grinned. "Maybe all my witnesses should be ten years old."

Kathryn promptly decided she had done a mediocre job, but Tita had been so good, it didn't matter, and Tom was too polite to say so. Deep in anticlimax, she was deposited back at her house with a casual wave of thanks.

The Chief of Police then drove off in high spirits to pursue a judge and a search warrant, leaving in Tita Robinson's mind, dormant and dangerous, the one piece of information he most needed.

CHAPTER 18

i

He sat at his desk at work. Not that he was working. But some sort of appearance had to be kept up. It wouldn't do to let anyone know how drastic, how desperate, the situation really was.

He had thought Monday afternoon was as bad as things could get. It could only get better after that. But the night had brought new horrors.

When he had looked at the cleaned kitchen, body and blood gone, white tile floor again spotless, he had had a sudden nightmarish thought that he had lost his mind. It had never happened at all, he had imagined the whole thing. He must be cracking up.

The worst thing was that he had no one to talk to, no one he could trust, no one who would understand. He had never realized how much you could miss your wife. That was the thing about wives, you took them for granted. They were always there. But not now. Now she was gone.

ii

What had she done? What had she said? Too much, probably. It had seemed harmless enough. Why not talk to that nice cop, whatever had happened to Mrs. Kimbrough, it could have nothing to do with Bill, after all. Not dear Bill. Never.

But the cop had come back and this time he wasn't nice. Dragging poor Bill away like that, when anyone could see he wasn't well. Why he had come to work at all, she could not understand.

It did not occur to Vickie—naturally—that Bill Stanley had come to work to escape his house, with its ghosts in kitchen and basement. Not that it did him any good, because the Chief of Police had come for him and taken him right back there. Bill had tried to just give the man his keys and tell him to go ahead, but the cop had insisted he had to be there.

"Regulations," Holder had lied. Actually, the C.S.I. team would have preferred to have the house to themselves, but the Chief had maintained it would be more nerve-racking for the suspect to be forced to witness the search, and he intended, if necessary, to rack every nerve in Bill Stanley's body.

He needed a confession. No matter what they found in the house, they'd have trouble making a homicide charge stick if they didn't have a body; if Stanley had been even halfway efficient or imaginative about hiding it, they might look for a year and not find it.

The Chief of Police and his prime suspect had been sitting on the sofa in the Stanley living room for about thirty minutes. The search in that room had been completed. The D.A.'s squad had been over every inch of it; they were rapid, thorough, and utterly cold-blooded. They put Tom Holder in mind of a plague of locusts.

Tom flicked a glance at Officer Rocko Pursley, sitting patiently across the room in one of the fragile-looking chairs. Apparently that admirable young man had not breathed a word at the station about his Chief's verbal seduction of Glamorous Gloria on Monday night. This being Thursday afternoon, that made almost three days of heroic restraint, so Tom had rewarded Pursley by bringing him along for the arrest. Not that it looked like much of a reward at that point. The suspect, instead of providing any excitement, was giving a good imitation of taking a nap.

Bill Stanley had leaned his head back against the sofa cushions and closed his eyes. Holder wondered if it might be bad policy to let him withdraw from what was going on, and decided to shake his tree with a couple of questions. "Mr. Stanley," he said, "you know we've been unable to get through to your wife in San Francisco."

Stanley made a sound in his throat.

"We've established that she caught her plane all right, but there was something kind of odd about it; maybe you can explain it to me. The guy at the check-in desk said she didn't check any luggage, and she didn't carry any, either, which seemed pretty strange, since she was going to be gone for most of a week. Do you know anything about that?"

Stanley had opened his eyes and turned to him. His face was expressionless. He met Holder's gaze without apparent difficulty for several seconds, then said, "I'm sorry, could you please say that again?"

Holder obliged him.

There was another silence, longer than the first; finally Holder asked, "Doesn't your wife usually take a suitcase or something with her when she leaves town for a week?"

Stanley covered his eyes with his hand for a moment, then dropped the hand and looked at Holder once more. "I'm sorry," he said again. "I'm sure you understand that this is—is difficult."

Holder made a listening noise.

Bill swallowed, and took an audible breath. "Sunday night," he said, "Carolyn packed two bags, a small suitcase and a hanging bag. That is, she put a few things in the hanging bag, in the compartments, I mean, she always leaves the dresses till the last minute. Anyway, they were both there in the bedroom when I left for work Monday morning."

"And were they still there when you came home from work with the flu that afternoon?" Holder asked with a microscopic touch of irony on the word *flu*.

Stanley stared at him blankly and stammered, "I, uh, I don't know. I mean, I didn't notice. Uh, you know I fell asleep here." He indicated the sofa they were sitting on.

"Well, they're not there now, are they? Flu or not, you would surely have noticed yesterday, or today, if they were still there?"

"Um, I guess so, I mean, I might . . ." He was patently unsure.

"Tell you what, Mr. Stanley, why don't we go upstairs and look?"

The suggestion did not appear to alarm Stanley, who rose unsteadily to his feet, murmuring, "Sure."

On the stairs Holder hung back, giving his suspect plenty of room to hang on to the banister, which he did, as if it were life and reason. Upstairs they turned left down a carpeted hallway and entered a large bedroom that overlooked the backyard. The first thing Holder noticed was twin beds. One was neatly made up, with a cover of lavishly flowered chintz; the other had been slept in at least once and left unmade.

Stanley stood in the doorway, looking around vaguely. "They were—I think they were on her bed," he said with an ineffective gesture.

Holder pretended to look at the room while covertly studying Bill Stanley. What he had really wanted was to see how Bill stood up to a visit to his bedroom; if it were the scene of the crime, or even the scene of his last tryst with Grace, surely it would rattle him. But Bill Stanley wasn't rattled. He remained in the semi-daze he had been in when they were sitting on the sofa, his face still sickly pale but not apparently traumatized by the bedroom or anything in it.

Holder shrugged and led the way back downstairs and across the front hall toward the living room. Down at the end of the hall the kitchen door opened, and a man stepped out and said, "Chief? Could you come in here, please?"

Holder, ever courteous, turned to Stanley to say, "Excuse me," but the words never got out of his mouth. There on Bill Stanley's face was the expression Holder had looked for in vain in the bedroom: It was the expression of a man who is looking undefended into the face of disaster. Holder took him by the arm and led him to the sofa and instructed him to sit down; Bill sat like an obedient child.

When Tom walked into the kitchen he saw immediately that the open dishwasher was the center of interest. He was puzzled until one of them stepped back to give him a better view. Then he saw the knife.

It was in the cutlery rack of the dishwasher, the long, triangular blade pointing upward over a black wooden handle with brass rivets. It seemed huge, but what made it remarkable was that the metal blade was as black as the handle, and flecked with rust.

Sid Garvey, who was in charge, said, "Something funny about this. That knife is one of this set here—" He waved a stubby pencil at a magnetic knife rack hanging on the wall nearby. Stuck to the magnetic strip were all the big knife's younger brothers, three of them, in graduated sizes. But their blades were mottled gray, not black.

"You see the difference in the blades," Sid was continuing. "Now, obviously, they're not stainless steel because they don't shine. My guess is these guys up on the rack here look the way they're supposed to, though why anybody would want a knife that looks like that, I don't know; anyway, the gray blades, I think, are normal. Now, the handles are wood, you see, and if you got some kind of special knife with a wooden handle, you don't put it in the dishwasher, right? But this one got put in the dishwasher and maybe that's what made the blade go all black. What do you think?"

"I think," said Harton's Chief of Police with a flicker of satisfaction, "that if you're cleaning up after a murder, you don't get too fussy about how you clean the knife."

"Little Tommy Holder, go to the head of the class." (Sid played poker with Tom and could get away with a lot.)

"Is there any blood left on it?" Tom asked, too eager for hard evidence to bandy insults with Garvey.

Sid shook his head. "Nothing I've got on me works on hemoglobin that's been cooked."

"Will you be able to get anything back at the lab?"

"Watch me," said Sid, and started giving orders to his team. One he dispatched upstairs with the command "Brush hunt," which meant, Find a hair follicle for DNA comparison. Two others were deputed to remove and pack up everything in the dishwasher that was removable, including the pieces of broken plate down in the bottom, the drain, and the rubber lining around the door. "And when you're done there, let's see what we can get from the floor."

"Good." Holder nodded. "Anything else?"

"Christ, we give you the weapon, whaddaya want?"

"The body," Tom sighed, and went back to the living room.

Stanley once more was leaning back with his eyes closed, and Tom wished he could do something creative like wave the knife in front of him, but he knew better than to screw around like that. So he sat in silence.

About twenty minutes after boredom had well and truly set in, another of the Trenton squad stepped into the room and indicated with a jerk of her head that Holder was wanted in the back hall. When they got there, Sid Garvey gave Tom a sour look and said, "No body, O.K.? But this"—his plastic-gloved hand held up a woman's handbag—"was in a box of Christmas ornaments in the basement. What a dumbass."

The bag was of some rough brown fabric with bits of leather trim. Garvey put the bag down on a narrow hall table and picked up a plastic bag containing a leather billfold. "This was in it," he announced, holding it up in front of Tom. The wallet had been put into the plastic bag unfolded; Tom saw some slots with credit cards peeking out of them, and a leather-framed window of clear plastic displaying a driver's license.

It was Grace Kimbrough's.

"Well, that about takes care of it, doesn't it?" said Tom.

Careful to touch only the fabric of the handbag, he took it from Sid and went back to the living room. "Mr. Stanley," he said. The man did not stir. "Look at this, Mr. Stanley."

Stanley opened his eyes and looked at the handbag. There was hardly a flicker of surprise.

"Can you identify this?"

No response.

"Come on, man, speak up. Whose is this?"

Bill was silent six seconds, then replied in a hoarse whisper, "Grace's."

"That's right. Would you like to tell us how it got into a box of Christmas decorations in your basement?"

Bill again closed his eyes.

"Would you like to tell us why you hid her handbag in the basement and took her body somewhere else?"

No response.

"Would you like to call your lawyer?"

No response.

Holder sighed. "O.K., you're under arrest. You have the right to remain silent. You have the right—"As Tom went through the Miranda rights, Bill Stanley slowly opened his eyes and stared at Holder with his first visible surprise. At the end of the little speech, Stanley giggled. Then he broke into great heaves of hysterical laughter, clutching his sides as if in pain.

"What in hell?" Holder muttered, and then to Pursley, "Cuff him."

Being handcuffed seemed to sober Stanley somewhat; he stopped shaking with laughter and turned his face away, refusing to look Holder in the eye.

Sid Garvey, who had come up behind Holder, said, "What's so funny about getting Mirandized?"

"You got me," Holder replied, annoyed with himself for not understanding what had just happened.

He was still annoyed at four o'clock that afternoon, when Bill Stanley was locked up in Trenton and refusing—God only knew why—to summon a lawyer, and the call from San Francisco came in.

The police there reported first, in some dudgeon, that they had been misinformed, that the woman they'd asked about in three dozen other hotels had checked into the Mark Hopkins— carrying a small Hartmann suitcase in mint condition—on Monday night, about an hour after Holder had supposedly ascertained that she wasn't expected there. The second part of the report was less satisfactory. Carolyn Stanley had checked out of the hotel at five-thirty on Tuesday morning, since which time the San Francisco police could discover neither hide nor hair of her.

CHAPTER 19

So the Chief of Police, who had blithely expected to be brushing up the crumbs by the end of the day, was left instead with the uncomfortable conviction that he didn't know what the hell was happening. He decided he needed beer and sympathy, and after a brief struggle with his conscience decided to see whether these commodities were to be had at Kathryn Koerney's house. They were.

This time he was entertained in the kitchen, and the silver was nowhere in sight. (Kathryn engineered this by the simple expedient of not telling Mrs. Warburton he was coming.) She waved her dispirited guest toward a chair at the breakfast table and informed him he looked like he could use a drink. He admitted that a beer would be welcome, and Kathryn, letting her fresh-brewed tea grow cold in the pot, fetched two beers and two plain glass tumblers. Sitting down opposite him, she looked him over with more curiosity than sympathy.

"Last I saw you," she said, "you were dashing off to get a search warrant, and fire-breathing dragons had nothing on you. I take it you've hit a snag."

He took a long swallow and set his glass down. "I don't know what I've hit." In tones of undisguised frustration, he began to tell her everything that had happened since their interview with Tita Robinson. He was looking for consolation, not assistance, but he got lucky. It happened at the very end of his story, when Kathryn got confused.

"Wait wait wait!" she laughed. "I had these people straight last time but I've lost it." She started to draw diagrams on the table with her fingers. "Grace is married to George. *Was* married to George. Grace was having an affair with Bill, who lives next door. Bill's wife is the cousin and business partner of Grace's husband. Bill has killed Grace, and his wife is God knows where in California. Yes?"

"That's it."

"Ye gods."

Tom grinned. "Cozy, ain't it?"

"Cozy? It's positively incestuous. How do you tell the players without a program?"

"Well, I've got a program, sort of," he admitted, putting his beer down and reaching toward the adjacent chair for the now-familiar vinyl folder. He dug through it for a few seconds, and produced a snapshot. "I asked George for a recent picture of his wife, and he gave me this. That's all four of them."

The photograph had been taken at a party; the two couples were holding cocktails and looking appropriately jovial. They were of that indescribable age that is too old to be called young but young enough to make the designation "middle-aged" seem premature. The women were both brunettes, but there all simi-larities ended. One was tiny, a voluptuous elf who had poured herself into a dress that invited admiration of her most obvious attributes; the tall one was what used to be called statuesque, and had draped a lot of chiffon over her elegant bones.

The men, too, were strikingly different. One was striking, pe-riod. Very tall, youthfully trim, generous waves of unreceding hair, handsome face, handsome grin, handsome suit. The other lacked both the height and the hair of his friend, and if he had ever had a youthful figure, he had lost it; glasses sat on the pointed nose of a pleasant, innocuous face; he looked like a near-sighted mouse.

"That's Bill Stanley," said Tom, pointing at the figure that loomed largest in his current concern. "He did the murder, and this is his wife, Carolyn, who's in California but God knows where. This is Grace Kimbrough, who's been killed by Bill, who is her next-door neighbor and lover, and this is George, Grace's husband, who reported her missing."

Kathryn's jaw sagged. "Oh!" she cried. "Carolyn! You didn't tell me her name was Carolyn! Stanley! Stanley, oh, my God, Stanley, of course her name is Stanley!" Kathryn was rocking back and forth in her chair, her hands clutching her head. "And her hus-band's name is Bill! And she's in business with George! Oh, oh, stupid, I'm so stupid!"

"You *know* these people?"

"Know them? They did this house! They're decorators, Tom. Elton Kimbrough Interiors. If you'd told me Bill's wife was named Carolyn!"

Tom stared at her briefly while something inside him did somer-saults. He was vindicated. It was Divine Providence, not his own embarrassing fantasies, that had decreed he should involve Kathryn in this thing. She actually knew the people. That was bound to be useful. Most of the guilt he had been feeling about this covert flirtation was instantly transformed into gratitude for the benignity of God. He dragged his happy mind back to the point and said, "Great! Just how well do you know them?"

Kathryn sat back in her chair, ordered her thoughts, and began to tell stories.

CHAPTER 20

It was June of the previous year. It was only eleven in the morning, so the sun was merely enthusiastic and had yet to become really offensive. But no amount of time in her native Texas had taught Kathryn to enjoy heat, and as she walked up Alexander Street she was grateful for the huge pools of shade created by the old maple trees.

In fact, she was grateful for quite a lot at that point. She had just spent forty-five minutes going over the deceptively plain-looking white clapboard house whose keys had been handed to her at the mortgage company's office at ten. She had pondered each bare room, trying to imagine it filled with comfort and color, so she would have some ideas—however vague—to convey to the decorator. In all this activity she was concentrating hard on the pleasure and excitement she felt and the gratitude those feelings induced, chiefly to drown out the small puritan voice of panic that bat-squeaked from the back of her brain, "Are you out of your mind? Who do you think you are, Rockefeller?—spending that kind of money on a house! And are you sure this is appropriate for a priest?"

Since the inheritance from her father was in fact ample to support the purchase of the house, not to mention the decorator she was about to hire, the question that niggled most seriously was the one about what was appropriate for a priest. The only thing that muffled this particular niggle was the reflection that she was giving to certain charities amounts whose total equaled the value of the house. But the bat-squeak was still faintly audible.

She turned right on Mercer Street, walked past the pretty, wooded grounds of the Episcopal church she would later know well, and emerged suddenly—as one does in Harton—from the residential neighborhood onto bustling Main Street. She waited for the light to change, glancing at the businesses across the road, and saw the decorators she'd been told about, Elton Kimbrough Interiors. It was an understated shop front whose very modesty proclaimed that it catered to wealth. A minute later she walked in their door.

She found herself standing on an Oriental rug in a small room containing a beautiful old wooden desk and a few marvelous chairs. There were three people there, engaged in efficient conversation that they broke off at the sound of the opening door. All three looked at Kathryn, performing the same split-second scan on her that she was performing on them.

Kathryn, for her part, cataloged a simply dressed and severely beautiful receptionist/secretary sitting at the desk, and an elegant couple standing near it: a diminutive woman, dark, curvaceous, and pretty, and a good-looking man, also dark, but very tall. The woman was wearing an exquisite rose-colored silk dress over which was draped a stunning scarf in lavender and white. The man was impeccable in an understated navy pinstripe suit that must have cost every penny as much as the clothes the woman was wearing, but made less noise about it. As Kathryn favored the unobtrusive, she was predisposed to prefer the man, the more so as the woman was wearing a face that had taken her forty-five minutes to put on and four hundred dollars to pay for. Kathryn decided (correctly, in fact, though she was never to know it) that inside the woman's dainty Italian shoes, her toenails were painted pale pink.

The Elton Kimbrough team were equally accurate in their evaluation of Kathryn: an attractive young woman of about thirty, chestnut hair expensively cut, and a classic shirtdress in a blue and white cotton print of stylized flowers that made both the Kimbrough women think, "Saks." They were perhaps slightly puzzled by her, as she was decades younger than their average customer, but she obviously represented money—her own or possibly her parents'—so she was welcome.

The man spoke first. He smiled winningly, wished Kathryn a good morning, and asked if he could help her, with a hopeful expression that clearly indicated that if he couldn't, it would ruin his day. Kathryn smiled back and said diffidently that she'd just bought Number Thirty-four, Alexander Street, and she was looking for—

The rest of it got lost in the general enthusiasm. The partners exclaimed and actually clapped their hands with pleasure ("Oh, wonderful! Congratulations! How superb! My dear girl, it's the Real Thing, but of course you know that—1753, I was told!") and even the alabaster receptionist raised her shapely brows and almost smiled.

George Kimbrough brushed past Carolyn Stanley, and seizing Kathryn's hand offered his full name as if it were a gift, then tossed in "and this is Carolyn"—effectively making her sound like his assistant. He began to draw his prize toward one of the two doors in the back wall, but Kathryn resisted him long enough to shake hands with Carolyn and look inquiringly at the ice princess at the desk.

Carolyn smiled with genuine warmth and said, dropping a hand on the princess's shoulder, "And this is Patricia Clyde, who keeps us organized." Kathryn shook hands with Patricia as well, noting out of the corner of her eye George's momentary impatience. A twentieth of a second after it would have been grossly rude to interrupt the handshake, George gently pulled Kathryn's elbow in the direction of his office again, using his other hand to give a couple of pats to that shoulder of Patricia's that Carolyn's hand had just vacated. Kathryn saw Patricia stiffen.

About fifteen minutes later, Kathryn had come to several conclusions. The first was that God was punishing her for her extravagant materialism. The second was that George Kimbrough had nothing to recommend him but his tailor and his dentist. She wondered how she could ever have thought his smile winning. In fact, she thought, warming to her theme, the chief trouble with George was that somebody had once told him he had a wolfish grin and he had taken it as a compliment. She had further concluded that he lacked the brains God gave geese.

These reflections gave her small comfort as she gazed despairingly at a sample of silk wallpaper in stripes of cream and gold that would not have been out of place at Versailles, and started for the third time to say, "I don't think I'm making myself clear." And for the third time, she got no further than "I don't think" before George interrupted her to assure her that he had lots of experience with pre-Revolutionary houses. He didn't quite go so far as to say that he would do the thinking for her, but his whole manner made it clear that she would be extremely sensible to allow him to do so.

At first Kathryn did not recognize the brief knock and Carolyn's murmured apology as her salvation, perhaps because she was too busy glaring at the cream-and-gold wallpaper. But Carolyn, come to fetch a sample book, heard George say that Ms. Koerney said she wanted something simple, took one look at Ms. Koerney's face, and promptly staged a rescue.

She looked pensively at Kathryn and said, "You know, my dear, I think I've got a wallpaper that looks just like your dress."

Kathryn looked up. This sounded altogether more promising. She started to say something, but unsurprisingly, George beat her to it.

"Like that dress?" he said with knitted brows, obviously displeased. "I don't know of any wallpaper like that."

"I can't remember quite where I saw it. . . ." Carolyn shut her eyes and laid two fingers across her nicely powdered nose in a good imitation of attempted recollection. Kathryn could never quite remember how the little woman had managed it from there, but within a few minutes she was in Carolyn's office with the door shut against a baffled and irked George, and listening to Carolyn utter magic words: "You don't want it to look like it was done by a decorator, do you?"

And so it was that Kathryn got just what she wanted for her house, and over a couple of months developed a sizable respect for the woman whose polished perfection had initially repelled her. Not that she found her a kindred spirit; Carolyn was far too

fond of saying "my Mercedes" when "my car" would have suf-
ficed, and Kathryn could have done without the artfully casual
references to "when I did the Governor's Mansion."

But Kathryn forgave her these lapses, not merely because she
was awfully good at her job, but because one day Carolyn took
her to lunch at Leboeuf's, examined the bill afterward, called the
waiter back, and said, "You made a mistake in the addition.
You've undercharged me twenty dollars."

(At this point in Kathryn's narrative, Tom Holder wondered
dizzily how large a lunch check would have to be before somebody could make a twenty-dollar error in it.)

But for Kathryn, whose parents had reared her in standards of
financial honesty that would have made the Boy Scouts look lax
by comparison, the point was that Carolyn would not take advantage of the waiter, who might have had to make the difference good out of his own pocket if the mistake were discovered.

Tom, however, could not figure out how honesty and professional ability could account for Carolyn's mysterious disappearance in San Francisco, and he said so.

"Actually," Kathryn confessed, "that one completely stumps
me. I can't picture Carolyn failing to meet her professional oblig-
ations. Very unlike her."

"That suits me fine. I'm working on the idea that she either
witnessed or helped with Grace's killing, and has run away so we
can't find her. I mean, if you've got a murder on your mind, you
probably wouldn't give a damn about your professional obliga-
tions, would you?"

"I simply cannot imagine Carolyn killing anybody."

"Happens to people. They reach a breaking point, get into a
rage—"

"That's what I can't picture. Carolyn in a rage. She's always completely in control. Of herself, and of everybody else."

"Well, O.K., she didn't do the killing, but she knows her husband did, or thinks he did, so she runs away to escape from a situation she can't face up to."

Kathryn shook her head. "There's something sort of, I don't know, iron-clad about Carolyn's honesty. I can't believe she wouldn't stay and face the music."

In his years on the job, Tom had heard a lot of people say they couldn't believe that so-and-so could possibly do what so-and-so had obviously just done. He said, with ever so slightly conspicuous patience, "Well, you've never seen her react to watching her husband kill their next-door neighbor, have you?"

Kathryn felt singularly foolish. Tom must think her naive, if not totally dim. She gave him a rueful smile. "You'd have to show me movies of it."

"Only wish I had some," he said, unaware of the dent he had made in Kathryn's oversensitive ego. He stared for a moment at the bottom of his empty glass, but waved her back to her seat as she rose, offering him what would have been his second refill. "No, no, I don't need any more. What I need is for you to tell me you know Bill Stanley, too."

Alas, Kathryn and Bill had met only once.

It had been a golden September afternoon, but Kathryn had had little time to appreciate it. It was four forty-five in the afternoon, she was up to her ears in papers that needed grading, and instead of grading them she was rooting through the chaos sprawled across her eighteen square feet of desktop, looking for some fabric swatches she seemed to have irretrievably lost. She had faithfully promised Carolyn that she would return them by

Thursday afternoon at the latest so George could show them to another client on Friday. While she searched, she upbraided herself for her procrastination (she should have looked for them earlier in the week), her untidiness (how could she possibly have gotten her workroom this messy in the five weeks she had lived in the house?), and her absurd optimism (she should have known that the house would never be finished before classes started at the seminary).

When she finally found the little sheaf of fabric squares (she had used them as a bookmark in a large volume of patristic theology), she looked at the clock and mildly swore. It was seven minutes past five, and experience had taught her that there wasn't the slightest possibility that Elton Kimbrough Interiors was still open. Swearing again, Kathryn began another search, this time for the small card on which Carolyn had written her home telephone number. Fortunately this was not buried as deep as the fabric swatches, so it was only about five-thirty when Kathryn pulled her Audi to a stop in front of Carolyn's mock-Tudor house in Canterbury Park.

The doorbell was answered by a short, slightly pudgy man in glasses and a denim apron who gave her a delighted smile and said, "So this is Kathryn the Great! Do come in, Kathryn, we're just back in the kitchen, pretending to be cooks, come help us get to the bottom of the cooking sherry, oh, sorry, I'm Bill, how do you do, no, no, I insist, you can't just run away, Carolyn would never forgive me if I let you go, besides, she's told me all about you and you've got to give me the chance to find out how much she's been exaggerating."

Kathryn laughed and submitted to this cajolery, allowing herself to be led past an exquisite pastel living room in which everything looked fragile and feminine (*Pure Carolyn*, Kathryn thought) to a spacious white kitchen at the back of the house, where the lady in question was chopping parsley with a large and familiar-looking knife.

"Come in, my dear, come in," Carolyn said warmly. "Thanks so much for bringing those wretched things, George might otherwise have gone distracted, just put them over there on the breakfast table." She waved the knife at the table, and her husband pretended to fall back in terror. She gave him a tolerant smile.

"Don't worry," he said, "she's not really dangerous, she's just trying to let the parsley know who's boss." He was pouring a glass of sherry, which he promptly pressed into Kathryn's hand. "Letting me know, too; that's a holy terror of a knife she's using, you wouldn't catch me coming near it; here, sit, sit, no, I'm for stainless steel, shiny and blunt."

Kathryn declined to sit, instead walking over to where Carolyn had just put down the knife, and picking it up. "Carbon steel Sabatier," she said appreciatively, running a finger along the flat of the blade, which was gunmetal gray and mottled with use—as any well-used carbon steel knife would be—but ever so lightly oiled, which meant Carolyn took good care of it. "I have a set of these myself, and I have never found a stainless steel knife that can take an edge the way these can."

"What did I tell you?" Carolyn crowed triumphantly over Bill, who clapped a hand to his forehead and groaned, "Oh, God, not another one!"

"Another one what?" Kathryn asked.

"Knife snob," said Bill in a voice eloquent of despair. "But I forgive you," he added magnanimously to Kathryn, "chiefly because I want to stay on your good side."

"And why do you want to do that?"

"I know!" Carolyn chimed in. "He wants to see the inside of your house."

"He is most welcome to do so." Kathryn bowed graciously to Bill, who instantly bowed back, murmuring, "Thank you, kind lady."

"I'm throwing a party as soon as Carolyn gets through making it gorgeous. You're both invited, of course."

This produced little cries of pleasure from both of them, which turned to cries of disappointment when Kathryn put down her scarcely touched sherry and announced she had to be leaving. They both followed her to the front door, and she was halfway down the walk to her car before they finally gave up imploring her to stay longer.

Come the evening of the party, however, Carolyn arrived with the ice princess instead of her husband: "Patricia's standing in for Bill, I knew you wouldn't mind, he's got some business thing he can't get out of." So that was all Kathryn had ever seen of Bill Stanley.

CHAPTER 21

It wasn't much. Tom, forgetting his manners, said so, making Kathryn feel singularly useless.

She had tried to impress him that morning, and apparently failed; now she had failed again. She felt suddenly cross and tired. "I hate this business anyway," she complained. "None of it makes sense, and it's obvious I'm the world's worst judge of character and I never knew these people at all. Here's Carolyn, who is a monster of rectitude, running around San Francisco, hiding from the police; here's her husband, who looks like the proverbial guy who wouldn't hurt a fly, murdering his next-door neighbor; and look who's the innocent bystander—the unspeakably obnoxious George Kimbrough!"

"You know, I'm glad to hear you say that, because I've been feeling kind of guilty for not feeling sorrier for him about his wife."

"I'm astonished that you didn't immediately prefer him to Bill Stanley as chief suspect."

"Do you know, that never even crossed my mind?"

"Why on earth not? He's so smarmy, I'd have thought it would be your first instinct."

Tom thought for a moment. "I guess it's because I've talked to killers, and I've talked to people who've had family go missing. They're different. It isn't just that one is guilty and the other isn't. It's something like, the killer knows too much and is trying to pretend he doesn't know it, and the guy whose wife or kid is missing doesn't know *enough*. He's confused, he keeps asking questions, he keeps saying things like 'I don't understand, I just don't understand.' And that was George all over when I talked to him on Monday night. He just didn't understand, he just didn't know where the hell she could be, he just didn't know what was going on."

"And you believed him?"

"Oh, yeah, it was real. Trust me, on this one I'm the one who speaks with authority and not as the scribes. George Kimbrough called us Monday night because he had no earthly idea what had happened to his wife. And he calls the station three times a day because he still has no idea, and it's driving him crazy."

"O.K., if you insist," she sighed.

"Who's insisting? I'm stuck with it." He sighed, too. "I guess I really ought to be rolling." He stood up reluctantly.

Kathryn, rising, was reluctant, too. He was leaving and she hadn't impressed him a bit. "Well," she began unhopefully as she walked him to the door, "I haven't the foggiest idea what Carolyn is up to, or why Bill thought getting arrested was so hilarious, but I admit that what really baffles the hell out of me is the two bags in the bedroom that turn into no bags on the plane that turn into one bag at the Mark—" She simply stopped. The only motion she made was to close her eyes. *Oh, God,* she thought, *give this to me.* After a few seconds she opened her eyes and said carefully, as though afraid movement would frighten the thought away, "The bellboy at the Mark Hopkins, he said the bag looked new. And Carolyn was late getting to the hotel. Bill expected her to have been there when he called. What time does that flight get to San Francisco, and was it on time?"

"Five minutes after seven, and yes."

"Lots of department stores and shopping centers stay open till nine these days."

Tom was grinning at her. "I'll make you an honorary sergeant. She went from the airport to a store and bought a new suitcase—"

"And pajamas and a toothbrush," added Kathryn triumphantly, "and a change of clothes. Possibly several changes of clothes."

"So she ran off to California without her luggage and bought some more when she got there. Now make my day and tell me *why* she did that."

"Haven't a clue. But it makes slightly more sense than her running off with half her luggage and leaving the other half in the car and lying to the airline clerk. Wait a minute—there was something funny about the car, wasn't there?"

"Come again?"

"Monday night, you said something to Bill Stanley about the car—"

"You mean when I asked him if he drove his wife to the airport, and he said she drove herself, and then he practically fainted."

"Right. It seems to me that oddities are collecting around that car. Stanley faints at the mention of it, Carolyn puts her bags in it, then goes off without them. Have you gone over it? Is there anything picturesque like bloodstains on the upholstery?"

It was Tom's turn to feel like a fool. "No," he admitted. "I didn't think Carolyn's car mattered, since we know Bill put Grace's body in the van. You know, I believe I'll just call the airport police again and ask them to have a little look around the long-term parking lot." He moved purposefully toward the front door, but Kathryn didn't mind. It was all right if he left now. She had the remark about honorary sergeant, and she planned to cherish it.

"Thanks." He waved as he went down the walk. "I'll let you know if we find anything interesting."

"Do that." She closed the door and turned to call up the stairs, "Warby! You have been exquisitely thoughtful and stayed out of the kitchen for an hour, but hadn't we better rescue the roast?"

They had barely finished dinner when the phone rang, and Kathryn leapt to get it.

"Hello?"

"Well, you were right."

"About what?"

"She left both her bags in the car, the small suitcase and the hanging bag. In the backseat."

"Now all we have to do is figure out why. Anything else about the car?"

"Nothing unusual. It's a white Mercedes, brand new, blue upholstery, no bloodstains."

"Now, who," Kathryn asked, momentarily diverted, "would drive a white car in this climate? I thought better of Carolyn."

"The bags are white, too. Blue trim. Like the car."

"My color-coordinated friend. I wonder if I'll ever get my life that well organized."

"I don't know about organized. The car is in short-term parking, not long-term. And she's gonna be gone for most of a week. Jesus, can you imagine what that's going to cost her?"

There was no response to this.

"Hello? Kathryn? Are you still there?"

"Sorry. I was just thinking."

"What about?"

"Carolyn. Oh, never mind. I'm sure it's nothing. Thanks for calling. Keep on keeping me posted, won't you?"

He promised he would, and they hung up. Kathryn, who normally helped with the supper dishes whenever she wasn't rushed for time, wandered out of the kitchen, deserting Mrs. Warburton, and found herself in the library. There she sank into a large oxblood-leather chair and proceeded, to all appearances, to spend twenty minutes studying the brass knob at the top of the left andiron. At the end of that time she decided she knew why Carolyn was eluding the San Francisco police.

CHAPTER 22

Some dim voice inside her protested, producing a niggling feeling of discomfort, but it was overcome by the immensely gratifying knowledge that she was being very, very clever. Tom would be thoroughly wowed. She couldn't wait to call him. She started to rise from her chair, then hesitated.

It was so far-fetched. It seemed plausible to her; would it seem so to Tom? What if it didn't, what if he said it was the silliest thing he'd ever heard, and—horror of horrors—what if he turned out to be right? The longer she thought about it, the greater the possibility for acute embarrassment loomed in her mind. She leaned back in her chair and drummed her fingers on the leather arms, making a faint, steady patter.

Suddenly her eyes opened wide.

It was a bold notion, and at first it seemed preposterous. But the more she thought about it, the more reasonable it began to look. She could certainly afford it. And chief among its advantages was that if she turned out to be wrong, Tom Holder would never know. And if she were right—what a coup! Yes, she would do it.

She looked at her watch and ticked off time zones on her fingers. Four-forty in San Francisco, good. But how to find an agency, and would they accept a job on the basis of a long-distance phone call? Three seconds' thought brought her an answer to both these problems.

She got up, marched into the workroom that stretched long and narrow across the back of the house, went to the enormous expanse of her desk, and fished her address book out of the clutter that Mrs. Warburton was forbidden ever to tidy. She consulted an entry under R, punched eleven digits into the phone, waited for an answer, and asked for Father Ryder.

There was a short pause, then a click, and a mellifluous voice announced that it was Geoffrey Ryder.

"Geoffrey, my love! Kathryn Koerney."

"KATE!" cried Father Ryder, one of the three people living who could get away with abbreviating Kathryn's name to one syllable. "Good God. The prettiest Kate in Christendom, my superdainty Kate," he chanted in Shakespearean tones, "never tell me you're in town!"

"Alas, no, I'm in New Jersey, more's the pity, it's just a good connection. How's life with the Bishop?"

"Oh, His Grace and I are getting along swimmingly, my dear, simply swimmingly. I can't tell you what an unspeakable relief it is to escape from parish life."

"Overdose of Altar Guild, Geoffrey?"

"And terminal overdose of the Daughters of the King. My dear, you wouldn't believe!"

"My dear, I do!" said Kathryn, who got along fine with the Daughters of the King. "Listen, sweetness, I would love to chatter endlessly with you, but I've got a rather interesting problem that needs to be addressed without further loss of time."

"Speak, speak! My ear is open like a greedy shark to catch the tunings of a voice divine."

"You've been reading Dorothy Sayers."

"But constantly, sweet Kate! How quick of you."

"The stimulus of talking to you, dear boy. Geoffrey, I need a private detective."

A burst of laughter met this announcement. "My dear, you are magnificent. As always."

"I'm serious. I need a private detective in the city of San Francisco, somebody who specializes in missing persons. Have you got a yellow pages handy?"

"Dear me," said Geoffrey, suddenly subdued. "One of your teenagers?"

"I'm not doing teenagers anymore, I'm doing fourth-graders, and to the best of my knowledge, they're all where they're supposed to be."

"Oh, for pity's sake!" Geoffrey was disgusted. "Have you got one of those Neanderthal rectors? It never fails, does it? Three years in seminary, and they stick you in Sunday school because it's Woman's Work."

"Six years in seminary, Geoffrey, and I asked for it. I like kids. Are you looking?"

"I'm looking, I'm looking. You *asked* for fourth-graders? Lawsy mercy me, will wonders never—here we are. I'm just skimming the big ads, here. Divorce seems to be the specialty of the house in most places. Who is the missing party, then?"

"A woman in her middle forties, whose next-door neighbor has just been murdered."

"Jesus, are you serious?"

"Yes."

"Lummy. Oh, here's one. Divorce, of course, but also Missing Persons and Runaways. Got a pencil?"

"Shoot."

"Charles Bradford, Inc., Investigators, 435-0763."

"Great. Now, Geoffrey, I need to trespass on your kindness a bit further. I'll have to hire this guy over the telephone, and just in case he wants some assurance, before he runs around investigating, that I do pay my bills, may I give him your name, rank, and serial number? And will you vouch for me?"

"But of course, darling. I vouch beautifully."

"Of course he might just take a credit card number; I really have no idea how these people work. I'm just trying to cover any eventuality."

"Count on me, my dear, I'd be thrilled. But you must promise to tell me all about it whenever you reach your thrilling conclusion. You're not by any mad chance doing a Lord Peter, are you?"

"The comparison shames me. Geoffrey, I must go."

"Yes, darling. Happy hunting, and be warned: If I die of curiosity I shall come back and haunt you."

"You'd be welcome. God bless. Bye."

"Good-bye, sweet Kate. Parting is such—"

But Kathryn had already hung up.

At Charles Bradford Investigators she got the man himself, and instantly suspected that the S at the end of "Investigators" was strictly for show. In this she wronged Mr. Bradford; his firm boasted five detectives and a secretary. The secretary had told him that "a woman who's a reverend" was calling from New Jersey, and Bradford, intrigued, had taken the call himself.

Kathryn, annoyed to feel a rush of nervousness come over her, managed nevertheless to describe the situation coherently to Mr. Bradford. She was obliged, she thought, to warn him that he might find himself tripping over the police in the search for Carolyn Stanley, which further obliged her to tell him why she didn't think the police were going to find the missing woman.

If Bradford was amused or skeptical—and Kathryn thought he had a right to be either or both—he tactfully refrained from saying so. He made note of Kathryn's two references, and after he had hung up checked the local number with the phone book. Yes, it was the diocesan headquarters of the Episcopal church. He made the call, and asked for the Bishop's chaplain. After a moment he found himself in conversation with a young man who assured him earnestly that if Kathryn Koerney's check bounced, he (Father Ryder) would eat his chasuble and dance naked on the high altar.

Bradford decided that aside from the murder angle, which really had no bearing on what he'd been asked to do, it was a rather routine case. He handed it over to one of his subordinates and went home to his dinner.

CHAPTER 23

i

Thursday. Where the *hell* was Grace? She had been missing since Monday night, and not only had the police not found her, they had arrested Billy for murdering her. Billy, for Christ's sake, murdering Grace! What a bunch of morons they were! He had tried to tell them they had it all wrong, that Billy couldn't possibly have killed Grace, he wouldn't hurt an ant, and even if he would, what reason could he have to kill Grace? She'd never done him any harm. But they wouldn't listen to him. They just told him they were sorry for his loss. His loss, what bullshit! And the moron cops were saying Carolyn had gone to San Francisco, but now they couldn't find her!

He had a headache. He *never* had headaches. It was all Grace's fault, how could she have gone off like this? For a fraction of a second he wondered if the cops were right, that something had happened to her. Not Billy killing her, of course, because that was

just stupid, that could never have happened, but maybe something else?

No. No, it couldn't be, what was he thinking? He must be going crazy. It was the stress, of course. He felt like screaming. He
felt like throwing things against the wall. But the ice bitch would
hear him. Suddenly he sat up straight. Now *that* was something
he could take care of.

ii

He didn't mind being in jail. If only they would leave him
alone. If only they wouldn't drag him out of the bare cell and off
to that room for questions. God, the questions. And when the
cops weren't asking questions, the lawyers were. He had told
them he didn't want a lawyer, but they had gotten one for him
anyway. But of course he didn't tell the lawyer anything, any
more than he told the cops, so the lawyer had given up and gone
away. And then they had sent him another one.

Somewhere deep inside him something knew that if only he
could get enough distance between himself and what was happening, it would be funny.

But it wasn't funny now. He had laughed, of course, when they
arrested him, but that was because of the surprise. But there
were no surprises now. Just all these damn people asking him
questions, over and over the same questions. And over and over
he told them that he didn't want to answer their questions. And
he was sticking to that. It was the least he could do for her. It was,
apparently, the only thing left that he could do for her. So he
would go on doing it.

iii

It was lunchtime on Thursday when Jim Robinson came by the station to deliver, somewhat sheepishly, his daughter's "Detective Notebook." Tita had remembered it on Wednesday, after the policeman and his lady assistant had left. She hadn't told them about it. And she was sure they needed to see it. Once again her father had made her a promise, and once again he was going to keep it, damn the embarrassment. And once again, fortunately, the sympathetic sergeant was at the front desk.

Sergeant Fischer, with a grin, had handed it to the Chief. The Chief, safe from Fischer's satire in the privacy of his office, had perused it. The first couple of pages contained a scrupulous and uninteresting log of everything the child had observed from her bedroom window on the previous Saturday and Sunday. As soon as Tom had grasped the nature of the contents of the book, he turned in some excitement to the page for Monday.

Here he was disappointed. The last entry was for shortly after eleven A.M., a time at which all his principals were accounted for and none of the entries concerned any Stanleys or Kimbroughs. Then he remembered that the Stanleys' house and yard could not be seen from Tita's bedroom window anyway. Nor the Kimbroughs', for that matter. Oh, well, it would have been too much to hope for. He turned to Tuesday, and found, surprisingly, nothing. He had expected an account of Tita's Monday-night adventure, but there was no entry on Tuesday. Wednesday's reports were as irrelevant as Saturday's and Sunday's.

He closed the notebook. Useless. On second thought, no, it wasn't. He could use it as an excuse to go to Kathryn's: "Here, Nancy Drew!" he would say. "*You* read it!" Since he couldn't fool

himself into thinking this errand was business, he waited until after four-thirty.

He told her everything, which was not much. She told him
nothing at all. She was still waiting for the call from California
that would tell her she was right. Then she could dazzle him. She
scolded herself: very childish, this sort of thing. But she had abandoned the hope that she would ever grow out of it; an obsessive
desire to score points with authority figures was a habit she had
contracted at the age of four, within three days of her enrollment
in kindergarten and her realization that the teacher was the most
important person in the room.

The call finally came on Friday.

iv

When she let herself into the office at nine twenty-five on Friday
morning, she was surprised to find that George had apparently not
yet arrived. Normally he got in first, because, she was sure, it gave
him a sense of superiority. But she had the place to herself. It would
have been pleasant if she hadn't been so worried about Carolyn.

On her desk was an envelope with her name on it. George's
handwriting. She sat and opened it.

Dear Patricia, it read. *I'm sorry to have to inform you that
Carolyn and I have decided to terminate your employment with us
effective immediately. We discussed it before she left for California.
We have met a young man who has both secretarial skills and experience in interior design. Of course you lack the latter, which is why
we have made this decision. He will be able to contribute more to the
firm than you and will work for the same salary. In lieu of notice you*

will find enclosed a check for three months' salary. Please remove all your things from the office today and when you leave, lock up, then put the key through the mail flap. Thank you for your four years with us. I will not be in today; please leave any messages on my desk. Sincerely, George Kimbrough.

Long before she got to the end of the letter, her mouth was hanging open. Impossible. Incredible. It was a lie, of course. And the insult! To be fired without notice! Who did he think he was, bullying her this way? He would pay for it. Oh, God, was he ever going to pay for it.

v

"And now we come to everybody's favorite sin," said Kathryn, her expertly pitched voice reaching without difficulty to the back corners of the lecture hall. "The last of the Seven Deadlies—" Here she paused, dropped her voice an octave, and pronounced lusciously: "Lust."

One hundred and twenty-seven seminary students laughed, and so did the professor in the back row under whose aegis Kathryn was delivering this lecture. Some of the junior faculty had a lot to learn about how to talk for fifty minutes without putting everybody to sleep, but this girl, he thought, was a born performer. He wondered how long they would be able to keep her; she joked about being the token Anglican in a Presbyterian seminary, but he sometimes suspected she felt a trifle isolated.

"Now, as I made clear in the beginning," she was continuing, "the order of the Seven Deadly Sins is neither arbitrary nor accidental. Lust is last because lust is least. According to the medieval

Church, lust is the least deadly, the least offensive of the Seven. Why? Because it is the only sin that contains within it some element of love. In Dante's *Inferno*, the lustful are near the top level of Hell, the least horrible place in Hell, and they have the easiest punishment of all the damned: They are light, wispy creatures, like dry leaves, and like dry leaves they are continually tossed about by great gusts of wind. This is to signify the way in which, in their mortal life, they were tossed around by their passions."

Kathryn leaned across the podium with a confidential air. "I know what you're thinking," she said in a stage whisper. "You're thinking, if lust is the least of the major sins, then why is the Church so obsessed with sex?" This got another laugh. "Well, boys and girls, there are two theories to account for this unhappy state of affairs. One is that we can blame it all on St. Augustine. St. Augustine, bless his cotton socks, was what we call a late convert. He spent his youth—"

Kathryn kept talking with scarcely a hitch, although her attention had been snagged by the opening of the door at the back of the large room and the totally unprecedented appearance there of Mrs. Warburton. Warby made no attempt to find a seat, but merely stood patiently against the back wall.

"—which means that if you go over to the university chapel," Kathryn was saying, "you will find St. Augustine pictured in the stained glass window dedicated to Truth rather than the one dedicated to Theology—a nice distinction if there ever was one, I'd love to talk to the guy who designed the windows, I suspect he was a Congregationalist—" There could be only one reason why Warby was seeking her out on the seminary campus in the middle of the day; there must have been a call from California. Frabjous day!

"—and if you can come up with a better system for classifying every conceivable manner of wrongdoing, I will personally buy you a fifth of scotch. Of course, if you don't drink scotch"— Kathryn paused, eyeing the large clock on the back wall; five seconds to go—"I want nothing to do with you." The bell rang before the laughter died away.

Plowing through the departing clamor of students, she made her way down the aisle to the back of the room.

"They've found her," said Mrs. Warburton.

Kathryn's heart skipped a beat. "Bradford called?"

Mrs. Warburton was hiding a smile. "Not Mr. Bradford. One of his detectives."

"What did he say?"

Mrs. Warburton's smile came out of hiding. "It's a she." Kathryn grimaced. She was not often caught in accidental sexism, and although she knew that Mrs. Warburton had deliberately laid the trap, she blamed only herself for walking straight into it. "Don't smirk, Warby, it's unbecoming."

Mrs. Warburton chuckled. "She called from Hoskin, which is a little town about a hundred and twenty miles north of San Francisco."

"And that's where our missing lady is?"

"Yes, at a motel, I've got the address. The detective—Miss Withers—says she shows no signs of leaving, but just in case, you should check with Mr. Bradford for a message when you get to San Francisco. I've got his home number."

Kathryn looked suspicious. "I didn't tell you I was going to San Francisco."

"Well, you didn't know you could, did you? What luck that the news came just when you have the whole weekend. I got you a seat on the three o'clock plane, but I thought I should come and tell you right away in case you weren't coming home to lunch."

"Warby."

"Oh, come now, Kate. You can't pretend you were going to turn her over to the police."

"That's the obvious thing to do," Kathryn countered unconvincingly.

"Nonsense. You're going to go out there and fetch her and bring her back to your policeman friend tied up in a bow."

"Oh."

"Well, that's what you want to do, isn't it?"

Kathryn sighed. "I have a lunch date I can't possibly break and I'd have to leave the house by one."

"I'll pack for you."

"You can't do that."

"Why not?"

Kathryn opened her mouth and closed it again.

Mrs. Warburton rolled on. "You'll only be gone overnight, after all. You won't have time to change before you leave, but I'll put in something comfortable for tomorrow. And all your night things, of course."

"I have papers to grade," said Kathryn stubbornly.

"Oh, you can do that on the plane," said Mrs. Warburton, maddeningly complacent. "You'll have lots of time." She nodded at Kathryn, and sailed away, down the now-empty hallway, on a wave of efficiency.

"Warby!" Kathryn called after her.

"Yes, dear?"

"Isn't this the part where you're supposed to pat me on the head and remind me to wear my mittens?"

Mrs. Warburton laughed.

CHAPTER 24

When she got off the plane in San Francisco, Kathryn was met by the pilot who was to fly her to Ukiah Municipal Airport, which was as close as airplanes got to where she was going. The man introduced himself as Fred, and stood looking bored while she phoned Charles Bradford to confirm that the quarry was still in Hoskin.

Fred then led Kathryn mutely through the scurrying crowds down the concourse, through the main body of the terminal building, and out another concourse, down an unmarked flight of stairs, out a door, and into a mild, clear night that was a blissful change from New Jersey. The pilot headed for a single-engine plane with a V-shaped tail, and Kathryn cried with real pleasure, "Oh, it's a Bonanza!"

This prompted Fred to regard her with more approval than he had previously accorded her, him not being—as he had told his boss—much for lady ministers. "You know planes?"

"I know this one. My uncle used to fly one."

"Pilot?"

"No, he was a rancher. His ranch was a seven-hour drive from nowhere in South Texas, so he used the Bonanza to get into town."

A couple of minutes' further conversation on this topic amply demonstrated that Kathryn's uncle Jesse had taught her everything her childish mind had been able to absorb about flying, and she hadn't forgotten it. Fred unbent a little. She was even forgiven for admiring the lights of San Francisco, a sight the pilot had seen too often to find inspiring.

The lights below first thinned, then became intermittent. Eventually Fred identified a cluster of them as Ukiah, and once past it they began their descent. They landed and taxied up to a small building. Fred remarked that you couldn't see much of the place in the dark, but then, he added with the only evidence of humor Kathryn had glimpsed in him, there wasn't much place to see even in the light.

She paid him with about a third of the cash Mrs. Warburton had withdrawn from the housekeeping account that afternoon, thanked him, and firmly reclaimed her bag and briefcase from his reluctantly cordial grasp. Bypassing the minute terminal building altogether, she walked directly to the taxi she could see waiting. "Are you for me? Koerney?"

"Yes, ma'am. Sunset Motel, in Hoskin?" The driver clearly thought there was some mistake.

"That's right," she assured him. She relinquished her gear to the driver and settled into the backseat, wondering if rich people— she still could not think of herself as one—moved through their whole lives with this sort of well-oiled efficiency.

The driver, after a brief attempt to persuade her that she'd like the Holiday Inn better, drove her to the shabby motel on which, Kathryn decided after one look, the sun had set a long time ago.

Faulty neon announced "ACANCY." The door to the office was flanked by a Coke machine and a cardboard box inhabited by a gloomy black dog of uncertain parentage. *The woman behind the desk*, thought Kathryn, *will have bleached-blond hair in curlers. And a cigarette hanging out of her mouth.*

She walked into the office, set down her things on a faded carpet of hideous green, and suppressed a grin. "Hello," she said to the middle-aged improbable redhead—in curlers—who was lighting a cigarette off the butt of the last one and concentrating heavily on an ancient black-and-white television in the corner of the room. "My name is Koerney. I'm looking for a Ms. Withers."

Not even the clergy collar earned Kathryn a second glance. "Number seven," said the redhead out of the corner of her mouth. "But she's over at the café. 'Cross the street. You can leave your stuff here if you want."

Kathryn, surprised by this unexpected graciousness, decided Ms. Withers had greased a palm, and availed herself of the offer. She then crossed the two-lane highway to Bart's Café, which despite its unpromising name appeared to be several degrees closer to civilization than the Sunset Motel.

She stood in the door, looking around and looking conspicuous. A dumpy, comfortable-looking woman of around forty-five, in a hairdo several decades out of date and a polyester pantsuit, waved to her. Kathryn advanced dubiously. "Ms. Withers?"

"Sally. Sit down and stop looking surprised."

Kathryn smiled, and sat. "Sorry. You don't look like a detective."

"That's my fortune, honey. But you should talk." The detective gestured at Kathryn's priestly attire.

Kathryn smiled again. "You've got a point. But don't keep me in suspense. You've found her?"

"I think so. It wasn't a cinch without a photo, but the woman in that back corner booth—don't look, she'll see you, she's looking around for the waitress. I'll tell you when. That woman there, she caught a taxi five blocks from the Mark Hopkins Tuesday morning at five-thirty-five. Taxi took her to the bus station, bus brought her here. It stops just outside this place. She went across the street and got a room at that motel, if you can believe it. Been here ever since. Must be bored out of her mind. I know I am, and I've only been here since this morning. Now." She nodded.

Kathryn turned quickly and looked in the direction indicated. At the booth in the corner, there she sat, elegant and unmistakable, looking, despite the pallor of despair, like a lily in a field of dandelions. Kathryn turned back to Sally Withers. "Brilliant, just brilliant. That's her all right. I don't suppose she's still using the name Stanley, is she?"

"Nope, Ellison. Maiden name, probably."

"Mmm. O.K., this is where I do my stuff. You know what the situation is. If she tries to get away, stop her."

"With a flying tackle."

"If necessary, yes. Here goes." Kathryn stood, and stumbled a little as she edged out of the booth. She found that she had something like stage fright. She bit her lip, clenched her fists, and said a brief, urgent prayer. Then, schooling her face to calm, she walked down the tile floor to the back corner booth and stood there. The woman looked up inquiringly.

Kathryn drew a careful breath and said in the most non-threatening voice she could muster: "Mrs. Kimbrough? Grace Kimbrough?"

CHAPTER 25

Grace Kimbrough continued to look inquiring for perhaps another second. Then Kathryn could see the realization hit her that she had been addressed by her own name; there was shock in her eyes, and fear.

"I thought perhaps you would like to know," said Kathryn diffidently, "that the police in New Jersey are looking for you—well, you already know that, of course, but I imagine you don't know that to find you they're dragging rivers and looking under bushes. Bill Stanley has been arrested for murdering you."

Fear gave way to blank astonishment. "Murdering *me*?"

"Yes, I thought that would surprise you. It was Carolyn he killed, wasn't it?" Some flicker of hope still remained in Kathryn that there was some other explanation, that Carolyn—Carolyn the capable, the exquisite, the honest—was not dead. But she saw the fear creep back into Grace Kimbrough's face, and knew that she had been right. Satisfyingly, ego-boostingly, terribly, sadly right. She needed to sit down. Grace still stared at her, wordless. Kathryn slipped into the seat opposite her and stared back, reading Carolyn's death in the frightened face of her friend. Satisfaction ebbed away, leaving Kathryn feeling suddenly tired and wondering why on earth she had thought she would enjoy this, this playing detective. But she couldn't quit now. She had work to do.

"Excuse me," she said gently. "I should perhaps introduce myself. My name is Kathryn Koerney. I've just come from Harton. I hired a private detective to find you. The San Francisco police couldn't find you because they were furnished with a description of Carolyn, and I imagine they've been asking around for a diminutive brunette with a well-rounded figure and short, curly hair." Kathryn's eye swept over Grace's smooth shoulder-length hair, and the bone structure that would normally establish her beauty but now only underlined her fatigue. Her height, thanks to the posture that even disaster had not touched, was evident still as she sat. "You drove Carolyn's car to the airport, didn't you? And used her ticket?"

Grace, uncomprehending, nodded almost imperceptibly. "But I never meant—why did they—"

"Bill moved Carolyn's body in the middle of the night—God only knows to where, he's not saying. He's not saying anything, in fact, not even to his lawyers. So, consider it: Carolyn is known to be leaving for California. She leaves her office after lunch to go home to get her luggage and go to the airport. That evening, the police are called in, not to look for Mrs. Stanley, who has apparently driven to the airport and caught her flight exactly as arranged, but for Grace Kimbrough, who wasn't supposed to be going anywhere and has vanished without a trace."

There was a pause. Grace managed to murmur, "How stupid of me."

"Not necessarily. You had no reason to assume that Carolyn's body would disappear. Drink your coffee, it's getting cold."

This considerate admonition startled Grace out of her trance. She looked at her cup, then carefully, using both hands, picked it up and drank. She set it back in the saucer as though relieved to have negotiated a difficult maneuver successfully. Her hands stayed on the cup, and she looked at them, not at Kathryn.

As Grace studied her hands, Kathryn became aware for the first time of the noises of the café: the clink of forks on plates, the clatter of dishes, a babble of conversation, the waitress's shrill, good-humored voice calling out an order for a Bart's burger and fries. They had been talking with a concentration so absolute that it had blanked out all other sounds and enclosed their booth in a capsule of silence. Suddenly Grace, too, seemed aware of her surroundings. She looked about with a kind of helpless irritation, as though the commonplace activity in the café were an affront to the magnitude of her distress.

Kathryn observed, "It's not the best place to talk, is it? Let's go somewhere else." She scooted out of the booth and held out her hand invitingly, almost as though to assist Grace to rise. Grace moved slowly but with determination. She stood, looked vaguely around her for an instant, then reached back across where she'd been sitting and grasped her handbag. She looked at Kathryn again.

Kathryn picked up the check that Grace had forgotten, glanced at it, calculated the tip, dug in her own handbag, and produced a dollar and some coins. Grace, saying not a word, watched Kathryn as she placed the money next to the plate containing the limp remains of a club sandwich.

Kathryn, who had expected a protest and an apology for absentmindedness, looked at Grace and with some surprise recognized the expression on her face: It was that of a child—not a happy one—who was waiting for the grown-ups to take care of grown-up things. When told to come along, she would come. Grace had abdicated; she had placed herself in Kathryn's hands. Kathryn had wanted to be in control of the situation, but this much authority frightened her. She summoned a reassuring smile and gestured for Grace to precede her; they walked to the cashier's stand by the door, Kathryn paid the bill, and they both stepped out into the night.

Across the parking lot to their left was a supermarket whose lights proclaimed that it kept late hours. Kathryn looked at Grace. "What do you drink?" she asked.

Grace lost a few seconds to astonishment, then answered, "Scotch."

"Good girl," said Kathryn. "Come on." They walked over to the store, and as Kathryn held the door open for Grace, a backward glance told her they were being followed by Sally Withers. Kathryn sketched a salute.

She bought Chivas Regal and soda and, because she doubted the amenities of the Sunset Motel, a package of plastic drinking cups and a bag of ice. Back at the motel, Grace asserted herself enough to lead Kathryn to her room. She fumbled with her key and got the door open, and they went in.

Kathryn wrinkled her fastidious nose, but it was no more—or no less—than she had expected. There was a lumpy-looking bed, an armchair upholstered in grim vinyl with two cigarette burns in the right arm, and a small plywood table, painted orange, next to the chair.

Kathryn waved at the chair and Grace sank into it. Kathryn mixed drinks at the table.

She handed Grace a scotch and soda that was mostly scotch, and went to put the ice in the bathroom sink. She returned with the expression of one who is determined to rise above her surroundings, picked up her own drink, kicked off her shoes, and sat cross-legged on the bed.

"Drink," she suggested, and did so herself. She watched Grace follow suit, and waited for the question that would tell her Grace's brain was back in some kind of functioning order. Eventually it came.

Grace rested her cup on one of the cigarette burns and focused on Kathryn. Her eyebrows contracted in puzzlement. "Who did you say you were?"

Kathryn explained who she was and how, because she was friends with the Chief of Police, she became involved in what was basically none of her business. She gave Grace a minute or two to digest this information, then asked the classic counselor's question: "Do you want to talk about it?"

Grace drew a breath, let it out, and drew another breath. She did want to talk about it. But how to convey the chaos of emotions? She remembered the initial shock, then the guilt, then the anger. Some of the anger was gone. She had gotten rid of it with Mike What's-his-name; she found she didn't want to remember his name. But in the end that had only produced more guilt, more of the feeling of having become something unrecognizably loathsome. She shook her head, as though trying to dislodge the thought.

The story. She could tell the story. Maybe that would be enough. Enough for what, she wasn't sure. But she began.

"It was all so fast. So sudden. At one o'clock that afternoon my life was normal. At one-thirty—" She made a small, helpless gesture.

Kathryn said, "At one-thirty it was a disaster, but let's start back at one."

"Yes, one o'clock. I was making out the grocery list." Grace actually achieved a shaky laugh. "I was about to look in the refrigerator to see if we had enough broccoli or whether I needed to buy some more. Can you believe it? Broccoli!" She started to laugh again, but the laugh slipped out of control; her whole face puckered, and she began to cry. She hadn't cried since that night in San Francisco. Since then, the other emotions had blocked the grief, but now it broke through like a thwarted river sweeping away a dam. Her whole body shook with the sobs.

Kathryn went over to her chair and sat on the arm, laying a hand on her shoulder. Grace leaned against her and wept without restraint. Kathryn, with an assurance born from long sessions with crying students, put both arms around her and patted her consolingly. At the right time she fished a tissue out of her pocket and offered it to Grace, then another one, then a third.

After what seemed a long time, the sobs subsided. Kathryn plucked the last wadded tissue out of Grace's hand and offered her a fresh one. This was accepted but not put immediately to any heavy-duty service, and Kathryn judged it time to return to her seat on the bed.

"I'm sorry," said Grace, "it's just so—so—"

"I'm sure it's perfectly horrible," Kathryn said calmly. "I'm sure I can't even imagine how bad it is."

Grace, for some reason, took strength from this admission and started again on her story.

CHAPTER 26

S he was reaching for the handle of the refrigerator when the phone rang, so she picked up the kitchen extension.

"Grace?" said a distraught voice.

"Carolyn? What's the matter?"

"I need you to drive me to the airport if you can."

"Yes, of course, but what's wrong?"

"I'm too upset to drive myself." As Carolyn's voice was quavering, Grace had no difficulty believing this, but she couldn't tell whether her friend was angry or sad or both.

"Yes, Carolyn, but what's upset you?"

"I can't tell you now. It's too awful. I've just had a hell of a row, I can't *remember* when I've been so angry."

Grace felt a flicker of apprehension. "What, uh, what's made you angry?"

"Well, I don't want to talk about it on the phone, I'll tell you in the car. Oh, God, you love someone, you trust someone for years, then they betray you. Everything's changed. Everything. My world has just—I can't even stay at the Mark, Patricia is canceling my reservation, my whole life is just—" She stopped, at a loss for words.

Grace's heart sank even as a flush rose to her cheeks. She couldn't make head or tail of the bit about the hotel, but the word *betray* was all too easy to understand. She stammered something, she hardly knew what.

Carolyn asked, "Can you leave in ten minutes?"

"Sure, sure, but, uh, my car's in the shop."

"That's all right, you can drive mine. Ten minutes?"

"Ten minutes, yes. Bye." Grace hung up the phone and saw that her hand was trembling. Carolyn had obviously found out. "But why on earth," Grace asked herself out loud, "isn't she mad at *me*?" She found a chair in the living room and almost fell into it. At first her brain just repeated the question dully, but eventually she began to think. After ten minutes the only explanation she had produced was that somehow Carolyn had found out Bill was having an affair, but she hadn't figured out who he was having it with. Grace could not imagine how she was going to share a car with Carolyn all the way to the airport without giving herself away. But she didn't have any more time to pull herself together; it was one-twenty.

She left her house by the front door, crossed her yard and the Stanleys', and let herself in their front door with her key. She called Carolyn's name but got no answer. Thinking she must still be upstairs, Grace went up to the bedroom but found it empty. "Carolyn?" she called toward the open bathroom door, but there was no response. She went back downstairs, walked through the dining room, and entered the kitchen. The earth stopped.

She did not scream, but that was only because she could not catch her breath. She stood in the doorway, her mouth frozen open, as waves of nausea hit her like breakers. The nausea passed. A short eternity passed. She dimly realized that she was moving forward on legs that did not seem to belong to her.

She knelt on the floor beside the body. Not to see if Carolyn was dead—she knew that already—but because something terrible inside her drew her down for a closer look.

The blood had stopped flowing. It lay in perfect stillness on the white tile floor, a glistening scarlet halo around the upper torso of the dead woman. The dress was white, too—or had been before the knife went through it. The knife now lay on the floor beside the body, oddly inconspicuous amid a gory miscellany of flatware and small utensils; every implement was as wet and as red as if it had been dipped in crimson paint.

The door of the dishwasher hung limp on broken hinges, pointing downward toward the body as if in mute apology. Three of the four small plates in the lower rack had slid from their places and lay in an untidy stack, facedown, where the cutlery rack had been before it had fallen to the floor. Like everything else within arm's reach, the rack and the plates in it were liberally splashed with blood.

She looked at the body, at the blood, at the knife. She thought she ought to feel something—anger, pity, remorse, anything—but no feeling came. Nothing except a fine buzzing that hummed in her ears and danced all over her body, as though an electric current ran through her skin. She did not seem to be able to move.

For how many minutes she remained kneeling, numbly gazing at Carolyn, she did not know.

Neither did she know how long Bill had been standing in the

doorway to the hall. She had not heard him come. His presence had crept into her senses gradually, through the buzzing, until there came a moment when she knew, unsurprised, that he was there.

She tried to look up, but she did not want to see his face; her eyes instead found his hands, and that somehow was worse.

He started to say something, but only a voiceless whisper came. He stopped, cleared his throat, tried again, and this time spoke. But what she heard was a thin, pinched travesty of his voice, the ghost of his voice.

It said, "Do you have any of the blood on you?"

For some reason the pedestrian practicality of the question offended her. The flicker of anger broke through the buzzing paralysis, or at least loosened it slightly. He was cool? So would she be.

"There's a little on my skirt."

"Stand up before there's more of it."

She stood up. Too suddenly, for the room heaved; she put out a hand to steady herself.

"Don't touch that!" he cried.

She snatched her hand back from the countertop, half-expecting to see a bloody handprint on the white surface. *Like Lady Macbeth!* she thought wildly. Then reason reasserted itself. "Don't be absurd. My fingerprints are all over this kitchen. All over the house."

He made a motion in the air in front of his face, as though to clear something away. "Of course," he said. "I— Yes, of course."

There was a silence. She could no longer look at the body now that he was there.

"I think you had better leave," he said.

"Yes," she replied, still not meeting his eyes. "Yes, I believe it's time." She moved stiffly, carefully, toward the back door.

Carolyn's Mercedes stood in the driveway. The driver's door was open. It seemed like an invitation. Grace got in, shut the door, started the engine, and drove. She moved automatically, as though she were running through some prewritten script.

She wasn't quite sure at what point she came to herself. Perhaps it was when she realized she was driving toward the airport. Perhaps it was when she stopped at a red light, and a police car pulled up beside her.

Oddly, her first thought was that she was driving without her license. She was to wonder about this later; surely the sight of a policeman should have made her think of the scene she had left behind in Harton. But no, instead, she thought, *Oh, God, I don't have my driver's license with me.* Instinctively she looked at the passenger seat, where her handbag would normally have been. And there was Carolyn's blue lizard handbag. She thought she must have dropped hers when she saw Carolyn's body. And she had left the house without it.

Sticking out of Carolyn's handbag was a colored folder with a travel agent's name on it. Of course. That would be Carolyn's plane ticket. And maybe a confirmation of her hotel reservation. The one now canceled.

The light turned green. Grace drove to the airport, parked close to the terminal building, took the blue lizard handbag, and tried unsuccessfully to take the luggage out of the backseat. Leaving it, she walked into the terminal and got herself onto Carolyn's flight to San Francisco. The plane was over Kansas before she figured out what she was doing. She was running away.

CHAPTER 27

Y ou're probably thinking that was a stupid thing to do," said
Grace, looking into her plastic cup and finding it empty.

"Not at all," Kathryn replied, rising to pour refills for both of
them. "I think it was an eminently reasonable thing to do. You
wanted to get away—and God knows I don't blame you. And
there was an escape route right in front of you. The only problem
was that the trail would be fairly easy to follow, so at five o'clock
the next morning you decamped and headed in the unlikely direction of the bus depot."

To Kathryn's considerable surprise, faint color stole up Grace's
throat and cheeks, and she stared at her scotch, not offering any
reply. At last she said, "Um, yes," but she would not look up.

Kathryn decided on boldness. "Is there something you're not
telling me?"

Grace lifted her head. Her cheeks were still pink. "Yes. But it has nothing to do with Carolyn or—any of this disaster. It's just something private."

Inspiration hit Kathryn, and before she could stop herself she said, "You had to get away from a man."

Grace was stunned. "How did you know?"

"I once left a place at dawn to get away from a man myself."

"Oh. But you're—" She gestured toward Kathryn.

"Don't let the collar fool you."

"Oh," said Grace again. There was a pause, then she said, "There was something—I don't know why I did this, I told him I was Carolyn. I mean, I told him my name was Carolyn Stanley."

Kathryn considered a moment. "I think that adds up. You were trying to escape, right? Trying to get away from everything? Well, if you used Carolyn's name, you could escape from yourself, too, after a fashion. Whatever you did, it wasn't you doing it."

To Kathryn's dismay, the flush stole again over Grace's face, making it painfully clear what the "it" was that Grace had been doing. Kathryn, possibly the more embarrassed of the two, plunged into a different topic. "Let me try another of my theories. Tell me about your suitcase." She nodded in the direction of the bag, which was sitting on an antiquated dresser under a cracked and somewhat grimy mirror.

"What? Oh. Well, since I came out here with nothing but Carolyn's handbag and the clothes I had on, I took a taxi from the airport to a shopping center and got just enough to keep me for a few days."

"Including a suitcase rather like the ones you've got at home."

"Yes." There was another pause while Grace's mind, the worst of the ordeal over, recovered sufficiently to rise to curiosity. "How did you know that?"

"Kidneys," said Kathryn solemnly, tapping her forehead.

Grace attempted a laugh. "No, tell me. Tell me how you found me, too. I mean, how you knew it was me."

"Well, it's the same story, actually. Miscellaneous bits from my friend the policeman." Kathryn started to number them on her fingers: "One: The missing Grace Kimbrough is presumed dead because a runaway takes her suitcases, and Grace leaves hers behind—all seven brown tweed bags with leather straps. Two: Carolyn Stanley checks in at the airport with no luggage. Three: Carolyn arrives at the Mark Hopkins with one brown Hartmann. Four: Carolyn's car is found in the parking lot at the airport with luggage in the backseat. Hypothesis: Carolyn, knowing or suspecting that her husband has murdered Grace, is in such a panic to get on the plane that she forgets her luggage and leaves it in the car. Obviously I got that bit wrong, but it didn't matter in the end. So she leaves the luggage, then, when she gets to San Francisco, she takes a taxi to a late-night store and buys a respectable suitcase, with contents, to take to the Mark Hopkins. But then my friend the policeman drops it on me that the luggage in the car at the airport—like the car itself—is white with blue trim. And this reminds me of Carolyn herself, who likes 'fragile' colors, and wears nothing but white and pastels, even in the winter. How much of a state would Carolyn have to be in to buy a *brown* suitcase?"

Grace knit her brow. "But you can't mean—is that all? Just what color the suitcase was?"

Kathryn stopped herself from saying "What bothered me to begin with was that I couldn't believe that Carolyn would have run away." It would sound like a criticism of Grace, and there was no point in chastising the woman. So instead she said, "The color of the suitcase told me it wasn't Carolyn. And there was only one other woman unaccounted for, so it had to be you."

"But—but that's—" Grace was incredulous. "That's just silly. If Carolyn was in a state, she'd buy anything, the color wouldn't matter. I should know, because I was the one doing it. I just pointed at the first thing I saw and said, 'I'll take that.' "

"But because it doesn't matter, you do what's automatic, and what's automatic is what you're used to. You bought the first thing you saw, and it just happened to be brown. But if it had been Carolyn, the first thing she saw would probably just happen to have been blue or white or even pink. You were eating a club sandwich over there across the street, or trying to. What did you order for lunch?"

"A club sandwich."

"And what do you normally order when you go out to eat a light lunch with your friends?"

Grace smiled faintly. "I see your point."

"But I really ought to admit," Kathryn continued, "that there was one other telling detail, besides the color of the suitcase, which made sense only if it was you in California, not Carolyn."

"Yes?"

"When they arrested Bill for the murder of Grace Kimbrough, he cracked up laughing. The police didn't know what the hell to make of that."

Grace looked measuringly at Kathryn. "You know," she said, "you must be awfully clever."

Kathryn attempted to smile modestly. "People have occasionally told me so," she replied. "Let's see if it's true. Let me try to guess why you're in this godforsaken excuse for a motel."

Grace actually chuckled. "It's awful, isn't it?"

"It's incredible. You are here because it was the first thing you saw when you got off the bus, and you were beyond caring."

"That's partly it. I wanted somewhere cheap, too. There was five hundred dollars in Carolyn's handbag, but I didn't know how long I'd be—uh, out here, and I didn't want to use her credit cards anymore. I'd used her American Express card at the store and the hotel, and nobody questioned it, but it made me a little nervous. I really didn't want to go on doing it. And besides—"

"You had decided it was time to drop the Stanley in favor of your maiden name."

"Well, some name besides Stanley, anyway. I decided on my maiden name only when the woman out there—" She broke off and stared at Kathryn in undisguised awe. "How did you know it was my maiden name?"

Kathryn perceived that she was being credited with omniscience, and shook her head, laughing. "No, I'm only fair-to-middlin' bright. If you want clever, really clever, I shall have to introduce you to Ms. Sally Withers!—which I ought to do about now, anyway, so the lady can call it a night." Kathryn was feeling better now. She had handled the conversation well; she had gotten out of Grace everything she needed to hear. It hadn't been fun, but she had done it, and she had done it right. She tossed off the last sip of scotch in her cup and stood. "Now, Mrs. Kimbrough—that's ridiculous, I'm going to call you Grace, and my name is Kathryn, in case you've forgotten. Grace: I propose to take you back to New Jersey on an eleven o'clock flight tomorrow morning. O.K.?"

Grace set her jaw. "O.K."

"Meanwhile," Kathryn continued in her finest steamroller manner, "I propose to take you away from all this. I have plenty of plastic, all of it legally mine, and you and I, my dear"—she laid a hand lightly on Grace's head—"are going to spend the rest of this rather awful night in the Holiday Inn. I'm told there actually is one, little though you might expect it from what you've seen of this town so far. One of God's little surprises."

CHAPTER 28

i

Something had to be done. Something. Anything. He couldn't just go on waiting. But what could he do? It would have been easy if he'd actually been a killer.

But of course he wasn't a killer. What had happened, that was an accident. Well, half an accident. He had moved the knife, yes, but that had been, well, a sudden temptation, a split-second act, he had done it without thinking. Crime of passion, heat of the moment, that sort of thing.

Besides, it might not have killed her. He pushed her, yes, and the knife was there where he put it, but it was possible, wasn't it, that she could have fallen sideways, or caught herself, or something? It was just a chance, just bad luck, that she had died. No one could blame him for that. It was almost like the thing had happened by itself. Like fate or something, nothing to do with him.

But fate, or luck, or whatever it was, had now deserted him.

He couldn't think of anything he could do. Besides wait. So he waited.

ii

They had to find her. They had been house-to-house in the neighborhood. They had combed the bushes in everybody's yards, front and back. They had talked to her mother over and over again and it was always the same: During that brief spell of sun in the morning, she had let Tita go outside for five minutes, just to sit on the swing, just for a little breath of fresh air; she was watching her through the kitchen window. But the phone had rung, and when she looked out the window again, her daughter was gone.

The Chief of Police was out beating the bushes with everybody else. No one was surprised. After all, when a child goes missing, the Chief is not going to sit back at the station, waiting for reports, he's going to be out there with his men. And women. Not just *his* men and women, either; they had called for reinforcements from West Windsor and Plainsboro. When that hadn't been enough, they called in Hopewell and Pennington and Lawrence. Private citizens, students from the university, all sorts of people had called in offering to help. So obviously the Chief was out there with everybody else.

What no one knew except the Chief himself was that he wasn't there out of duty or for community relations. He was there out of guilt. He didn't even notice that the day had once more become overcast and dismal. The other searchers were encouraged to take breaks from time to time; people went around with thermoses of coffee, but the Chief wouldn't take a break. His guilt was a consuming fire.

He had missed something. That much was clear. He thought he had gotten everything the child had to tell him, but he was obviously wrong. Disastrously wrong. If only he could talk to Kathryn about it, ask her to help him to remember, maybe together they could figure it out. But Kathryn had left town for the weekend, and that woman, Mrs. Warburton, said she had tried to get hold of her and couldn't; for some reason Kathryn hadn't stayed at the motel whose name and number she had left with her housekeeper. So there was no help there.

The thing that was driving him crazy was that the murderer was already in custody. The killer was cooling his heels in a cell in Trenton when the little girl went missing. So nobody took her, she'd just wandered off. She had to have just wandered off. That had to be it.

But he didn't believe it for a minute.

iii

Since there was nothing to do but wait, he did a lot of thinking, a lot of remembering. He wished he could stop himself from doing it, because it hurt so much. But the more it hurt, the more he remembered.

The day they discovered they both loved Shakespeare. He had dug out his copy of the sonnets and read to her. That stolen afternoon they went to see Kenneth Branagh's *Hamlet*. How they had squabbled amiably over it; he had liked the way they did the "Get thee to a nunnery" scene, she hadn't.

Hamlet.

Oh, yes, indeed. To be or not to be. He had never expected to find himself so deep in despair that suicide looked attractive. Oh, that this too, too solid flesh would melt . . .

Of course—he thought with a mordant flash of humor—that was just the problem, wasn't it? It was too, too solid flesh that had gotten him into this.

CHAPTER 29

On the eastern face of the Rockies the weather had turned foul, and Grace and Kathryn found themselves in an interminable delay at the airport in Denver. They ate a late lunch in the restaurant, and lingered over coffee.

They had a table by a window overlooking the runway, which Kathryn thought was fortunate. When two strangers share a meal, it helps to have something to pretend to look at when conversation languishes. But Grace was beginning to want to talk.

She said, "You must think I'm terrible."

"What, for running away? I already told you—"

"No, not for running away. For— Because of Bill."

"Oh." Kathryn shrugged. "Not necessarily."

"Why not? It's a sin, isn't it? Adultery?" Grace spoke the word harshly, as if determined not to spare herself.

"Grace. I am well acquainted with your husband. Your only choice was adultery or homicide."

Grace laughed in the middle of a sip of coffee, and choked.

"Sorry," said Kathryn hastily, thinking belatedly that a joke about homicide was probably in bad taste, given the circumstances.

Grace recovered. "But you wouldn't do it, would you? Commit adultery, I mean."

Kathryn privately believed that she was as likely to commit adultery as she was to commit murder, but then, ten years ago she would have said the same thing about divorce. So she said, "It's a temptation that hasn't come much in my way. I've been luckier than you in that respect."

"What a very kind thing to say."

"It's true."

"You mean you've never been tempted?"

"When I was married I was too busy being miserable, I think, to have the leisure to fall in love with anybody else. After my divorce—well, there was a married man, a friend, offering sympathy. I got drunk and depressed and got as far as kissing him. If he'd been patient, who knows, he might have succeeded in seducing me, but he was all over me in two seconds, and I broke and ran. And that's when I left town at dawn to escape a man. I still have nightmares about it. All of which makes me more cautious than I used to be."

"So now you're"—Grace looked for a word—"safe from it?"

"From the deed itself, I think." Kathryn flashed a smile. "But like Jimmy Carter and just about everybody else, I've committed adultery in my heart many times."

Grace smiled back, and, emboldened by Kathryn's frankness, asked, "Your policeman friend?"

"Who, Tom? Heavens, no!"

"You don't find him attractive?"

"Well, yes and no. To tell the truth, we flirt with each other in an understated sort of way, but it's not serious. I don't have fantasies about luring him away from his wife."

"Why not?"

"Good question. Let's see. It's not because he's fifteen years older than I am, and I really don't think it's because he's forty pounds overweight." She squinted out the window at the fog-bound planes. An uncomfortable thought occurred to her. How did one say it without sounding like the most god-awful snob? Kathryn sighed. "I feel reasonably sure he wouldn't recognize a quotation from *Hamlet* if he heard one."

She was still looking out the window at the runway, but after several seconds in which no response came, she turned to look at Grace. She saw to her surprise that Grace's eyes were filling with tears.

"I know exactly what you mean," said Grace. "George wouldn't either. But Bill does. We were both English majors. He reads—he used to read the sonnets to me."

Kathryn tried to picture a real estate agent who read Shakespeare's sonnets to his lover, and failed. "Tell me about Bill. If you like."

Grace dashed a hand across her eyes. "I don't think I can. I obviously don't know a thing about him." She shook her head, baffled. "I'd have said he wouldn't hurt a fly. He was always the kindest, most considerate—everybody loved him, everybody."

"Including Carolyn?"

"Yes. I'm sure of it. But—" She stopped, and looked at Kathryn, considering. "Yes, I'll tell you," she decided. "Something happened to Carolyn. Bill wanted her to see a doctor, but she wouldn't. She just lost interest in sex. It was about three years ago. She had twin beds put in their bedroom, wouldn't let Bill touch her. Bill said she was very polite about it, she kept apologizing, but she was set on it. She just turned their marriage into a platonic relationship."

Kathryn digested this for a moment, then asked, "If that's true, why would she have had such a fit when she found out that Bill was—"

"I don't *know*!" Grace cried. "And it haunts me! I always thought she knew, and that she didn't mind."

"You thought she didn't *mind*?"

"I swear to you! She would make it easy for me and Bill to be together, she would actually suggest things we could do together, and she would smile at me as if she knew, as if it were—oh, some special joke that we shared. You don't believe me."

"I believe that's what you think happened. But I think you may be deceiving yourself. You wanted her not to mind, so you convinced yourself—"

"No! No, I'm sure of it. She didn't want him anymore, and she didn't want to be a dog in the manger. She wanted him to be happy. She was a very decent person."

"Yes, I know she was, I've often thought so. But however decent she was, last Monday she had a hell of a row with Bill, who, she said, had betrayed her. And she canceled her reservation at the Mark Hopkins, presumably to go to another hotel, which must mean—because I can't figure out what else it could mean—she didn't want Bill to know where she was staying. She was afraid. Just being clear across the country wasn't safe enough."

"But that's impossible!" Grace protested vehemently. "She

could not have been afraid of Bill. He never even raised his voice to her."

"But, Grace—he killed her. Within the hour. She had put him into a fury, and she knew it. There's no other explanation for her behavior."

"But why did it happen *now?* How did she find out?"

"Maybe she found out from George. She was apparently acting quite normally until she had lunch with George. Then she returned to her office in a rare state and started making agitated phone calls and told Patricia to change her hotel reservation."

Grace was shaking her head firmly. "George doesn't know."

"How can you be sure of that?"

"Because he hasn't said anything. Believe me, if George knew, my life would not be worth living."

"All right, then, could Carolyn have gotten it from Patricia?"

"Patricia? How could she have found out?"

"God knows. It occurs to me only because my friend the policeman says Patricia knows something she isn't telling, and it's about Carolyn's private affairs."

The instant she said "affairs," Kathryn understood. *All the times I've seen them touch each other when they didn't have to,* she thought. *Why did I never see it before?* It explained the twin beds. Carolyn, operating under a peculiar version of monogamy, had stopped sleeping with her husband in order to be faithful to her lesbian lover.

Grace was about to ask why Kathryn was looking so struck, but as Kathryn would never have told her, it was fortunate that there was a sudden diversion. After three and a half hours, their flight was being called.

CHAPTER 30

Tom Holder was not pleased. Kathryn sat with sinking heart and realized that she had erred disastrously. She had upstaged him. He had invited her in to help a bit, and she had taken over the show and outdone him. That could be the only explanation for the grim mouth and the hard eyes with which he listened to Grace Kimbrough's story. Grace was clearly terrified of him, and Kathryn didn't blame her.

It was just after nine o'clock on Sunday morning. The flight had landed closer to midnight than to its scheduled eight P.M. Mrs. Warburton, who had whiled away the evening with an unusually witty historical romance, was disgustingly fresh, and said with a cheery smile as Kathryn and Grace got into the car, "Where to, boss?"

Kathryn looked at her watch and groaned. "It'll be after one before we get there. Oh, hell, Warby, take us home. We've spent all day in airports and airplanes, and I don't know about you," she said to Grace, "but I am stiff as a board, and I think that tomorrow morning is plenty of time to tackle Tom Holder."

Grace had heartily agreed. She had further agreed to spend the night in Kathryn's guest room. "I don't really want," she said faintly, "to face George." Kathryn had thought it high time Grace informed her unfortunate husband that she wasn't dead, but when she had suggested as much while they were still in California, Grace had stated unequivocally that George would be happier thinking her dead than knowing she was having an affair. "If I'm dead, you see, it doesn't bother his pride." This was said not bitterly, but in the manner of disinterested assessment. Kathryn let the matter drop.

On Sunday morning she had called the police station, ascertained that Holder was indeed there, and asked the officer to tell the Chief that Kathryn Koerney would be there in fifteen minutes with something he would find useful in the Stanley-Kimbrough case. Since it was only three blocks, and the threat of rain was not entirely convincing, they set off on foot beneath the dripping maples. On the way they stopped at the church so that Kathryn could tell the Rector she might not be there for the ten-thirty service, though she was hoping to be—which was why she hadn't let Grace sleep until noon.

As they went through the lobby of the City Hall toward the glass partition that said *Police*, Kathryn was too intent on her errand, and much too pleased at the prospect of Tom's appreciation, to wonder why the place seemed a bit heavily populated for a Sunday morning. She ushered Grace through the glass door, stepped up to the desk, and said, "Kathryn Koerney. To see Chief Holder." As the officer waved them toward an open door on his left, there was a stir behind them, the glass door was flung open again, and several people tried to crowd through it. A woman's voice, excited and almost incredulous, shrilled, "Excuse me, aren't you Grace Kimbrough?" As Kathryn and Grace both turned to look at her, two camera flashes in rapid succession caught them full in the face. Momentarily stunned, neither attempted to answer the questions that were being hurled at them by the woman and her media colleagues; Kathryn regained her wits, thrust Grace through the door into the hallway, gave the reporters a firm "No comment," and slammed the door on them. Grace looked rattled, but Kathryn felt all the more like a hunter bringing home a twenty-point buck.

She waltzed into Holder's office, indicated her companion, and said with all the smugness of a fundamentalist warbling "Meet Me in the Rapture," "Tom, this is Grace Kimbrough." She had been unable to suppress a triumphant smile.

The immediate reaction had been everything she'd hoped for. Tom rose from his chair with mouth agape, then tried to frame a question but couldn't do better than an unfinished "What in hell—" and Grace, looking suitably solemn, was apologizing for all the trouble she'd caused them. Tom stayed dumbfounded through most of Kathryn's brief explanation, but toward the end, when she was telling him how she'd gone out to California to fetch Grace, the wonder began to fade, giving way to an uncharacteristic grimness. He gave Grace a long, measuring look in which no sympathy could be detected, picked up his desk phone, and snapped into it an order for a tape recorder, and then, on an obvious second thought, growled at Grace, "I suppose you want a lawyer?"

Grace cast a frightened glance at Kathryn and met a blank, unhelpful look. "I—ah— No," she said. "No, I just want to get this over with."

Holder told her to sit down, and sat himself. Kathryn, who had observed his reactions with increasing dismay, began to edge tactfully toward the door, but was stopped by his bursting out aggrievedly, "For God's sake, you're not leaving, are you?"

Kathryn swallowed. "Not if you don't want me to," she said carefully.

Holder, his mouth a thin line, stabbed a finger toward a chair. Kathryn sat in it and gripped the edges of it with fingers that went white. An officer walked in with a tape recorder and proceeded to set up the machine on the Chief's desk. Kathryn wondered how on earth she had so misjudged her friend: She had thought him that rarity, the man with an unassailable ego. She realized that she had assumed, because she didn't scare him under normal circumstances, that she could do something extraordinary and still not threaten him. *Stupid*, she thought; *I should have known better.*

So Grace told her tale into an unfriendly chill. Holder interrupted her from time to time with a question, but not often; besides the trial run to Kathryn in the Sunset Motel, Grace had had Saturday's interminable cross-country flight during which to rehearse this speech, and by that point she had it pretty well organized. She finished, and there was a brief silence. Holder switched off the tape recorder and studied Grace.

"You realize there are about half a dozen things we could charge you with," he said.

"Yes," she answered, and closed her lips tightly. Holder's mouth was tight, too, and he regarded Grace with narrow eyes. "I take it you intend to be cooperative?" he asked.

"Yes," Grace said again.

The hard gaze went to Kathryn. "How about you? Can you spare a couple of hours?"

"Sure," said Kathryn briefly. She was grateful not to find herself banished into outer darkness, but her apprehension remained. Tom was so obviously far from pleased.

Had she but known it, Holder was not resentful of her coup, he was only desperately disappointed. It didn't help. Victim and witness had changed places, but it just didn't help. Kathryn had brought off something really brilliant, but he was still faced with a calamity he couldn't explain and couldn't fix. He wasn't going to tell her, not yet, because she might be able to help him with Grace and Bill. Besides, let her enjoy her triumph a little while longer. He was in too much turmoil himself to notice that she wasn't enjoying it at all.

He pushed his chair back with a grunt, and rose. "Wait here a minute," he said, and left the room. The two women eyed each other nervously. Kathryn stretched out a hand and grasped Grace's forearm. "You'll make it," she said. Grace gave her a rather pathetic smile.

Holder came back. "All right, now," he said to Grace. "We're going to Trenton to talk to Bill Stanley."

Grace stiffened, but Kathryn thought Tom was actually being rather polite; he could, after all, have said something cutting like "to see your boyfriend." He was keeping the lid on something that looked suspiciously like anger, and he was not taking it out on Grace. Kathryn began to be intrigued, and to hope that she had not, after all, alienated him for life.

CHAPTER 31

Grace and Kathryn were bustled out the back door of the
police station and into a waiting car. They had the backseat
to themselves, Holder riding in front with the uniformed driver.
Nobody spoke a word. They rode through the gray, early winter
beauty of the New Jersey countryside, and eventually arrived at
the unappealing urban sprawl of Trenton. They threaded through
streets unfamiliar to Kathryn, and finally pulled up at the back entrance of a large and unmistakably institutional building.

Here they were bustled again, Holder all but encircling them
with his arms, for all the world like a hen with two chicks. He
was afraid some chance passerby would blurt out the news that
would ruin their concentration for the interview to come. He
could not guard their ears with his physical bulk, but to make the
attempt was instinctive. Kathryn wondered what he was pro-
tecting them from; Grace thought only that she was about to

confront Bill, and would scarcely have noticed if Holder had led her by the earlobe.

There were doors, a corridor, an elevator, another corridor, more doors. At a couple of points Holder spoke to people. A tall, stooped man with acne scars attached himself to their little cavalcade, and Holder introduced him as Assistant District Attorney Somebody, Kathryn didn't catch the name. At last they reached a bare, ugly room containing a rectangular table and six mismatched chairs. A pudgy young man rose from one of them, greeting Holder and the Assistant District Attorney with handshakes but looking past them at the two women. "This had better be good, guys. Sunday morning, for God's sake." But a smile played about his mouth, and behind his glasses his small eyes were alive with interest.

Holder shook his hand and said guardedly that it was worth a try, anyway. "Kathryn, Mrs. Kimbrough, Harry Beeton—Bill Stanley's lawyer."

Grace greeted him with nervous courtesy. Kathryn, who had heard from Tom how Bill Stanley had been going through lawyers, smiled at Harry Beeton and asked if he was number three.

He grinned. "Number four, and the stubbornest of the lot. Looks like it's about to pay off."

The door opened, and they all turned. A uniformed guard with a gun on his hip ushered into the room a shabby version of a man who had been a respectable citizen a week earlier. His clothes looked slept in; he was ill-shaven, and behind the lenses of his glasses there were dark shadows under his eyes. When he saw Grace, he stopped dead and his pale face turned a shade whiter. Beeton stepped over and took him by the elbow.

"All right, Mr. Stanley," he said in a voice that deftly combined kindness and sarcasm. "Just sit down right here. We got tired of asking you to talk, so for a change we're just going to ask you to listen. You know Chief Holder. He's brought Mrs. Kimbrough here and she's going to make a statement." At this, Bill looked across at Grace with something like alarm, and made half a gesture toward her, but stopped himself. Beeton continued smoothly. "All you have to do is listen to it. When it's over you can talk if you want to, or you can go right back to your cell, or you can go into another room with me and we can talk alone. I strongly advise you to do the latter. The lady in the collar is a priest from St. Margaret's Episcopal Church. She brought Mrs. Kimbrough back from California, and she's here as a courtesy to Mrs. Kimbrough and Chief Holder. All right. Chief?"

Everybody had sat down during this speech except Beeton, who sat once he had concluded it. He and his client were on one side of the table; Holder, Grace, and Kathryn sat on the other. The Assistant District Attorney leaned against the wall.

Grace had glanced at Bill fleetingly, almost furtively, and after that had not looked at him again. She sat with her hands clasped on the table in front of her, her right thumb rubbing the base of her left thumb, studying this activity as though it absorbed her entire attention. Bill, showing no signs of wanting to speak, stared across the table at Grace. When Kathryn saw his face, she looked away; even Tom Holder found somewhere else to put his eyes. Only the lawyer, who had spent too many days trying to coax something out of this man, looked at him steadily and without apology.

Holder didn't think Grace was going to feel like making a statement, but he thought it only fair to ask. "Mrs. Kimbrough," he said, "would you like to repeat what you said in my office?"

Grace, who had had the wits to see this coming, did not look up. The small, nervous motion of her hands continued. She took a deep breath, then a deeper breath. Finally she said in a weak, desperate voice that would have stirred pity in a stone, "I don't think I can."

Holder, considerably softer than stone, did not push her. Instead, he reached down to the battered briefcase he had brought with him and pulled a portable tape recorder out of it. He set it on the table, took a cassette out of his breast pocket, and inserted it in the machine. "All right, then, Mrs. Kimbrough, we won't ask you to repeat it, we'll just play this recording of it. All you have to do is verify that this is in fact the statement you made." He punched a button, and a tinny version of Grace's voice, stronger than the live voice that had spoken a few moments before but still more obedient than confident, spoke out: *"It began at about one o'clock Monday afternoon, when I received a phone call from Carolyn. She was at her office . . ."* The disembodied voice continued, with a rumble of interruption now and again, to tell the terrible story.

At the point where Grace got to the discovery of the corpse, Kathryn risked a glance at Bill Stanley and found his face no longer an embarrassment of bleak despair. He was staring at Grace with what looked like surprise, and the beginning of a suspicion of hope. As Grace's voice dully recited the tally of gory debris on the floor, the hope grew stronger, and then broke into ungovernable relief. Tears welled in his eyes and rolled down his cheeks. They continued to fall all during Grace's description of her flight to California, and they were still falling when the voice trailed off into silence and Holder leaned forward to push the stop button on the machine.

Bill Stanley sniffed inelegantly, gulped, and said, "Grace."

The movement of her hands stopped. She raised her head and looked at him.

He burst into giggling sobs. "Grace, Grace, oh, Grace!" he cried, flinging himself forward across the table and reaching toward her. "Oh, Grace!"

She regarded him with astonishment, and drew back slightly so that he could not reach her. But she continued to stare at him, and something like faint hope appeared in her eyes.

Tom Holder looked from one of them to the other, and finally past Grace to Kathryn, with an expression that clearly asked if she could figure out what was happening. Kathryn made a face that just as clearly responded "Don't look at me," but then the light dawned on both of them at once.

Tom said, "He thought—"

Kathryn said, "That she did it."

Grace gaped at Kathryn, then turned back to Bill and gaped at him.

"Grace, listen to me," Bill said, still reaching urgently toward her. "She called me—"

"Hold it right there, fella," Harry Beeton interrupted, reaching across Bill and trying to tug him back. "Let's go have a little chat first, you and me."

But Bill pushed his attorney away and reached again across the table, imploring Grace to listen to him; Beeton grabbed him again and loudly besought him to shut the hell up; meanwhile, Holder bellowed at Stanley a reminder of his rights and simultaneously turned the cassette over, switched the machine to "record," and shoved the corner of it that was the microphone in Stanley's direction; Harry Beeton instantly stopped shouting at Bill and lunged for the tape recorder, yelling, "You can't do that!"

and shut it off at the same time that Grace finally found her voice enough to stammer Bill's name with a question mark after it, so it was quite noisy for about thirty seconds.

Stanley finally turned to Beeton and yelled, "Oh, for Christ's sake, shut up, I'm not about to confess to murder or anything!" and Beeton flung up his hands and cried, "All right, all right, so talk if you want to."

"Grace," said Bill into the sudden stillness, "she called me at the office; she didn't say she'd talked to you, but it must have been about the same time, about one o'clock. She said she thought she should let me know she wouldn't be staying at the Mark Hopkins"—Stanley made no sign that he remembered pretending to Holder that the change of hotel was a surprise to him—"because she said she didn't want to be bothered. She wouldn't explain what she meant, said she'd tell me when she got back, but she did say the same thing she said to you—about having a horrible row, and not wanting to talk about it over the phone, but it was terrible when someone you loved and trusted betrayed you. So of course I thought that was just her way of telling me—that she knew—she knew"—here he grimaced, as if in apology, glancing quickly at his all-too-public audience for this utterance—"about us. So I—I couldn't stand the suspense, I had to know before she left, I couldn't wait a whole week. So I went home. I thought I could just catch her there before she left. When I pulled in the driveway, her car was still there. The door was open, like you said. I ran into the house—the back door was open, I thought she must have just gone back in for a second to do something she forgot—and I went in and got to the kitchen and—and—there you were! And—I didn't know why you were there, I mean, she hadn't told me she'd asked you to come over to drive her . . ." He faltered and stopped, and his eyes were begging for forgiveness.

What was happening on Grace's face was more complicated. During Bill's story, hope had struggled with anger and disbelief. Toward the end, hope appeared to be winning, but just as Bill stopped speaking, she was struck by a thought as obviously as if someone had slapped her in the face. And what the thought produced was a slow blush that crept across her cheeks and down her neck, coupled with a look of such dismay that in any other circumstances it would have been comic. She uttered a tiny, choked cry and buried her face in her hands.

This utterly mystified everyone in the room, from Bill Stanley to the Assistant D.A., but after a moment Kathryn uttered a soft "Ah!" of understanding. Grace's escape in San Francisco had included a man; some sort of repudiation of Bill, Kathryn guessed, because at that point Grace believed Bill had murdered Carolyn. Bill was a scoundrel, therefore she had betrayed him. And now it turned out that he was innocent of everything except an attempt to protect her.

She's ruined it, Kathryn thought. *Now she can't go back to him. He did all this for her, and now she can't go back to him.*

"Grace? Grace, what's—" Bill had been about to say "What's wrong?" but so many things were so spectacularly wrong that the question seemed absurd. People had begun to turn from Grace and look back at him expectantly. He couldn't think of anything constructive to do other than to continue to explain to her what had happened, so, somewhat hesitantly, he did so. "Um, later," he said, "later, when they came around asking about where you were"—he stopped and swallowed audibly—"I had put her in the basement by then; I was going to pretend she'd gone to

California after all. I was hoping they'd look for her out there. I was an idiot. I forgot the car. The car would still be there. I didn't think of it until you"—he nodded at Tom Holder—"asked me if I drove her to the airport. I suddenly realized the car must still be in the driveway. But it wasn't," he said to Grace, "because you had taken it. I figured that out finally, after they'd left."

Holder was rising, and indicating by a jerk of his head to Kathryn that she should accompany him out of the room. He held the door for her, followed her, and shut the door. "Well, what do you think?" he demanded.

"Of Bill?"

"Yeah. Do you believe him?"

"Believe him? For heaven's sake, Tom, you heard him. If that's acting"—Kathryn shook her head—"I resign. I'll burn my collar and take up computer programming."

"Yeah, that's what I was afraid of, but I wanted your opinion, too."

"Tom, I know you've lost your prime suspect, but do you actually need a suspect?"

"Hmm?"

"I mean, isn't there just a snowflake's chance in hell that Carolyn died *accidentally*? She goes back into the house for something—maybe just to wait for Grace—and she's in the kitchen and she slips on a wet spot on the floor and falls backward onto the dishwasher door, which has a ten-inch carving knife sticking out of the cutlery rack. She falls off the dishwasher door, taking the cutlery rack and everything in it with her, and winds up on the floor in a pool of blood and kitchen utensils. Straightforward accidental death, only Bill Stanley louses it up by moving her body. Which reminds me, aren't you going to ask him where he put it?"

"Right now I don't give a damn where he put it, and Carolyn Stanley did not die accidentally."

"Oh, what a dunce I am! I forgot that that knife wouldn't be in the dishwasher."

"It's not just that." Holder wiped his face with his hands, and sighed. He looked old and weary. "I didn't tell you," he said. "I didn't tell you because I wanted you to listen to that in there and I wanted you to have a clear head for it."

"Didn't tell me what?"

"It's the kid, Tita Robinson. She's missing. She's been gone since about noon yesterday."

CHAPTER 32

Kathryn stood with her hand over her mouth, as though to hold back her own horror, her eyes asking questions she didn't dare put into words.

"She was just about well," Holder said. "Her mother let her get dressed and go outside for five minutes. She didn't come back. None of her friends or playmates had seen her, none of the neighbors. Her parents called all the obvious people, then reported it to us right away; they didn't waste time sitting and waiting. They think it has something to do with this killing, with her giving evidence. They don't believe it's a coincidence. I don't blame them. I don't believe it, either."

A cold wire had tightened around Kathryn's heart. She leaned against the wall for support. "But her evidence was against Bill Stanley, and surely he's been here, locked up?"

"Exactly."

"And Grace was in California."

"Right," Tom said. "So it has to be George."

"Does George fit?"

"Sure he fits." Tom began ticking off points on his fingers. "He lives in that neighborhood, he's been home since Wednesday afternoon, Carolyn started talking about that 'hell of a row' just after she'd had lunch with him, the row was with somebody she loved and trusted, she said, and that could be George, and if he was in business with her, he probably had the opportunity to betray her somehow. Right?"

"Yes, that all makes sense."

"So now we get another search warrant," Tom concluded.

She would have to say it. She hated it, she hated herself, but she had to say it. "Tom. Patricia Clyde is someone she loved and trusted, and she probably keeps the books for Elton Kimbrough. And the first evidence we have of Carolyn being upset is when she was back at the office with Patricia. Of course, Patricia doesn't live in Canterbury Park—no, I take that back, I don't know where she lives."

Tom stared. "You think Patricia Clyde killed Carolyn?"

"No, I'm with you, I think George did it. But going only on what we know and ignoring my personal prejudice, you can't leave Patricia out."

Tom considered her agitation and diagnosed it correctly. "You know something you're not telling me."

She couldn't tell him. Any insight she had had been triggered by her conversation with Grace in the Denver airport. Grace had obviously spoken in the belief that the conversation was private and would stay that way, and to a priest that was sacred. Kathryn would have considered violating that trust only to save a life.

And no life was at stake here; it was already lost. Tita had disappeared almost twenty-four hours ago, and unlike Grace, she was not going to turn up alive and well in California. Kathryn fixed her attention on a crack in the plaster on the opposite wall, and said, as though she were very tired, "No, Tom, I don't know anything. My ignorance is frightening."

There was a silence of a few seconds before he replied, "You know, that was pretty good. I think most people would've believed it."

She looked up at him, and to her utter astonishment he leaned over and kissed her on the cheek. "So I'll get two search warrants," he said.

Her surprise at his reaction was interrupted by the sudden remembrance of what the first search warrant had revealed, and a wave of nausea ran through her. She looked up and down the corridor, but there was nowhere to sit down.

"Are you all right?" he asked.

"Yes. No, of course I'm not all right." She waved him away. "Go get your search warrants."

He looked at her intently for a minute, then turned away and started down the hall. But after five steps he turned and came back. "Listen, Kathryn, if it hadn't been for you, I wouldn't have this much." He patted her on the shoulder. "That was good work."

She nodded her acknowledgment of this, not trusting herself to speak. Tom patted her shoulder again and strode off down the corridor. Kathryn stood there, battling against a trembling lip and gathering tears, and losing. A woman walking down the corridor glanced at her curiously, and walked on. Kathryn realized she was standing around in a public building somehow connected to law enforcement, wearing her clericals, and crying. She dug in the pocket of her overcoat, found her scarf, and with shaking hands wound it twice around her neck, covering all traces of the white collar.

It occurred to her that she had come with Tom, that he had gone God only knew where, and she had no way to get home. Grace was in the same boat. Kathryn looked at the closed door and clenched her teeth. She found her handkerchief, wiped her eyes, blew her nose, straightened her face and her spine, and went back into the room where Bill was informing his impatient attorney that he wasn't going to go anywhere or talk to anyone until Grace spoke to him.

At the moment that seemed most unlikely, as Grace still had her hands over her face and was shaking her head slowly, but when Kathryn called her name, she was surprised into looking up. "Grace—I'm taking a taxi back to Harton, do you want a ride?"

The way Grace said "yes," it was clear that she considered this offer an answer to a prayer, but before she reached the door, Bill was crying out in real anguish, begging her to stay.

Kathryn was motivated partly by pastoral concerns and partly by her urgent desire to be alone with her emotions; she didn't really want company on the taxi ride home. She blocked Grace's exit from the room and spoke quietly in her ear. "Do you think you should leave him like this? Don't you owe him something?"

"I can't tell him. I *can't*."

"Then don't tell him. But don't leave him. You can't just keep running away, you know."

Grace hesitated, and Kathryn glanced at Harry Beeton, who recognized his cue instantly. "Mrs. Kimbrough, I can take you back to Harton, if you like. As soon as we're through talking to Bill."

Slowly Grace turned, then walked back to the table and sat down where she had been sitting before, across from Bill. The blush had long gone, and she was very pale.

Kathryn started out the door but turned back. "Grace. I don't think you should go home to George."

Grace managed to speak. "That's the last thing I want to do."

"Come back to my place."

"I shouldn't impose on you. But I can't think of what else to do right now, so I guess I will. Thanks."

Kathryn told Harry Beeton her address, stepped out of the room, and set out to find the front entrance to the building. She found it, emerged onto a main thoroughfare, and eventually spotted and hailed a taxi. As the driver whistled his way out of Trenton, Kathryn collapsed in the backseat and sank into a misery like quicksand.

She felt as if her ego spread through her like a cancer, contaminating the whole of her. Across her mind came a line from the old form of the General Confession; the Prayer Book revisers had judged it theologically unsound and had changed it, but to Kathryn at that moment it seemed written for her: *"There is no health in us."*

She had gloried in herself, fancying herself a sort of Peter Wimsey with a few credits in pastoral counseling; she had wanted to be thought clever, she had wanted to impress. Well, she had succeeded. The Chief of Police had patted her on the shoulder and told her she had done well. And that child, that engaging, delightful child—

Oh, God, don't let her be dead, she prayed, but she knew it was a foolish prayer. If Tita had disappeared because she was a dangerous witness, she would not be hidden or held for ransom, she would be silenced. Kathryn felt sick.

Suddenly in the black depths of her guilt a new pit yawned at her feet: Could she have prevented it?

It was bad enough that she had been playing ego games while a child was being murdered, but in her first wave of horror it had not occurred to her that her guilt might extend to actual responsibility for Tita's death. It occurred to her now. She was no longer sick, she was stunned. It was several minutes before her brain struggled out of its paralysis and began to attempt to deal with the question.

She had put off getting Grace and her story to Tom Holder in favor of a good night's sleep. But Tita had vanished long before their plane had landed—about twelve hours before, in fact. About the time she and Grace had been waking up Saturday morning in the Holiday Inn. But what if she had called Tom when she'd found Grace, told him her story then and there? She hadn't done so because she had wanted to be onstage when he learned about Grace; she had wanted to watch his amazement.

And of course there had been no urgency; Carolyn Stanley was dead, and the murderer, supposedly, in custody. It had simply been a matter of getting straight who the victim had been. She had been wrong. She had been congratulating herself on being the only one who had it right, and she had been disastrously wrong.

She didn't notice they were approaching her house until the cab actually stopped. She paid the driver, and somehow got herself out of the car, up the walk, and in the front door. The house was silent. Mrs. Warburton would still be at church; the Presbyterians drank coffee until well past noon. Kathryn dropped her handbag on the first chair she passed and her coat and scarf on the second, and flung herself onto the sofa. Now that she had the privacy for a good cry, she seemed to have run out of tears. Or perhaps the matter had gone beyond tears.

She was still rehearsing, dully, alternate sequences of events. If she had called Tom Friday night. If she had told him what Grace had said. But what would Tom have done? Would he not have assumed, as she had, that the value of Grace's story was its damning evidence against Bill Stanley and the likelihood that it would provoke him to confess? Would Tom have done anything other than wait for Grace's return to arrange a confrontation between her and Bill? Impossible to tell. But he might have done something else, and it might have made a difference. She would never know now. It was too late.

CHAPTER 33

Eventually Kathryn began to wonder how long it would take Tom Holder to get his search warrants. Was he at George's even now, or at Patricia's? How long would it be before they found something, something they would have to report to Tita's parents?

Tita's parents.

Duty summoned Kathryn out of despair. There was very little she could do for the Robinsons, but that little must be done. It was an obligation. There was nobody in the world she wanted more to avoid, but she would go to their house and wait with them until someone came to tell them what had happened to their daughter. She went upstairs to replenish her supply of handkerchiefs and pocket tissues, and thus supplied, got her car from the garage and drove to Dickens Street.

James and Julia Robinson opened the front door together, their faces stiff with dread and the shreds of unkillable hope. Kathryn looked at Julia and said immediately, "I don't have any news. I've just come to be with you while you wait."

Tita's father, of course, had no idea who she was, and in the state Tita's mother was in, it took her a moment to recognize Kathryn.

"Oh—oh, yes, of course, you're the policeman's friend from church, the Sunday school teacher. Uh, Jim, this is, uh—"

Kathryn told James Robinson her name; he told her his, trying automatically to smile, and invited her in.

They turned to lead Kathryn to the living room, and saw a group of anxious faces in the doorway. "It's nothing," Julia told them, "I mean—it's not news. Uh, this is Kathryn Koerney, she's been helping the police. My mother, Mrs. Selby; our friends, Bob and Sheila Holtam, Ruth Childs."

They all shook hands and made little murmurs at each other. Awkwardly, they found their seats again, James bringing forward a chair for Kathryn. There was silence.

"Have they—" Tita's mother began, and stopped. "No, you said—no news. It's just—it's just that we can't understand, because Bill Stanley's in jail, isn't he? And isn't he the one who killed Grace?"

The question startled Kathryn; she had forgotten how little the Robinsons knew. She hesitated. She was privy to information Tom would surely not want publicized. On the other hand, certain basic facts—like who was still alive and who wasn't—would be public knowledge by the following day, if only because of her own stupidity in steering Grace right into a flock of reporters. That cat was already out of its bag; it couldn't hurt to describe it to the Robinsons and their friends.

Kathryn reflected that if she did this right, she could make it last a half hour or more. Or until Tom came. So she gave them a carefully edited account of everything that had happened the previous Monday, and how it had come to light. She omitted the details that pointed to George Kimbrough or Patricia Clyde. No one seemed eager for her to get on with the story; they accepted her snail's pace as though they, too, knew that all that could be done was to pass the time in any way it could be passed.

Finally, however, she ran out of things to say. There were a few halfhearted responses. Somebody said, "How terrible for Mrs. Kimbrough." Then a clock-ticking silence fell.

One of the friends announced that she would make some coffee, and began to make a great business of taking orders.

Somewhere in the brittle exchanges—"Let me help you"—"Oh, it's no trouble"—"Black, with sugar"—Kathryn's mind wandered off the track; people and voices faded into a gray silence in which a ginger-haired child sat on the sofa and spoke in a small, sure voice, and said, with complete confidence—something that was wrong. No, not wrong when she said it, it was wrong only later. Later when? At the fence. At the fence and at the window, it was wrong. "Julia," said Kathryn rather too loudly.

The bustle about the coffee died instantly, and every eye in the room went to Kathryn. She looked at the anxious faces and thought, *Oh, God, if I say anything, they'll think it might help; they'll start hoping.* Still, something stirred in her, and it would not be quiet; it insisted that she discover it. And in that insistence there was an urgency she did not understand, but responded to as if to divine command. "Julia, could I—would it—" She stopped, then forced herself to speak firmly. "If you don't mind, I'd like to go look at the backyard again."

Julia blinked, stared a moment, then said, "Sure. This way." She led Kathryn out of the room and through the kitchen to the back door. Kathryn thanked her and stepped outside.

It was exactly as it had been when she and Tom had been there last Wednesday: the same damp yard, the same wet swing set, the same still trees, under the same November sky. Kathryn walked across the soggy grass toward the back fence. As she approached it, the feeling grew in her that there was something to notice, something to remark. Something, perhaps, Tita had noticed but had thought unimportant, or had forgotten, and so not told them? For one thing was certain: Tita had not been killed because of what she had said in her statement on Wednesday. That damage was done. It profits nothing to dispose of a witness who has already revealed what needs to be kept secret. The witness who is dangerous is the one who has seen something but has not yet spoken of it. *What had Tita seen, and not recognized as important?*

Kathryn climbed a few boards up the fence and looked over it into the Stanleys' backyard. Oddly, she had the feeling that she had been closer to seeing what she was looking for before she had mounted the fence. The sensation of trembling right on the brink of discovery had been strongest a few feet away from it; once she touched the boards, the intuition fled. It was like trying to sharpen an image in a telescope by turning the focus ring, and then turning it a fraction too far. The clarity had been there for a sliver of an instant, but now it was gone. She descended to the ground and stepped back a few feet. The fence stood blankly in front of her. She turned, walked several yards back toward the house, turned again, and once more approached the fence. Yes, it was that blank wall that was trying to tell her something. But what? That something didn't fit, something wasn't right. But it eluded her.

She walked back to the house, noticing, for the first time, the little audience that peered hopefully out of the living room window. Taken aback, Kathryn shook her head. They thought she was looking for Tita, when all she was looking for was answers.

Julia met her at the kitchen door. "What is it?" she asked softly.

Kathryn laid her hands on the woman's shoulders. "Please. You mustn't—you mustn't get your hopes up. I'm just trying to figure out *why*." She dropped her hands. "But I'd like to see Tita's bedroom again."

Julia nodded, and again led the way. Leaving the group in the living room in a kind of suspended animation, they went upstairs to Tita's bedroom, crossed to the window, and looked out. It was somewhere outside, whatever was bothering Kathryn. Somewhere out there with the lawn, and the trees, and the fence.

Kathryn stared out the window at the commonplace suburban view, but it stubbornly refused to yield anything to her. There was nothing there to see. Absolutely nothing. But that was the problem, surely? Should there not have been something? Something the window did not offer, that she had rightly expected to find?

Tita's mother started to speak into the obviously barren silence, but Kathryn made an abrupt noise and flung up a hand to ward off the interruption. Neither woman was in any condition to notice that she'd been rude. Julia held her breath, and Kathryn stood frozen, her hand still splay-fingered in midair, her face contracted in a fury of attempted recollection.

Suddenly she covered her face with her hands and a voice inside her cried desperately at God, *Show me!* Then she lowered her hands and looked again.

And saw.

CHAPTER 34

I t was so obvious, she could not imagine how she had failed to see it.

She turned to Julia Robinson and asked, "Did Tita often stand on the fence, looking into the Stanleys' backyard?"

"I—ah, don't know. I don't think—I ever saw her do it."

"But you have to climb the fence in order to see into the Stanleys' backyard."

"Uh, I guess so. Yes."

"You can't see the Stanleys' backyard, or their back door, while standing on the ground in your backyard, because the fence is too high."

"Yes, that's right." Her voice rose on the last word, making almost a question.

Kathryn pointed out the window. "But you can't see the Stanleys' backyard, or driveway, or back door, from this window, either, because of those two trees."

"Yes?" Definitely a question.

"Then how does Tita know how Bill Stanley goes up his back steps? She described it exactly. Hand on the rail, two steps at a time. She said he *always* did it that way. How does she know that? She was sure of it, like she'd seen it a dozen times."

Julia stared blankly. "I don't know. . . ."

"Does Tita go over there to visit, to their yard?"

"No, I don't think so. They don't have any children."

"Then how did she get to be so familiar with Bill Stanley going up his back steps?"

"I can't—oh! Maybe the attic? That's higher, but I'd have thought the trees would still be— Let's look," she said suddenly, and hurried from the room.

With Kathryn hard on her heels, Julia Robinson made for a door at the end of the hall, threw it open, and ran up the narrow flight of stairs to the attic. In five swift strides she crossed to the little living area by the back dormer, and leaned over to look out of the low window. Behind her, Kathryn dropped into the armchair, slouched down to what might be a child's height, and looked past Julia's elbow out the window. From this high vantage point there was a space in the evergreens. And there, neatly framed by branches, was an unobstructed view of the Stanleys' back porch.

Kathryn stared at it for a moment, then looked up at Julia Robinson's face in time to see the hope die out of it and the dread come back in a wave. They had not discovered a clue to Tita's whereabouts; they had found only a horribly good reason for her disappearance.

"Was she—" Kathryn cleared her throat and tried again.

"Was she up here that afternoon? Last Monday? She was sick, re-member."

"I can't—I can't think." Julia's eyes had seen too much and had gone blank with fear.

"It was Monday night when she woke you up talking about Bill Stanley and a body."

Julia stifled a sob, and swallowed. "Yes, that was it. I remember I thought she shouldn't have come up here, because it had obvi-ously made her worse."

"What time was it, about?"

Julia thought a moment. "I think it was just after lunch."

Kathryn was looking around on the bookshelf and the floor by the chair. "Did she have a separate notebook for up here?"

Tita's mother heard the past tense, and reached out to the back of the chair for support. "No," she said in a tight voice. "I gave her only one."

"And she didn't use it up here."

"Yes, she did. She had been writing in it when I found her here."

Kathryn protested: "All the entries in the book say 'From the Bedroom Window.' "

Julia was clutching the chair back, slogging through the con-versation by sheer strength of will. "But I could have sworn I saw a page marked 'From the Attic.' I'm sure—well, I'm pretty sure, that it said something about the attic."

"What else did it say?"

Julia shook her head helplessly. "I didn't really look that closely. Is it important, do you think?"

"I have no idea. But I'm going to find out." Kathryn discovered, as she followed Julia Robinson downstairs and took hasty leave of the people in the living room, that the unidentifiable urgency that had propelled her to examine the back fence and the bedroom window still had hold of her. If anything, it was growing more acute.

She hurried down the walk to her car, and drove home at a speed that would have shocked Tom Holder—indeed, would have shocked herself if she had been in any state to notice. At Alexander Street she burst through the front door past a startled Mrs. Warburton and sprinted down the hall and into her workroom.

From under a pile of papers she snatched the spiral notebook she had not looked at since Tom Holder had given it to her the previous Thursday. Too excited to sit, she stood over her desk, breathless, her hands shaking as they scrambled over the pages, looking for the right day.

She found it. Just as Tom had said, at the top of the page: *"Monday, November 7th. From the Bedroom Window."* Then a short list of activities that had taken place that morning in the Robinsons' backyard and that of the Hensons, next door. Nothing else. The next page was blank, and so, apparently, was the rest of the book.

Tita's mother was wrong.

Kathryn was baffled. Tita's big adventure had been Monday night. Why was there no word about it? She had had the book all of Tuesday and Wednesday before handing it over to her father Thursday morning to take to the police. Why had she abandoned her game just when it got interesting?

Kathryn fanned the pages of the notebook, a swift succession of blank sheets her only reward. She flipped through them again, a little more carefully. Two thirds of the way through, she thought she caught a fleeting glimpse of writing. She paged back to it. The spiral was of the variety that is divided into three sections by two pages of stiff colored card, and this was the first page of the third section. It tended to cling to the divider, so that when the pages were fanned rapidly, only its blank verso was visible. This page contained a paragraph, unheaded, that began: *"Last night in the middle of the night I heard funny noises in the Stanleys' garage."* It was a less-official version of Tita's statement. Kathryn scanned it; it contained nothing new. The next page was blank. She flipped back to the first page of the second section, which also hid its written face against the divider that preceded it. She opened it out.

And there it was. On the top line was written *"From the Attic."* The first entry was at 1:04 Monday, and concerned Joey Henson playing in his sandbox. At 1:05 something called Mephistopheles (creatively misspelled) had crossed the backyard.

And at 1:12 things had started to happen on the Stanleys' back porch.

CHAPTER 35

Kathryn read with a thudding heart, and then reached for the telephone book. Tom would go to George's before he went to Patricia's, but he might stop at the station before he did either. She found the number and punched it into the phone.

"Hello, is Chief Holder there? Has he already gone to the Kimbroughs' with a search warrant?" The officer could not take it upon himself to say where Chief Holder was, but if the caller would like to leave a message? Kathryn hung up on him and grabbed for the phone book again.

This time the voice that answered was more familiar.

"May I speak to Chief Holder, please?"

"You have the wrong number," said George Kimbrough testily.

"Mr. Kimbrough? Don't hang up, I'm looking for the Chief of Police, this is his office calling." She could hear her heart beating.

"Well, I don't know why you think he's here, because he's not."

"Oh—I see." She took a careful breath. "I understood he was going to make a routine inquiry concerning—ah, concerning the homicide," she extemporized, "and I somehow got the impression he was going to see you, but obviously he wasn't. Sorry to have bothered you." She put down the receiver with an emphatic "Damn!" She paged hurriedly through the phone book once more, picked up the receiver again, and punched out another number.

"Why 'damn'?" asked Mrs. Warburton from the doorway.

"Oh, I may have spooked him," Kathryn said fretfully. "That was probably a dumb thing to do— Hello, Patricia? Kathryn Koerney. Are the police there yet?"

"You mean they're coming?"

"Yes, but don't worry about it. It's George they're after, but they don't know it yet. I have to go, bye." She hung up without ceremony and called the police station again. "This is Kathryn Koerney, and I have an urgent message to get through to Tom Holder, who is in Trenton, trying to get a search warrant, can you tell me whose office I'm likely to find him in?"

The officer was unable to tell her that, but if she would like to leave a message?

"No, you don't understand, this is urgent, he's trying to get a search warrant," Kathryn babbled frantically, "and I can save him the trouble, I've got information here he can make an arrest on—"

The officer began to address her in the elaborately patient voice he obviously reserved for cranks, and repeated his willingness to take a message.

Kathryn slammed the phone down and said, loudly, a word her housekeeper had never heard her use before.

"My dear," said Mrs. Warburton, "you're shaking. Sit down."

"How can I sit down?" Kathryn wailed. "I've got to—I've got to"—she shook her hands in frustration—"*do* something!"

"Well, then," said Mrs. Warburton calmly, "do something."

Kathryn stopped shaking and stared at her. She took a slow, deep breath and made herself let it out smoothly. She picked up Tita's notebook, still open to the crucial page, and held it up in front of Mrs. Warburton. "All right, then. You take this thing to the police station, and by hook or by crook, come hell or high water, you see to it that the instant Tom Holder steps into that building, you give him this, give it to him yourself, personally, and tell him I said to read this page."

"Read this page."

"That's right. The minute he gets there, understand? Insist on it. Walk over people." She thrust the notebook into Mrs. Warburton's hands and headed for the front door. With her hand on the knob she stopped, considered a moment, turned, and ran upstairs. Two and a half minutes later she ran out of the house into a light drizzle, got into her car, and again made record time on the distance between Alexander Street and Canterbury Park.

Two blocks from the Kimbroughs' house, a silver-gray Mercedes coming toward her made a left turn, and as the car crossed her path, Kathryn recognized George at the wheel. She turned right and followed him. At the edge of Canterbury Park he stopped at a red light. Kathryn quickly pulled her car over, parked it at the curb, and jumped out. She ran to the passenger door of George's car and opened it.

"George!" she cried with a big smile. "Just the person I wanted to—"

George had jumped when the door was opened, and gaped at the intruder in wide-eyed panic. He stomped on his accelerator and roared through the intersection, laying rubber on the damp asphalt like a teenage hot-rodder.

Kathryn, who had freed her hand from the door handle barely in time to avert the loss of fingers, stared after him, open-mouthed. As he vanished around a corner, she shook herself out of her astonishment, dashed back to her car, and gave chase, thanking God fervently for expensive tires and good traction. The rain continued, faint but persistent.

There was no way George could know of her connection with the police. To him, she could be only a Kimbrough customer—a customer, moreover, whose favor he had always assiduously courted. But he had not hesitated an instant to leave her, without a word, in a cloud of exhaust. It was more than colossally rude, it was dangerous. She could have had half her hand wrenched off. She turned the corner and saw the Mercedes far ahead of her, speeding down the wet street.

Why such guilty terror? Why had he fled so precipitously from a mere acquaintance? An appalling revelation came to Kathryn: George had Tita Robinson's body in the car; he was on his way to dispose of it. Nothing else would explain such desperate determination not to be joined or delayed by anyone whatsoever. With her heart in her throat, she ran a red light, took a slippery thirty-mile-an-hour curve at forty-seven, and prayed for a passing police car.

Canterbury Park was close to the edge of town; within minutes they were out of the suburbs into a semirural area, where homes were placed two or three to a mile, far back from the road, in groves of pines. Kathryn, an inveterate explorer of country roads, realized thankfully that she was familiar with this one.

There was hardly any traffic. Kathryn nudged her windshield

wipers up to a faster rhythm, pushed her accelerator a tenth of an inch closer to the floor, took another curve at heart-stopping speed, and began softly to curse George Kimbrough through her gritted teeth. The curses were a prayer as surely as the appeal for a police car had been.

It was not her job to chase criminals, and what she was doing was dangerous—not only to her, which didn't matter, but to anyone who got in her way. But if she gave up the chase, George would slow down; he could proceed at a decorous pace, unremarkable and unhindered, off into the soggy gray countryside, until he found a suitably secluded spot.

Her knuckles were white and her grip on the steering wheel would have crushed anything less sturdy. There was a cell phone in her handbag. She thought fleetingly of calling for assistance, but dismissed the idea even as it occurred. At that speed it would have been lunacy to try to make a call on dry streets; on the rain-soaked roads she was traveling it would have been criminal. And probably fatal.

Besides, she would get help only if she got through to Tom Holder. If he wasn't at the station, all she would get was a replay of her previous frustration: That idiot would offer to take a message. By the time she talked to Tom, George would be long gone. He could hide poor Tita's body, return home, and play innocent when the cops came around. Kathryn didn't think the evidence in Tita's notebook would be sufficient to convict him if no other evidence turned up.

From one of the long driveways ahead, out from under the dripping trees, came a child crossing the road. Kathryn stood on her brake pedal and jerked her wheel to the left. The car, sliding over the wet pavement, went into a skid she could not control.

Eternal seconds later she came to a halt, skewed sideways across the road. She looked around. The child had retreated to his driveway and was yelling angrily at her. Unheard through her shut windows, she exploded at him, "What the hell are you doing out in this weather?" forgetting that she herself had spent un-numbered childhood hours walking in the rain. She drew her breath on a sob, pulled the car around, and took off down the road again.

Her heart was pounding so hard, she could feel her pulse in her fingertips, and at this point only one consideration kept her going: She knew it was no coincidence that George had gone on his gruesome errand this morning. God only knew why he hadn't gotten rid of Tita before now, but he was doing it now rather than later because of Kathryn's phone call. She had, in effect, warned him that the police were on their way to his house. If he got away with this murder, it would be entirely her fault.

Still, the incident with the child had seriously frightened her, and as she sped down the road she prayed furiously: *Do something, dammit, because in about three minutes I am giving this up before I run over somebody.* Kathryn had learned in seminary that God was the best and safest target for one's anger—after all, his feelings can't be hurt—but she had also been taught that it was bad theology to give God an ultimatum. At that point, however, she was more in touch with her feelings than with her theology.

In the next moment she took note of a couple of things she did not immediately recognize as an answer to her prayer. First, George was still in sight, which, given her brief delay, he shouldn't have been. Second, the reason he was still in sight was that he had lost precious seconds deciding, at a sudden fork in the road, which way to take. He had opted for the narrow lane that went off to the left. Just before she got to the fork, Kathryn realized that God had delivered George into her hands. She went to the right.

A half a mile farther on, there was a small road on the left that met the main road at a right angle. Kathryn pulled across it, her Audi blocking its entire width. George could still get around her on the shoulder, but he would have to do it slowly. That he would come to this intersection she was certain; on the road he had taken he could do nothing else. He would wind around for about a mile first, but if he was still traveling fast, he should arrive in less than a minute. Kathryn rolled down her window and switched off the ignition. She looked around her, praying now for privacy; for the next few minutes she wanted neither police nor passersby. The nearest house was a quarter of a mile away; with any luck its inhabitants were all inside watching television.

Kathryn opened the handbag that sat on the passenger seat and pulled out the item she had hastily fetched from her bedroom before she had dashed off to confront George. It was her uncle Jesse's gun.

It was an old friend, that gun, but now it seemed cold to her touch, and threatening. In the stillness she was aware of her heartbeat again.

It was against the law to carry firearms in the state of New Jersey. A conviction carried a mandatory prison sentence of one year. Yet Kathryn, in the grip of an urgency that was pointless if Tita Robinson was dead, and setting out in haste to challenge a murderer in his den, had been afraid to go without it. George had killed twice. She could have attempted to ensure her safety by telling him the police were on their way, but what if he hadn't believed her? It would be stupid for him to harm her, under the circumstances, but that was just the trouble: George *was* stupid. So she had brought the gun. And now she was going to use it.

The seconds dragged by. The steady drizzle whispered in the woods. Had he stopped? Turned back? Surely not. He could not know, on that winding road, that his pursuer was no longer behind him. "Come on, damn you," she muttered. She thought about what George was carrying in his car, and was filled with cold fury. As she watched that place in the trees where the narrow road disappeared, and willed it to disgorge her prey, she felt an antipathy like an incubating demon growing inside her. She realized suddenly that she could kill him here and simply drive away. Throw the gun away somewhere. A disused canal crept through the woods a few miles down the road. There was a place where you could drive to the water's edge and still stay mostly hidden in the trees. She wouldn't even have to get out of the car. Lean out the window, toss the gun into the canal, drive back to Harton. Justice would be served. George would be dead. No one would ever know.

The frost-colored Mercedes squealed around the bend.

Kathryn lifted the gun and took aim. Closer, closer. Through the windshield of the approaching car she saw George's face over the steering wheel. He was coming almost straight at her, and he had begun to slow down. An easy shot. She fired.

CHAPTER 36

The Mercedes skidded wildly, out of control. It came to rest in the muddy ditch at the side of the road, and George tumbled out of it to stare incredulously at his left front tire. It was not so much flat as destroyed. He looked up at the car that blocked his way, and saw Kathryn Koerney get out of it. She was wearing her clericals and the Burberry he had remarked upon five days ago, and she was carrying a gun.

"What in hell—" he thundered, starting toward her, but she lifted the gun, and he stopped.

"I'll tell you what in hell," she said savagely. "What in hell have you done with that child? Where is she?"

George turned the color of dirty snow and staggered backward a couple of paces. He bumped into the front of his car and leaned against it. The mist, now growing fainter, settled on wan cheeks already damp with sweat.

"Where is she?" Kathryn repeated, raising the gun to aim at his face.

George cringed and flung up a hand. "In . . . the trunk," he gasped.

Kathryn's gorge rose, and for a few moments she fought desperately to keep from being sick.

George, alarmed by the look on her face, and cowed by the weapon, attempted to placate her. "Shall I—" He gestured toward the trunk.

"No!" Kathryn fairly shouted. The last thing in the world she wanted to do was look in that trunk. She stood still for a minute, struggling for control. The drizzle unobtrusively stopped, but she didn't notice. All she knew was that she needed to sit down. "Get in my car," she ordered. "Backseat."

He walked unsteadily over to the Audi and got in. She went around to the passenger side, got in the front seat, and sat sideways so she could watch him. Making sure her captive could still see the gun through the space between the seat backs, and thanking God that George seemed not to have a clue how frightened she was, she dug into her handbag again and produced the cell phone.

Miraculously, she remembered the number of the Harton Police Station. Praying that she wouldn't get the idiot again, she got another miracle: Someone intelligent answered. Kathryn introduced herself as the woman who had brought Grace Kimbrough back from California, and then for good measure threw in that she was a personal friend of Tom Holder. With a clarity of thought and speech of which she would not have dreamt herself capable given her emotional state, she related the salient details of her situation, described with precision where she could be found, and concluded, "I'm holding him here, but I don't know how much longer I can continue to hold him, so I'd be deeply grateful if you'd send someone to take him off my hands."

The intelligent voice became curious. "How are you holding him?"

Kathryn wasn't about to tell the cops about her gun if she could help it. After a second's hesitation she replied evenly, "Sheer force of personality."

This riposte earned her a chuckle and a promise that Chief Holder would be notified and a patrol car dispatched without delay.

Kathryn turned her attention back to George. There was time to pass; might as well ask questions. "How did you find out that Tita had seen you on the Stanleys' back porch that day?"

But George had thought of something. "That's against the law," he said officiously, nodding at the gun. "You can get into trouble with that."

"Not as much trouble as you're going to get into."

"They'll send you to jail."

"I'll get out before you will."

George licked his lips again. "Listen, you can't be serious. You don't want to go to jail. Put that thing away and let me go, or I'll tell the police about it."

"Oh, I expect you to," Kathryn replied with a cool she was far from feeling. "But when they pull up, I'll put it back in my hand-bag and they won't see it. If you say anything about it, I'll laugh and say, 'Get him.' Do you think they'll search me on your word? Notice the collar, George."

George had no answer to this, and she asked him again how he had discovered that Tita had seen him on the Stanleys' porch.

"Who's Tita?"

Kathryn swore at him. "That little girl, you—" She couldn't think of a noun bad enough, so she let it go.

George shrank before her fury. "I didn't—I didn't ever plan to kill her," he whined. "I didn't want to hurt her. I just—just panicked. I had to get her safe, I mean, keep her quiet."

Kathryn had never hated anyone the way she hated this man, but for the second time that weekend, she spoke the classic counselor's line: "Do you want to talk about it?"

He was only too ready to do so. "I had gone over there to get some stuff for Bill, his lawyer had asked me to. Shirts and things. I was at the back door, and I heard this voice say hello, and there was this kid looking over the fence. She called me by name, but I didn't know who she was, I don't know the neighborhood kids. Anyway, she started to talk about how she'd gotten Bill arrested because of what she'd seen. And I encouraged her, you know, because I wanted to know what had happened, it's been driving me nuts, not knowing what was going on."

"That I can well imagine," said Kathryn. "You leave a perfectly good corpse lying around and some fool goes and hides it. Enough to make you give up murder, I should think." She found that the sarcasm was a useful vent for her feelings. If she kept it up, maybe she could keep from crying.

"But I didn't—I didn't *murder* Carolyn! I didn't mean to kill her. It was an accident."

"Oh, really?"

"Yes. I was just—we were arguing."

"What about?"

"Oh, nothing. Some misunderstanding."

"What, precisely, had she misunderstood?"

"Well, if you must know," said George, aggrieved, "she thought I'd made some mistakes on a couple of our accounts."

"I thought it might be that," Kathryn commented. "How much did you steal?"

"I didn't steal anything! It was all a mistake, I'm telling you—"

"Oh, don't tell me. I'd much rather hear about this *accident* of yours."

"Oh, that. Well, we were arguing. She started on me at lunch. I don't know how she found—I don't know what got her started. I told her she had it all wrong, but the stupid cow wouldn't believe me. She said she wanted me to refund—I mean pay her—sixty thousand dollars, or she was going to report me to the police. I ask you! So I told her to get stuffed and I left the restaurant. I started to go to the city, I had an appointment there, but then I thought—maybe I should try again, to get her to understand. So I turned around and drove home." George rubbed a hand across his face. "When I got there I went through the gap in the hedge to their house, and she was just about to get in her car to go to the airport; she was supposed to be going to San Francisco. I didn't want to have an argument there in the driveway, so we went into her house. She kept saying Grace was coming any minute to drive her to the airport, so she didn't have time to listen."

Kathryn reflected that it had been prudent of Carolyn to let him know someone was coming. That should have kept her safe. But Carolyn had forgotten that George was a fool.

George was continuing: "So we went in the kitchen and I was trying to explain, but she said she wasn't going to listen to me, and she actually turned her back on me and started to empty the damn dishwasher. Just to ignore me, you know, and I wish she hadn't done that, because that was what—well, it wouldn't have happened if she hadn't opened the dishwasher. Because she was going around the kitchen, putting the dishes away and not listening to me at all, and I was getting really piss—frustrated, you see. So at one point I shoved her, you know, just a little, to get her attention, just kind of—pushed her. Anyway, she lost her balance and fell over backward. She—she fell on this huge knife, it was in the dishwasher, in the cutlery rack, you know? Anyway, this knife—it was awful. She made the most awful noise, just lying there, across the dishwasher door. And the blood, my God. Anyway, I panicked. I ran away. I mean, you can understand that, can't you?"

"Yes. I understand it perfectly."

"It was pretty awful. And I was scared, of course. I thought people might think—well, you know."

"Yes, I know. People might think. You left her lying across the dishwasher door?"

"Yes."

Then he must have hoped it would be taken for an accident— just as she herself had suggested to Tom Holder. But in the minutes between George's exit and Grace's entrance, the hinges of the dishwasher door had given way, and Carolyn's body had rolled off. The knife handle, apparently, had brought the cutlery rack with it, while the pull of the cutlery rack had evidently loosened the knife, so that it fell free to become one item of the gory clutter on the floor. So the outlines of the "accident" were badly blurred by the time Grace and Bill had come upon the scene.

"This knife," Kathryn said. "It was the largest one from that set that hangs by the sink?"

"Yes, yes, it was."

"How do you know?"

There was a pause, and George Kimbrough's pale face flushed crimson. "Well, I, uh, I looked, of course. Uh, leaned over to see what, uh, what . . ."

"Yes, of course you did. And you recognized the knife?"

"Yes, yes, I did."

"They're Sabatier, aren't they?"

"What? Oh, I wouldn't know. Grace bought them for Bill and Carolyn a few years ago. There was something special about them."

He hadn't known, he still didn't know, what that something special was. So he didn't know that Carolyn would never have put one of those knives in the dishwasher.

George had put it there. He had waited until her back was turned, taken the knife from its rack, stuck it point up in the cutlery rack, and maneuvered Carolyn into the right position. And then he had pushed her. Kathryn wondered if he had held her down on it, and began to feel sick again.

George, watching her face nervously, repeated, "It was an accident."

"Sure," said Kathryn in a tight voice. If all he was trying to cover up was an accident, he would not have killed Tita. She said: "You were going to tell me about your conversation with Tita."

"Oh. Well, the kid was talking at me over the back fence about Bill and the body, and then all of a sudden she says she saw me, too, that day, when I was talking to Carolyn. Mrs. Stanley, she called her. 'You went in the house together and you came out alone,' she said. Well, of course you can see what that did to me. I panicked, like I said. I told her I'd show her something interesting having to do with the murder if she came in the house."

Kimbrough said this in the manner of someone offering plausible excuses for forgetting a lunch date.

"So she went into your house and you killed her."

"No, I didn't."

"You didn't?"

"No, I just put her in the basement. I didn't want to kill her."

"You put her in the basement?" Kathryn repeated, beginning to be puzzled.

"Yes, I was waiting for Grace to come back from wherever the hell she ran off to, I thought she'd help me. But Grace hasn't come back," he complained, "and now the police are saying Bill killed her, which is ridiculous, why should he?"

Kathryn struggled for speech, and found it. "How was Grace supposed to help you?"

"She could stay in the house and say I'd gone somewhere on a business trip, and I could take the kid to Mexico. I couldn't very well leave town while the cops were saying Grace had been murdered, it would have looked suspicious."

"Mexico?"

"Yeah. I figured I could maybe drug her or something, get her across the border, maybe just put her in the backseat and say she was asleep. Then I would take her somewhere and leave her where somebody would find her. Like a church or something," said George piously, "where they'd take care of her."

Kathryn realized that in thinking George didn't have the brains God gave geese, she had been overly generous. "They would call her parents," she pointed out.

"I figured some small town, maybe, where they wouldn't speak English—"

"How far do you think you have to drive into Mexico to find a town small enough that nobody speaks enough English to understand 'telephone' and 'New Jersey' and a string of numbers?"

"Well," said George uncomfortably, "I didn't have it all worked out, like I told you, I just panicked, and put her in the basement. But Grace hasn't come home yet, and here are the police saying Bill's hidden Grace's body, which can't be right because it had to be Carolyn's body, and why should he kill Grace anyway?"

It was the second time he had asked, and Kathryn, who had no pity for him whatsoever, decided to tell him. "Men have frequently been known to kill their lovers."

George started. "Grace and Bill? Lovers? That's ridiculous! That stupid policeman said so, too. I don't know where people get such stupid ideas."

"What's stupid about it?"

"Grace and Bill? Hah! He's thirty pounds overweight and blind as a bat. And he's two inches shorter than she is."

Kathryn regarded George with real awe, and wondered if it was possible to feel infinite contempt for someone. She pulled the conversation back to the point. "At any rate, you were waiting for Grace to come home and she didn't."

"That's right. And then this morning I got a phone call. Somebody from the police station"—George continued, unaware that Kathryn had turned to stone, and could hardly hear him for the humming in her ears—"they were kind of vague, but I got the idea somebody was on the way over, so I thought there wasn't any more time to lose, and I'd better get rid of the kid fast." He looked for some acknowledgment to this, but all he got was stony silence. "I didn't have anything to put her to sleep with," he went on lamely, "so I had—I had to knock her out, but I didn't want to hurt her. I tried not to hit her too hard." Silence. "I had to leave her tied up, but I was really careful, the way I carried her."

The humming in Kathryn's ears abruptly ceased. "You mean she's alive?"

George was exasperated. "Of course she's alive!"

"You didn't kill her?"

"For Christ's sake," George cried, "aren't you listening? I've told you a dozen times I didn't kill her!"

"I thought you meant—when you—" Kathryn gaped at George, then at the Mercedes. "She's in the trunk?"

"I *told* you she was in the trunk."

"You idiot!" Kathryn shrieked, waving the gun at him. "Get her out! NOW!"

George fell out of Kathryn's car and scrambled over to his own. He pulled the keys out of the ignition and fumbled them into the lock of the trunk while Kathryn stood over him with the gun, shouting at him to hurry up. The trunk popped open and Tita blinked dazedly up at them. She was gagged with what appeared to be a long sock, and bound hand and foot with thin cord.

Kathryn, tears of relief running down her cheeks, reached a reassuring hand down to grip the girl's shoulder, saying, "Tita, hon, it's all right. You're safe now. It's me, remember me? Kathryn. I'm with the police." To George she snapped in an entirely different tone, "Untie her."

"Oh, sure, of course," mumbled George, unclipping a tiny silver pocket knife from the key chain. He started to open the knife.

"Stop!" Kathryn ordered. "Lay it down next to her." George did so. "Now step back, way back, twenty feet." George obliged.

Kathryn laid the gun down on the floor of the trunk, picked up the knife, opened it, and cut the gag and the cords.

Tita began to weep. "My head hurts," she complained, clutching it. "He hit me."

"I know he did," Kathryn said, stroking her hair. "But he's not going to do it again. The police are going to arrest him."

"I want to get out," Tita announced, trying to sit up.

"I'm not sure that's a good idea, honey. It might be better for you to lie down for a while."

"I've *been* lying down," Tita rejoined unanswerably, "and I want to get out."

"O.K., then. I'll help you. Can you stand up? Careful, don't bump your head. Here, I'll lift you out." As she set Tita on her feet, she saw two police cars pull up alongside her Audi.

She caught her breath. She glanced down at the gun, lying where she had left it on the floor of the trunk. Her handbag was in her car. There was no way she could get to it without the gun being seen. Four members of Harton's Finest were emerging from the patrol cars. She didn't think the gun would fit in the pocket of her raincoat. It would show. *Dear God*, she thought. One of the cops was Tom Holder. All four of them were moving eagerly toward her. She closed the trunk, pulled the keys out of the lock, called, "George! Catch!" and tossed them at him.

He was startled, of course; he threw out a tardy hand, missed them, picked them up off the ground, and pocketed them. He looked nervously at the police, but the three in uniform, following their Chief's lead, had eyes only for the woman in the priest's collar and the little girl.

"My God, Kathryn!" Tom exulted. "You've got her! Is she all right?"

Tita had wrapped her arms around Kathryn's waist and buried her face in the folds of her raincoat, crying softly. Kathryn had an arm around the child's shoulders and with her other hand stroked the ginger-colored hair. "She's fine," she told Tom in an unsteady voice, then corrected herself: "Well, not quite; she's got a headache and ought to be checked for concussion. But it beats the alternatives."

"You ain't kiddin'."

The sound of an engine starting made them turn around. George was in Kathryn's car.

"Get him!" Holder barked, and the uniforms sprinted to obey, but before they could reach the car, George had pulled away in a storm of kicked-up gravel. The two officers who had arrived in the front car leapt back into it and roared after him. The police-woman who had driven Tom Holder looked at her Chief, who was saying under his breath the sort of words that used to be called unprintable. "No, you stay with me," he said. "Call the sta-tion and have them call the Robinsons, tell them their daughter's alive and O.K. and we're bringing her home, but they'll need to take her to the hospital emergency room just to be sure she hasn't got a concussion."

The woman nodded and trotted back to her vehicle. Holder turned to Kathryn and gestured politely toward the police car. "Climb aboard."

"Come on, Tita," she said. "Let's take you home." She led the child past Holder, who was kneeling to examine the ruins of George's left front tire.

"What happened here?" he asked.

Kathryn's heart contracted. She said woodenly, "He had a flat."

"How lucky can ya get?" Holder remarked.

Meanwhile, two miles down the road, at a curve that was sharper than it looked, George had wrapped Kathryn's car around a substantial tree. The pursuing patrol car screeched to a halt; the two policemen jumped out and ran to assess the condition of their recaptured suspect. They peered into the steaming wreckage and promptly wished they hadn't.

CHAPTER 37

Tom Holder had polished off two roast beef sandwiches and perhaps a bit too much of a very remarkable scotch. It was Kathryn's—trust her to have a bottle of something he'd never heard of and could not pronounce—and she had kept up with him, shot for shot. They were sitting in her living room at dusk, tying up loose ends.

They had settled the question of Patricia Clyde's guilty knowledge.

"She's the one who found out George had been fiddling with the books," Kathryn said.

Kathryn had had a long, tear-stained session with Patricia earlier in the afternoon. The police had dropped her at home, and she had borrowed Mrs. Warburton's car to pay, she had said, a pastoral call. Somebody had to tell Patricia about Carolyn.

In turn, Patricia had told her how she'd suspected George for months, finally proved it to her satisfaction, and told Carolyn that fateful Monday morning. Carolyn, disliking scenes, chose to drop the bomb on George over a civilized lunch at Leboeuf's. He couldn't shout at her there.

"But according to Patricia, George's reaction, even in the middle of Leboeuf's, frightened Carolyn. She came back to the office and collected the evidence to take it with her to San Francisco, because it occurred to her that otherwise it wouldn't be there when she got back. She had Patricia cancel her hotel reservation because she didn't want George to know where she was."

"And Miss Iceberg knew all about this and didn't tell me. I could wring her neck."

"Well, don't be too hard on Patricia. She thought she didn't have the right to tell you about George's embezzling, that was for Carolyn to tell you when she got back from California, and why should she tell you, anyway, since Bill killing Grace didn't have anything to do with George cooking the books?"

"Oh, speaking of books—I brought you a souvenir." He dug in his vinyl zipper folder, pulled out a sheet of paper, and handed it to Kathryn.

"All *right!*" she said, producing a tired grin. "I may frame it." It was a photocopy of the "Attic" page of Tita's notebook. A series of entries in the middle of the page read as follows:

> *1:12 P.M. Mrs. S. comes out of the house carrying two suitcases. Sounds of argument from Mrs. S. and somebody else. (Behind trees) Mrs. S. and Mr. K. go in the back door.*
> *1:18 P.M. Mr. K. comes out alone. He is in a hurry.*
> *1:24 P.M. Mr. S. goes in the back door.*
> *1:27 P.M. Mrs. K. comes out the back door.*

"When I think," said Kathryn, "that this was just sitting around! How can you say I've been anything but a dithering incompetent all along? After all, you gave me this to read, and I didn't."

"Oh, come on, Kathryn! You can't blame yourself for that. I didn't really expect you to read it. I gave it to you as a kind of joke." *It gave me an excuse to come over here.* The words were in his mind, but he kept them from his tongue. It would be too explicit. She would shut up on him like a clam, and things would never be easy between them again.

They had settled the question of Bill Stanley's future.

"Oh, community service, probably. Worst thing that will happen to him is embarrassment."

"Given the scope of the embarrassment in question, I'm inclined to think that's not a minor consideration. Where did he put Carolyn's body?"

"In the canal near the golf course."

Kathryn studied her scotch. "That will make messy work for some of your people," she said.

"Yes," Holder replied briefly, studying his own scotch.

"I know what I meant to ask you," he said, changing the subject. "What was going on with Grace back there in Trenton when she blushed?"

The fact that Grace had fallen into bed with (apparently) the first man she'd run into in San Francisco was, like Kathryn's intuition about Carolyn's sex life, something she had gleaned in confidence. So she said, "I can't tell you. It was nothing remotely criminal. It had to do," she said, picking her words carefully, "with how she chose to escape from the supposition that Bill had killed Carolyn, presumably over her, over Grace."

Tom looked at her for a moment. "You know, you're really good about not telling on people." Kathryn attempted to look blank, and failed. Tom continued. "You didn't tell me, in Trenton, that Carolyn and Miss Iceberg were lovers, and you're not telling me now that Grace cleared out of the Mark Hopkins at five A.M. to get away from some man she'd gone to bed with."

Kathryn gawked at him. "Now, how in hell do you know all that?"

"Even a dumb cop can read between the lines."

"Really? I don't know any dumb cops." She said it pointedly.

Tom hid his face in his scotch glass in an attempt to cover up how deeply pleased he was by this remark.

They then settled the matter that was secretly troubling Kathryn more than any other.

"Trenton tells me there was a gun in the trunk of George's car."

Kathryn's heart skipped a beat.

"Grace swears it doesn't belong to them."

A pause ensued while the Reverend Dr. Koerney utterly failed to find anything to say.

Tom continued as smoothly as though speechlessness from Kathryn were normal behavior. "It's an old Smith & Wesson .38 revolver, one shot fired. If it had been used in a crime, it would now be police property, but nobody's figured out where and when George could have used it. It's not registered in the state of New Jersey, but registration is voluntary for a gun that old, so it doesn't look like there's anything illegal that we could prove about it."

Kathryn was a fervent supporter of gun control, and she had always meant to register the .38 but had somehow never gotten around to it. She suspected this omission had less to do with indolence than with the sure and certain knowledge that Uncle Jesse would roll over in his dusty South Texas grave if she did anything as knee-jerk liberal with his gun as to go and register it with the dang police.

Tom was rolling scotch around in his mouth and trying to decide which he was enjoying more, the single malt on his own tongue or the paralysis on Kathryn's. He swallowed appreciatively. "So I was thinking. You told me you used to shoot rats in the barn on your uncle's ranch. Were you any good at it?"

Kathryn cleared her throat and managed to produce one syllable: "Yes."

"Well, then, you should have a gun of your own. Maybe you'd like this one," he suggested. "They tell me it's a nice old piece. Why don't I talk to Grace? I'll tell her the thing must have been George's and he just never told her about it. She won't want it, and she owes you a favor. I bet if I tell her you'd like to have it, she'll give it to you."

"Tom—"

"Of course you know you can't just carry it around any old where, you're only allowed to take it to and from a firing range, and you have to put it in the trunk when you do."

"Tom—"

"I'll talk to Grace and let you know."

She gave him a long look which he met with a seraphic smile. "Thank you," she said.

They next settled the question of George's guilt—and of Kathryn's.

"No, Tom," she said emphatically, "I was *not* a real help. I went barging in where I shouldn't have, and I damn near got that child killed."

"Listen, Kathryn. If you hadn't done anything, anything at all, except go help me with that talk with Tita, she would still have climbed that fence yesterday and talked to George and wound up in his basement."

"But she didn't wind up in the trunk of his car until I made that stupid phone call."

"Yeah, but he would have killed her eventually. He had to kill her."

"What I don't understand is why he didn't kill her in the first place."

"My guess is that he was squeamish. Notice the way he killed Carolyn. He didn't pick up a knife and stab her, he put the knife down and then pushed her down on it."

"He was trying to make it look like an accident."

"I think making it look like an accident was a second thought, and the real reason was that it takes less guts to push somebody than to stab somebody."

Kathryn pondered what she knew of George, and agreed. She added, "You don't believe that Mexico business, do you?"

"I think he thought about that, because he would've liked to have thought of something else instead of killing Tita, but he must have known it was a dumb idea."

"Not as dumb as thinking Grace would help him when she came home."

"Oh, yeah, Grace coming home, that's another thing I owe you."

"No, Tom, I refuse to take credit here. I was completely out of my depth, I was playing ego games when I should have left everything to the professionals, and any way you slice it," she said, determined in her self-deprecation, "nothing but a miraculous stroke of luck, or Providence, or whatever, stands between me and being guilty of Tita Robinson's death."

"Crap," said Tom succinctly. "If Tita had died, there would have been one person absolutely responsible: George Kimbrough. And if there's any guilt left over, you can spread it all over Bill and Grace. For God's sake, Kathryn, look what they did! They found a murder, and what did they do? They covered it up. What they should have done was pick up a phone and dial 911. If they'd done that, we'd have talked to Patricia Clyde within an hour, and found out about George and the money, and George would have been in a cell on Monday night instead of calling to tell us his wife was missing."

"Well, yes, I suppose, but at least they were trying to protect each other. There was some love in it."

"Love? They were trying to protect each other because they'd been boinking each other. Pardon me, I'm not an expert on these things, but the last time I looked, that was called adultery, right? If they really loved each other and their marriages were really hopeless, why weren't they honest about it? Why didn't they just divorce George and Carolyn and marry each other?"

Kathryn had to admit to herself that she hadn't thought of that. Nevertheless, at any other time she might have argued further, but she had had an exhausting weekend.

"Besides," Tom started again, then paused. Could he say it? Would she be angry? Maybe. No. Yes. To hell with it. "Besides, if you're claiming all the blame for yourself, when it's other people's fault as much or even more, isn't that the sin of pride?" (He had been paying attention when Kathryn had covered precisely this point a year ago in an adult Sunday school session on sin.)

Kathryn felt as if she had been hit with a wet towel. Oh, God.

It was true. Tom was right. Ego again. Her insatiable, terrible ego. After a long and horrid day, it was too much: She burst into tears.

Tom was aghast. "Oh, no!" he cried. "Kat, don't! I didn't mean it, I'm so stupid—" He reached a hand toward her, but stopped.

"No, you're not stupid, you're right," she hiccuped through her sobs. "You're right. I am eaten up with pride."

Tom sat paralyzed. Like Grace, looking helplessly at Bill across the chasm created by her own guilt, Tom sat glued to his chair, longing to go to her, put his arms around her and comfort her, but unable to do so. If he had been nothing but an honest friend, he could have done it. But he had looked upon her—in the biblical phrase—to lust after her; he had committed adultery in his heart. So he sat across from her, miserable, while she wept.

Finally she excused herself and left the room.

Tom had been taught by his upbringing, by his job, and by his years of stoically endured suffering at home, not to cry. So he sat with his elbows on his knees and his face in his hands and men-tally kicked himself.

He was doing such a ferocious job of this that he did not hear her come back into the room, so was surprised by a light touch on his shoulder as she walked past his chair.

"Sorry about that," she said quietly, taking her place again on the sofa. "It's been a long day."

"I'm so sorry—" he began, but she held up a hand.

"Hush. Not your fault. It's just that occasionally I despair of ever overcoming my . . . my flaws."

You and me both, he thought. He started to say "Nobody's per-fect," but it was so lame. He searched for a phrase, and surprised

himself by remembering one from the New Testament. He said,
" 'We have all sinned and fallen short of the glory of God.' "

It was perfect. She even smiled—a little. "How true," she replied, sniffing only slightly.

She had washed her face, but she was still red around the eyes. He had never seen her look less pretty or more desirable. He ached to touch her, but contented himself with smiling at her.

"Besides," she continued, "nobody's called me Kat since my father died. It was nice."

So he reminded her of her father. Great.

She fetched a huge sigh and performed an elongated stretch, like a cat. "Tom," she said. "It's Sunday."

"And?"

"I haven't been to church."

"Neither have I."

"I'm a traveling Eucharist, you know. I can make my own."

"Yeah?"

"I propose to amble up to the church, break into the sacristy, get a chalice and paten and wafer and wine, and offer a Eucharist in thanksgiving for the life of Tita Robinson and for the repose of the soul of Carolyn Stanley."

Tom pondered this a minute and found it good. "I'm with you," he said. "But shouldn't we include George's soul?"

Kathryn regarded him without enthusiasm. "You have from here to there to talk me into it."

It was a dark Sunday afternoon in November. The killer of Carolyn Stanley lay on a slab in the morgue in Trenton. His two accomplices after the fact lay exhausted in their separate beds, he in the jail cell from which his lawyer would shortly free him, she in a guest room in the house of a friend, trying to come to terms with what she'd lost.

But the two most urgently aware of their sins were the policeman and the priest who were walking toward the church in a wet dusk, pretending to argue about praying for the soul of a killer. They walked side by side but were careful not to touch each other. A fine mist fell on them, soft as a blessing.